Endorsements

Good storytelling in a unique way ... insightful, mystical, and enjoyable ... a mixture of reality and imagination.

—Ben A. Saathoff, Pastor, Retired

"Dead men tell no tales," unless Mr. Weatherby writes for them. The Frenchman's tale is a very readable story of intrigue and adventure. It is also a study of characters, cultures, morality, and the meaning of life.

Eat the fresh bread first. Read the story as light entertainment. But be prepared to be drawn into questions of purpose and ethics.

—Ray D. Stites, Minister,
former Bible college president

Like the Frenchman, I also landed on Saipan in 1977, and now the reality of that time and the tropical paradise are captured in the words written by Kent Weatherby. The story is a mesmerizing tale of the businesses, scenery, sailing, night life, politics, and personalities of the people who inhabited Micronesia.

—Robert V. Mulch, Judge, Retired

THE

FRENCHMAN

ATE

THE

FRESH

BREAD

FIRST

THE FRENCHMAN ATE THE FRESH BREAD FIRST

A NOVEL BY KENT WEATHERBY

TATE PUBLISHING *& Enterprises*

Published by Tate Publishing & Enterprises, LLC
127 E. Trade Center Terrace | Mustang, Oklahoma 73064 USA
1.888.361.9473 | www.tatepublishing.com

Tate Publishing is committed to excellence in the publishing industry. The company reflects the philosophy established by the founders, based on Psalm 68:11,
"The Lord gave the word and great was the company of those who published it."

Book design copyright © 2009 by Tate Publishing, LLC. All rights reserved.
Cover design by Lindsay B. Behrens
Interior design by Joey Garrett

Published in the United States of America

ISBN: 978-1-60799-019-2
1. Fiction / Action & Adventure
2. Fiction / Literary
09.05.04

There is a way which seemeth right unto a man,
but the end thereof are the ways of death.

Proverbs 14:12

Dedication

For my family and friends who lived and worked on Saipan in the tumultuous days before the Frenchman visited the island and then disappeared forever.

Acknowledgments

I would like to acknowledge the following people for their assistance in making this book of fiction a reality:

My family for their patience in putting up with my endless telling the story.

My cousin Hal who encouraged the development of Jonathan Cartwright as a character in the story.

Jaime McNutt Bode at Tate Publishing for helping make the story compelling.

Prologue

No one knew who he was, what his name was, or when he arrived on the island. He was first seen shortly after dawn on a calm summer Thursday morning before the heat of the day, walking south along Beach Road from Charlie Dock in the direction of the Continental Hotel, the largest and most elaborate building on Saipan. He was in his mid-forties, and his entire appearance had an unkempt yet quietly dignified air. He had shaggy brown hair, uncut for weeks, and wore dirty white deck shoes without socks, a clean white T-shirt, and mid-thigh faded blue shorts slightly frayed at the seams. He was lean and muscular with well-tanned arms and legs. His stride was rhythmic as one accustomed to days and weeks at sea, subjected to gentle swell, a handsome man who gave the appearance of knowing who he was, where he had been, and where he was going even if he wasn't exactly sure of the location. There was something about him that called out reckless danger; he was a confident man.

His boat, a double-mast forty-six-foot ketch tied to the dock, had slipped through the reef into the lagoon, passing Managaha Island during the night. No one can now recall the sound of her engine—not surprising since Charlie Dock is an isolated location in Tanapag Harbor. Only a few small buildings associated with harbor operations, a Mobil oil station, and the local Coca-Cola bottling plant were located within a half mile of where he tied the boat, a beautiful jade sailboat with the name "Monique" painted on the stern.

A lawyer in the Trust Territory Attorney General's Office returning home from an all-night poker party with friends on Capitol Hill, slightly intoxicated, picked him up in his rusting white Nissan and gave him a ride to the top of Navy Hill where his wife gave him breakfast, fresh mango and banana, orange juice, eggs, and coarse white bread.

He was slightly aloof at first, though friendly, speaking with only a faint accent, his English otherwise excellent. He was French. His first words anyone can now recall were at that breakfast; "Always eat the fresh bread first," he had said, a philosophy of life he wore as most people wear comfortable clothes. He lived for the present with no apparent regard for the past and little concern for the future.

As the days passed, the inhabitants he met variously believed him to be a doctor, a lawyer, clearly a professional man, possibly a banker. A few even speculated he was a criminal running from the law using the months aboard a sailboat in the oceans of the world as a cooling off period until it was safe for him to return to his native country. Some insisted he was a priest who had renounced his faith and rejected the church. He spoke only once of the church and avoided Mt. Carmel Cathedral as well as those who served God within.

He expressed a hostile disavowal of all matters relating to religion. If he had a spiritual life, he kept it well concealed. He had a taste for spirits, expensive wine, even beer, but he seldom drank distilled spirit except for cognac. After months at sea, he had a passion for good food, dining frequently at the Continental Hotel where his palate was satisfied. He otherwise shunned the comfort of air-conditioned rooms, preferring the shade of ironwood trees during the hot, humid days, cooled by the movement of a gentle breeze over his warm skin.

He never dined alone, paying in cash for whatever he wanted, always seeming to entertain one or more guests, sometimes young, single, tanned or dark-skinned ladies in brightly colored island dresses, Caucasian and native alike, who let their broad-hipped sensuality speak for them. They were the only people on the island invited aboard his boat.

He hired a driver, a young Trukese teenager of dubious reputation, who drove him wherever he wanted to go and was seen not with him but waiting for him on both ends and sides of the crescent-shaped island, at the beach, in hotels and Palauan bars alike, where the Frenchman occasionally bought drinks for the patrons and listened to the conversation, drinking in the culture as much as the libation served.

It was his third day on the island when a report of this enigmatic visitor's activities reached the high commissioner who two days later happened upon his path, by coincidence no doubt, in the restaurant of the Hafa Dai Hotel at noon where they spent a few minutes in conversation before adjourning to the high commissioner's office for another hour. No one now admits knowing what they discussed. A month later the high commissioner was overheard to remark, "How sad, such an opportunity, so much lost," when a cable concerning the stranger was received at the headquarters building.

What little the islanders did learn about him was he had sailed from the ancient Mediterranean Sea port of Toulon, or at least so it was rumored, embarked on a solo circumnavigation of the earth months earlier. His course had followed the prevailing easterlies wherever he found them, following both wind and current whenever possible, but first traveling west, going through the Pillars of Hercules, rounding the Cape of Good Hope, sailing on into the Arabian Sea, crossing the Indian Ocean, passing through the Strait of Malacca. Along the way, he stopped at small harbors where immigration and customs officials were scarce, inefficient, and susceptible to bribes. He had a radio receiver but no transmitter on board, and so he was incapable of communicating with the outside world while at sea. Whether he was making the trip for research purposes in contemplation of writing an adventure story or whether he was simply escaping from something, or someone, no one knew.

He disappeared just as he arrived, suddenly and without warning. On the morning of day seven, the *Monique* was gone. No one heard her engine or saw her leave the dock. He had simply departed sometime during the hours of darkness Wednesday morning. Everyone was surprised when they learned of his departure and surmised he intended to continue sailing toward the east, endlessly moving toward the sun.

Ten days after he left, the *Monique* stopped at Moen Island in Truk Lagoon, though he departed there even more abruptly. A month after leaving Saipan, a navy frigate found the derelict boat, fully rigged, sails reefed with sheets flapping harmlessly in the light breeze floating unattended south of the Marshall Islands. No one was aboard, living or dead, except for the decayed remains of a flying fish in the cockpit. Only a copy of Bernard Moitessier's book *La Longue Route*, open to chapter eighteen where the words *puisque je suis allé trop loin* were underlined, but scribbled in the margin *non— parce que je suis allé trop loin*, a tiny bloodstain on deck, a partially eaten loaf of stale bread, a half tin of moldy camembert cheese, and two empty bottles of expensive French Beaujolais testified to the presence of a living person having been aboard.

The Frenchman

I am dead as humanity understands the meaning of death, but even the dead, such as I, deserve to have someone tell their story. Since I cannot rely on anyone else to relate the events leading to my premature demise, I will have to tell you myself.

The old priest on Saipan prayed for a miracle, one that would give me hope for redemption, to escape from purgatory before the final descent into hell. He prayed that God would grant me the time to set matters right, and so now that I am caught up in a miraculous existence, where I am not totally dead, spiritually dead, yet not alive to the world, I see a small ray of hope before me though I am uncertain what is expected of me.

For me, there is no concept of time. I have been given a special gift of seeing events clearly without being constrained by time or place, seeing and understanding things beyond mortal ability to know them, the gaps in my knowledge made complete, seeing words, actions, and thoughts not as they appeared to be but as they actually were. I do not know how long the gift lasts, but if I am to have any hope of escaping damnation, I must use it before it is lost.

The lessons I have learned, the mistakes I have made, I hope to pass on so that you and I, if God wills it, may avoid the eternity otherwise awaiting me—the God I denied when breathing the air of mortal life. Nevertheless, if it is too late for me, perhaps others will benefit from the story I will relate. Unlike Lazarus in the bosom of Abraham before me, dead yet alive, I can speak to my living brothers that they might escape the torment across the abyss separating Lazarus and the rich man. I will speak to you of a life often misspent, sometimes tragic, that destined me to this place.

My name is not important—although the pseudonym I used was known—nor is the time and place of my birth and death; those details we mostly see on tombstones with the actual days of our lives being contained in the hyphen. In my case I am the only person, if I may properly refer to myself as such, who is likely to talk about the events of my hyphen leading up to a date that would otherwise forever be unknown.

Of all the people inhabiting the earth, it is my hope that you will personally benefit from the telling of my story. Physical death came suddenly and unexpectedly, but I would not have had it any other way, though that was not always the case. In hearing my story, you may discover a great deal about me while much will undoubtedly remain unresolved since the portion of my hyphen I wish to relate is only the last part of the dash. Yes, that may well be the proper word for it, my dash toward that final month, day, and year.

Chapter One

It is quite true my arrival on Saipan was sudden, unseen, and unforeseen. I had not planned to arrive in that manner. It is simply a matter of when the wind, current, and tides permitted. I sailed in the time-honored method, using sextant and chronometer, and had set a dead-reckoned course from the Philippine village of Aparri at the northern end of Luzon. I had stopped there to repair my potable water tank after my on-board supply of fresh water had become contaminated by seawater. Once the repairs were made, I immediately set out alone for my intended destination.

I enjoy the solitary life, or should I say enjoyed the solitary life, and so never minded living for weeks on end with only my thoughts and nothing, or no one, else. For that reason among others, I had undertaken the circumnavigation of the earth. For the most part, I traveled just a few degrees either north or south of the equator, sailing as much as possible either above or below those calm waters known as the doldrums, endeavoring always to stay well away from shipping lanes, assuring me of not only solitude but freedom from detection as well.

Monique and I passed time in the company of birds and porpoises without once seeing another human being. On occasion a flying fish following the boat would hurtle close by, a blur as it approached unannounced at over thirty miles per hour, its four-pound body having the force of a sledgehammer. Our very existence ceased except for the wind and waves.

Ocean travel under sail is an inexact science at best. Wind, tides, and currents take even the ablest of seamen well off their course, and I do count myself amongst the very best. At last, I had arrived in Micronesia, a third of the way around the world, though much farther by the route I had taken. Here were the islands Conrad had discovered and written about—Palau, Yap, the Marianas chain, Truk Lagoon and Ponape, not to mention the Marshalls. Among these far-flung islands and people, I surely would find adventure if not danger in the diverse culture, Western or Eastern Carolinian, blended at Saipan, some more violent than others, where piracy was practiced even then upon the unwary. It was a place I had heard about, read about from the time I was a child.

Most intriguing of all, Truk Lagoon beckoned, where Japanese power imposed on native tradition had resulted in defeat, starvation, and cannibalism. Even now, after all those years, Truk was still a place where a man could simply disappear and few people would ask why. Nevertheless, I planned to go to Truk, but before going there, I planned my first stop on Saipan, and that is where I should begin my story.

I retired on the night before I anticipated arriving at the Trust Territory of the Pacific Islands capitol having first set a course that should have seen my arrival sometime after dawn. It was therefore a surprise when I discovered the cable connecting my wind vane to the rudder had crimped, failing to control my passage properly, and I had drifted over forty miles to the north with the current. Upon awakening, I found I was nowhere near that lovely high green island.

I replaced the cable with a line wondering how I had ever been naïve enough to allow the use of metal alloy on the boat instead of flexible rope that had served seamen for centuries, wondering at what other point it would fail me. Since I did not have sufficient fuel on board to correct the drift in navigation with my engine, choosing instead to carry the weight normally allocated to fuel in the form of my well-stocked wine cellar, I beat into the freshening breeze, working against the current, and made my way down the archipelago to my destination. It was a disappointment to me when I reached the island after the sun had set.

I checked my charts and identified a broad channel into the lagoon, but in the poor light, with the moon moving from the first quarter to full, clouds obscured what little illumination it offered. I hove to and lay off listening to the sea rumble like rolling thunder against the coral until the first light of dawn, then motored toward the dock. In that soft glow, the island rose like a great pyramid out of the water, dark with only the sparsest lighting, a strip along the beach with pockets at Garapan and Chalan Kanoa, the kind of yellow glow you get from irregular voltage. Only the resort hotels had lights as brilliant as I remembered the seaside cities of France. It was too early in the morning for much color to show, and the island appeared in shadows and shades of black and gray and a deep musty green.

The high islands were always my favorites, evoking thoughts of the prison island where Papillon struggled to survive, solely for the purpose of escape, survival not being a sufficient reason to continue living. There were times when I saw my tiny boat as an exaggerated coconut raft carrying me away from the tortured imprisonment of my former life. But who was I, certainly not Papillon ... Dega? I wondered if all I had done by my journey was trade that small island, not the one I approached, the one I sailed, for the larger jail of Europe. Could it be that I was, after all, the perfect blend of tough, brave Papillon and the frightened Louis Dega?

I passed a small island in the lagoon, with the ruins of a small Japanese defense position and a few palm trees, midway between the reef and dock. The Philippine Sea behind me was bathed in sunlight, but Mt. Topachau held the western side of the island in shadow leaving me to imagine the harbor buildings more than see them. I came alongside the end of the pier carefully staying clear of the berthing place for any large vessels that might arrive later. There was no one around, and so, taking stock of the height of the dock, the location of the steel rings embedded in the concrete. I killed the boat's motor and leaped onto land with line in hand tying *Monique* securely to the island.

As I had approached land, I noticed the bright lights of a hotel were not more than a mile south. And so, I struck out with that swaying motion a man uses when he is accustomed to the pitch and roll, the swell of the sea, walking toward the lights dimming rapidly as the sun rose over the mountain top. The morning was cool and the pavement level, a rough, hard-surfaced road with coral as one of its chief components.

I had not walked more than a quarter mile when I sensed something catching up behind me. As I turned, an old Nissan, an automobile that had once been white, now faded and chalky with rust around the headlights, slowed and stopped. The driver was skinny—I say skinny, not slender, for George was truly a skinny man, one could say with impunity scrawny with a thin scraggly beard and eyes that had once been bright but even in the dim light were watery, a white man but brown nevertheless, his skin wrinkled and leathery from the tropical sun. He leaned a little across the passenger seat toward the open window.

"It's early. Want a ride? Where you going?" he said in a warm voice slightly slurred after a night of hard drinking.

"Down the road to the tall building," I replied. "Thought I'd treat myself to breakfast." I opened the door and started to sit.

"Watch out for the traps," the man said. His voice had a mixture of humor and cunning. "There is a family of shrews living in here. They get in through the holes in the floorboard."

Looking down, I saw the pavement was in fact clearly visible between my feet as I gingerly lowered myself onto the seat, careful to avoid a mousetrap on the console between the bucket seats and another on one of the few remaining solid pieces of flooring.

Noticing my gaze fixed on the floorboard, he continued, "That's how they get in. There is a whole nest of them, but I never see one except when in the trap. But for that and the droppings on the seat, you wouldn't know they were here." The explanation of the shrews behind him, he said, "Where'd you come from? What's your name? I'm George, George Rowley." He seemed to be a man who asked two questions for every statement.

"From the ketch; you can see her from here. I just arrived," I responded.

He looked over his shoulder at the receding image of the harbor and mast of the boat, his curiosity for my name lost with the view. "Well, there's no use going to the Continental Hotel this early. They won't have the breakfast buffet set up for at least another two hours. Come along with me. My wife, Beth, will fix us some breakfast."

He sped off down the road and reached for the CB radio. "Drifter to Home, come back Home."

The response from Home was affectionate but firm. "Drifter, where have you been all night? I was worried." Why she should have been worried I later discovered was a matter for little conjecture. Irresponsibility, gambling, and booze had become the hallmark of Drifter's life, costing him his job on the mainland as an Assistant District Attorney in the Los Angeles County prosecutor's office.

"Oh, you know, we got into a poker game after leaving the bowling alley and had a few drinks. I've got a new guy with me. He just got on island, and we could sure use some breakfast. Any hope? Come on back."

The voice at the other end sounded resigned to the fact of life and a little more tentative. "Yeah, I guess. Give me a second to get some clothes on. Out!"

The man who identified himself as both George and Drifter turned left at the hotel entrance and, after ignoring the stop sign on Middle Road, drove up a hill. Not more than a minute after the woman said "out," he made one last left turn, came around what appeared to be a ball field, passed a white concrete house, then suddenly swerved right and stopped beside the house. "This is it," he said flatly and opened the door to be greeted by the biggest dog I'd ever seen, its head the size of a small beach ball, thirty inches at the shoulder, at least forty-five kilos. "Stay down, Bear," he yelled at the beast as it jumped on him and began trying to take his arm in its mouth, a mouth wet with saliva.

I did not move. "It's okay. Bear's friendly; he's still a pup, not quite a year old. Well, he'll be friendly to you. I can't say the same for everyone. Bear doesn't much like dark-skinned people; don't know why."

We entered the house by the rear door just as the woman George called Beth came into the kitchen wearing a scoop-neck loose-fitting cover-up. Even wearing the dress, it was plain to see she was a well-proportioned woman, mid- to late thirties, possibly forty, appearing much younger than George, who I would have said was nearing sixty but later learned was only a few years older than Beth.

When she bent to get the eggs from the refrigerator, she removed all doubt of her figure; firm breasts and a pleasantly rounded midriff came into my hungry view. How long had it been? I used the long weeks at sea as a self-imposed abstinence, making my stay ashore an opportunity for orgiastic release. She caught my look as she turned back glancing to see if George had noticed. He had not, busily making three Screwdrivers with freshly squeezed orange juice, pouring the vodka from a half-gallon jug. She smiled, appreciating my appreciation.

We ate our breakfast with the massive Bear lying on the floor at Beth's feet. I inquired about life on the island, the people living there, the native culture, the way life adopted a rhythm, the same on all tropical islands yet somehow always decidedly different. The eggs Beth explained were fresh, coming from a Chamorro farmer somewhere to the south. The mango and bananas were locally grown. The coffee was black and strong. The cheese I found indifferent, and the bread, a coarse white bread carved from a partially eaten loaf baked two days earlier beside one with its hard bronze crust intact prompted me to remark, "You should always remember to eat the fresh bread first." When George looked at me with a puzzled expression, I continued, "To do otherwise is to always eat stale bread."

Chapter Two

It was after nine when George offered to take me to the hotel at the bottom of what I now knew was Navy Hill. Taking Beth's hand, with exaggerated formality I raised her fingers to my lips, "Thank you so much. I hope to see much more of you before I leave."

She smiled and replied, "Possibly but probably not so much as you hope."

I have always been a man who believed a kind rebuff to a friendly invitation was not a matter to take offense, so I merely paused and said, "Until we meet again." She said possibly. Ah yes, there was cause to hope, I mused. My libido aroused, I was certain to find a more receptive partner elsewhere tonight.

We left Bear following us, ever watchful of my next move as I once more negotiated my way between the open floorboard, the traps, and the seat. We retraced our path down the hill to the intersection of Middle Road where George turned to me, "How'd you like to see the island?" and without waiting for my reply, turned right and drove past several old derelict electric generators on our left, rusting beside the road, before coming to another road that led steeply uphill.

As we climbed this tree-canopied road, I knew we were ascending the pyramid I had seen from beyond the reef. The road twisted and turned, snails popping under the tires, as we steadily climbed a thousand feet above the lower road, all the time in the shade of a dense jungle inching forward to encroach on that ribbon of pavement leading I knew not where until, at the last turn, we broke out into an open plateau filled with buildings.

"This is the Trust Territory headquarters. In the old days, up until about fifteen years ago, it was a CIA installation. There are people on the island, mainly the locals, who still think it is," George explained and continued driving. A half mile farther along, we started our descent, more gently now and with more open space. "About halfway down there is a place where we can get some betel nut and local weed," he volunteered.

I nodded, reflecting that my small stash on board *Monique* was running low. The road curved, dipped, and rose again as it worked its way down the mountain. Coming around a sweeping left curve, George swerved suddenly right onto a narrow lane flanked by tangen-tangen jungle, a woody tangle too dense to walk through sown by the U.S. Navy to control erosion.

A hundred yards past the turn, he stopped in a clearing bordered by a huge breadfruit tree and several banana trees. There in the opening stood a house. I hesitate to call it house, for it was more of a semi-permanent shelter constructed from leftover war material, the sides and roof a combination of corrugated steel and wood that had not seen paint for years, if ever. Parked haphazardly beside the house was a rusted Toyota pickup and a late-model car with the name Dodge and Charger written on the trunk. Orange and shiny, it was the only indication of status in the entire clearing.

The area surrounding the building, which in other circumstances would be called a front yard, was devoid of toys normally associated with small children, although a lively brood of indeterminate number, ranging in age from four to twelve, ran about naked. A sturdy dark-skinned woman worn down by years of child bearing and work was sweeping the front stoop. She ignored the smaller children occupied in a game only they understood as we approached.

The house was otherwise occupied by a medium-height, stocky, muscular man George informed me was Trukese. The man's demeanor spoke of aggression, one might even say evil, accentuated by a drooping left eyelid and a scar that turned the corner of his mouth downward as if it had once been snagged by a huge fishhook then ripped loose. He was not a man to be taken lightly or underestimated.

The man looked in our direction with suspicion as we slowed then stopped. "George, what is the attorney general doing out here on a Thursday morning? Is that a cop you got with you?"

George was out of the car quickly. "Xarkus, you old fart. Why you makin' that woman do all the work?"

"Hey, man, what you expect? I got important things to do. This all woman's work. Maybe those kids help her when they get big. What you want?"

Ignoring the question for the moment, George

answered, "This guy's new on the island. He came in this morning on a sailboat all by himself."

Xarkus eyed me suspiciously. "Yeah?"

"Yeah, and we thought maybe you had some stuff for sale, you know, some nut and maybe a little pot."

"Maybe I know where you could get something, maybe not. This guy okay?"

"Xarkus, what'd you expect? They're going to send some guy on a fancy sailboat halfway across the Pacific to bust you for selling something everybody uses? Good grief, man, I am the law, and I've been one of your best customers for years."

Xarkus paused, thinking. "All right. Come on in; I'll fix you some nut and we'll smoke a joint. Maybe we will talk about it a little more. Move over, woman. Make way for these gentlemen." With that, he shouldered past his wife through the open doorway.

The house was much the same inside as on the out; old furniture smelled of sweat and decaying fabric, musty, dark, and humid, the heat of the day rising with the sun hardly lessened by the canopy of the breadfruit tree.

Xarkus waved us to seats on the rattan chairs while he went into another room in the small square house. When he returned, he had a box about the size for storing a pair of shoes. He first extracted three brownish-colored nuts, which he cracked using a pair of pliers. He laid these on three leaves and sprinkled lime powder over the top, carefully rolling them into small packets. He placed one in his mouth rolling it to his cheek as he handed the others to each of us. George promptly placed one in his mouth and nodded to me to do likewise.

Xarkus then removed a package of cigarette papers

from the box and a cloth sack containing the marijuana. He rolled a joint and lit it, taking a slow drag, pulling the smoke deep into his lungs and held it, closing his eyes and passing the cigarette on to George, who did the same then handed it to me.

By the third joint, the combination of marijuana and betel nut were beginning to have their full effect. The mixture provided an odd feeling of well-being, power, invincibility, and peacefulness, a sensation heightened by the sight of a fine veil of liquid sunshine through the open door. The scene I observed through the open doorway appeared surreal by the presence of the woman working on the stoop and the naked children frolicking in the yard not caring that a gentle rain was falling on their game.

Nothing had been said as we passed this time until Xarkus turned to me, "So, you want to maybe make some purchases?"

"Maybe; what I have on board my boat is running low, and what you have is excellent quality, though I have nothing to judge against the betel nut."

"It is the best. It is the type we get only from my home at Truk. It is much different from the kind they have in Yap and Palau. Ours is much better. It acts faster because it is not so hard."

Truk Lagoon, I thought. *Now there is a place I would like to see—so much history and adventure over the years.* I opened my mouth to remove the saliva-soaked quid.

"No good," Xarkus said. "Keep it in your cheek all morning. It makes you feel good for a long time."

I nodded and pushed the soggy quid to the back of

my right cheek. "How much for a bag of weed and a bag of nut?"

"Two hundred dollars American money," he answered.

"Too much, I'll give you fifty dollars apiece," I countered, reminded that much of my money had been confiscated only weeks before.

George stood by watching. He did not intend to get into the bargaining. His deal was his deal. I was on my own.

"No, no." Xarkus frowned. "Two hundred is my price, one hundred dollars for each bag."

The haggling continued for another ten minutes when at last I said, "Okay, my final offer is one hundred twenty-five for both bags. Take it or leave it. I've still got a stash on board. It may be running low, but I don't need yours."

In the end, Xarkus' greed got the better of him. His scowl deepened but he nodded in agreement.

I can now see what I could only then guess. He had gotten the best of the bargain. I looked at George, whose nod revealed nothing.

"Maybe later, when you see how good my stuff is, you'll want something better. I can get you anything you want. You want opium? I can get it."

"No. I never use anything but marijuana," I lied. "The other stuff is too dangerous. You lose control."

At that point, I wanted to get the conversation away

from the talk of drugs, recalling with pain the experience of my wife. "I'm going to be on the island for a few days, Xarkus. Maybe you could rent me your car?"

"No, but my son could drive you, if the price is right."

The haggling began again in earnest. We settled on a price of ten dollars per day. The son I learned was a young man in his late teens, maybe twenty, who had been on the stoop during some period of our visit.

"Hiroki," Xarkus yelled, "come in here."

The boy entered. He had the same droopy-eyed appearance as his father only slimmer, his hair in the Afro style of American blacks. "Did you hear?"

"Yeah."

"You do what he says. He's a friend of George. He's a friend of mine."

"Yeah."

I turned to him. "Hiroki, is that your name?"

"Well, you heard him call me that. You got a hearing problem?"

Xarkus struck the boy on the ear. "You don't talk like that. You hear me?"

The boy dropped his eyes sullenly. "Yeah, I hear you."

"Hiroki, I'm going with George. You pick me up at the dock at seven tonight. I'll give you five dollars at the end of each day. I'll buy the gas. The rest you'll get on my last night here. Got it?"

"Yeah."

George turned the Nissan around in the clearing and headed back up the lane to the main road. I looked at my watch. It was a quarter till eleven.

Seeing that day now, free from the limitation of human frailty, I know my trouble began almost the moment I set foot on the island. The accident of meeting George led me to meet his friends, among them Xarkus and the Trukese community living on Saipan. The instant Xarkus decided I was wealthy, events were put in motion, resulting in my fleeing the island.

Chapter Three

The backside of Saipan, the far side behind Mt. Topachau away from the Philippine Sea, if a tangen-tangen covered jungle island can be thought to have a backside, faced the Pacific Ocean. There was no lagoon on this side. The surf broke with power generated from the Marianas Trench a few miles off shore against coral at the very edge of land.

As I said, the road that led down from the mountain was gentler on the eastern side, winding, curving, first down then up as it slowly descended. From time to time, a narrow road appeared suddenly just after or before a sharp curve; no such features appeared on the steep side. The likelihood of a dwelling similar to that occupied by the Xarkus family on such a lane was great. These locations were marked in most instances with banana, mango, and breadfruit trees in the otherwise seemingly impenetrable woody growth sown by the navy after the war to control erosion. The plant had done its work; only now, it threatened anything left untended for even a few months.

The terrain may be different, but the rising heat and

humidity, the jungle where a man had trouble walking—
if he could at all without the aid of a machete—took me
back to the days of my youth. The difference, of course,
was here no one was shooting at me. The terror I had felt
then was absent now though not altogether forgotten.

I was grateful to George for driving me around the
island. The smell of earth and the shade of trees was a
welcome change from the days at sea where the sun beat
down unmercifully. Even though I relished the sense of
freedom, the lack of complicating relationships one gets
from being alone on a sailboat in the great oceans of the
world, after a few weeks a yearning for land overwhelmed
me. It is land, not the sea, that is our natural habitat, and
it is not the incessant nagging fear associated with being
blown by the wind, albeit under control, but loneliness
that eventually drives us all to terra firma.

"I've got a place I want to show you," George said.
"So far as I am aware, it is unique in all of Micronesia.
Hey, it may be unique in the whole world."

"What's that?"

"You'll see. It isn't far from here." With that, he
turned onto a path, not nearly as broad as the narrow side
roads we had been passing, and with the woody plants
scratching against the side of the Nissan, he drove about
three hundred yards to a spot where the tangen-tangen
became so dense it was impossible to go farther.

"We have to walk from here."

Without further explanation he left the car and
began walking along a footpath toward what I knew was
the direction of the ocean. I followed. The effects of the
screwdrivers, betel nut, and marijuana had me in such a
mellow state it did not occur to me there was any dan-

ger in where we were going. I was curious to see what George thought so spectacular.

We walked only a short distance, not more than a quarter-mile, but the going was not easy descending steeply in places. The brief rain shower, one of those light misting rains that fall while the sky overhead remains sunny, peculiar to tropical islands, left the ground damp and the way slippery. We scrambled down the slope through the wood until at last we came out onto a small beach where I was startled to find the disembodied head of a man. I say disembodied in the very loosest sense of that phrase for in this instance the head had never rested upon the torso of any man or woman. The head was perfectly formed with the features of a Pacific islander seen in profile, carved in stone, carved by unearthly hands, chiseled by wind and water, though how that was possible in such detail is beyond my comprehension. A hundred feet beyond the head the deep water of the Pacific broke on the reef not with a roar but with the deep rumbling sound one might expect from a sleeping giant, a giant without a body.

I stood in awe for a moment then said, "I've never seen such a thing."

"He's called 'Old Man by the Sea.' There is a legend that goes with him. It has something to do with Saipan always being protected from the sea as long as the Old Man stands guard. I can't help but wonder what would happen if a tsunami made landfall on this side of the island, a real possibility with the Marianas Trench just offshore."

The setting was beautiful with nothing in sight except what nature had placed there. The only sound the

loud murmur of the ocean made all the more pleasant
by the gentle breeze blowing in from the water cooling the warmth of the sun, the fearful power of the sea
held at bay by the reef a hundred feet off shore. In all,
it combined the ferocious power of the ocean with the
peacefulness and tranquility of land, a tranquility that I
would soon learn did not really exist. For several minutes
we sat on the beach, neither of us saying a word.

At last I broke the silence. "What's the story? It is
Thursday, and no one seems to be working."

"It's Liberation Day. Working on Saipan has its ben-
efits. First of all, no one here pays U.S. income tax even
though we are technically U.S. citizens. Then, by working for the TT government, we get all the U.S. holidays
plus all the local holidays. Liberation Day is a celebration commemorating the end of the Battle of Saipan in
1944. We also get the Fourth of July off. Most people just
take off the whole week. Yesterday wasn't a holiday, but
since today is, there were a lot of people having health
problems. Even more will call in tomorrow. We refer to
it as having an 'eye' problem. 'I' don't see any reason why
I should work." With the wink of an eye George enjoyed
his bad pun.

"So what happens?" I asked.

"There will be a parade of sorts, lots of picnics, even
sailboat races on Sunday. Nothing like the America's
Cup, mostly just Hobie Cats and a couple of other kinds
in the lagoon. Of course, there will be lots of politics.
It is a Northern Mariana holiday, but most members of
the Congress of Micronesia will be on island along with
dignitaries from the other districts, Palau, Yap, Ponape,
the Marshalls."

"It sounds like I got here at a good time. Maybe I'll stay for a week or so. There isn't much to see or do on some of the places I've stopped. After a couple of days, it is time to move on."

"Well, there will be plenty to do. On Monday, a Japanese cruise ship is calling. There will be legal gambling that night."

"What do you mean by legal gambling?"

"You know, there is always gambling, but organized gambling was outlawed after some unsavory sorts pilfered all the war reparations money from the local people who survived the battle. Now the tables are set up only when cruise ships stop. It's in the best tradition of fleecing tourists."

"How does that work? Who operates the games if you don't have casinos?"

"The Rotary Club, they get a special dispensation from the government. All the money they take in goes for their civic projects, stuff for kids, traffic safety, things like that. The games are completely honest. If anything, the players have an advantage since the folks working the tables are just local businessmen. Most of them like to gamble but don't know much about running the games. I suspect there is a lot of money getting away from them, but then they don't mind. The few times they have the games, enough money is raised for the work they do. After all, there are only about fourteen thousand people living on the island and less than seventy-five miles of roads. How much do they need?"

"Isn't the question how much can you win? It seems to me life is about winning. Money is just how I keep score. I like the thrill of experiencing the unknown. Not

Kent Weatherby

knowing if my hand is good enough but putting money on it anyway."

"I see what you mean. I too get a rush from the uncertainty."

"What about the excitement of seeing the other guy break; doesn't that get you?"

"No. We don't play for stakes that high; you can win or lose several hundred dollars in a poker game, but no one loses more than they can afford."

"You mean to say you've never seen a man desperate."

"Nervous yes; they have to face up to their family. But desperate, no."

"For me, the thrill is more than beating the other guy. The lower you put him down, the higher you go. It is the look of desperation, hopelessness in the eyes of another man that gives me a rush."

"What is the goal then?"

"Suicide; if you break a man far enough, if you truly ruin him, he'll do it, or kill. A man driven to despair will do one or the other."

"You can't mean that. There is enough of a high in just winning when more was at stake than you know you should lose."

"Of course I mean it. I've seen it. I've done it. I've seen men steal and in the process of stealing commit murder. I've known of men who, when cornered afterward, took their own lives." *Or run*, I thought. Sometimes winning and losing had nothing to do with gambling. It had to do with life, and if a man was pushed too far, he might not just kill, he might run as well.

"That's just bravado," George said, not willing to entertain that I was serious. "Let's smoke another joint."

42

I noted George's answer to unpleasantness was either alcohol or drugs.

"Fine, this one is on me," I replied, thankful for the change in the conversation. It bothered me that I'd already said much more than I had intended. With that, I took the makings out of my shoulder bag and began to roll a roach. I would say no more but first would probe George. "You mean to say you've never been pushed to the point where you wondered if taking your own life or killing someone else wasn't an option."

"No, that would be unthinkable."

I paused considering our circumstances. Here we were in the middle of the Pacific far from what others would consider civilization. George's answer sounded good, but something had brought, possibly driven, him here. Was he Catholic? Did he fear the unknown, eternal damnation, if there was such a thing? He certainly did not look like someone who had many options left in life. "Surely, George, there is a reason you have come all the way from the United States out to this all but forgotten outpost to live?"

"We like the quiet, the laid-back lifestyle."

"And nothing more? You are a long way from Los Angeles. Are you sure you aren't trying to get away from something?"

Now irritated, George snapped back, "What about you? It strikes me that you are farther from home than we are?"

"Ah, but my circumstances are different. I don't need to work. I can do whatever I want, and what I want is to enjoy life to the fullest, so I sail my boat stopping wherever I choose and partake of the culture, taking everything there is, often things not openly given, and then move on. I'm not tied to one place, to one person, to one job. I am free, totally and completely free in a way you don't understand."

George did not respond.

For the next half hour we lay back on the grainy volcanic and coral sand watching the clouds float by letting the warmth of the sun relax our bodies as the marijuana numbed our brains. My mind drifted with the clouds back to a time I had not mentioned to George, a time when I had close firsthand knowledge of the drive to kill. It was not always money that led men to kill.

It was half past twelve when we left the Old Man and walked back to the car. George continued his sporadic drive around the island stopping at local bars where he seemed always to be recognized as a friend. The bars we visited were mostly small, dark places with a half dozen shirtless, shoeless men drinking beer, frequently speaking a language I did not understand. At each bar I stood for drinks but was not accepted for anything other than the source of another round of beer.

I later heard talk about how I had been an observer of the culture. Do not believe it. I saw and heard nothing worth remembering with the exception of one American, a short, burly man in his mid- to late thirties who walked into one of the bars, picked a fight with the largest Palauan man present, and proceeded to pummel him into the dirt floor for no other reason than he was able to do so.

At last George said, "I suppose I really ought to take you over to the airport. The immigration and customs people will want to do their thing. It will go quickly since I'm with you. I doubt they will even want to go on your boat since it is a holiday. The only reason any of them is working is the Air Mike flight through the islands comes in today from Hawaii. They will be busy with those folks and won't want to waste their time with you."

George was as good as his word. The airport came as a surprise to me. Up till then I had thought of Saipan as just another of those out-of-the-way places that you only reached with great difficulty and then by small aircraft. What awaited me was a huge modern building, the newest on the island along with the Continental Hotel. Like the hotel, it took advantage of the tropical climate. Much of the building was open to the air with a beautiful bar on the second floor.

We parked in the landscaped parking lot, ours being one of only a dozen vehicles, and walked the few feet from the car to the terminal. The immigration and customs officer spoke to George as we entered the ground floor office, looked at the passport I gave him, stamped it, and returned it to me.

"Mr. Henri Gener, welcome to Saipan. I hope your stay with us will be a pleasant one."

I now see that we had no more than left the office when the man reached for the telephone and made several calls reporting my arrival. Good as my forged passport was, he had noticed a flaw in the document, a level of sophistication I had not expected on the island from what I believed to be a low-level bureaucrat. Even with his suspicions aroused, he saw no reason to deny my entry. After all, a member of the TTPI Attorney General's office accompanied me, and this was Saipan, where the granting of favors was commonplace. Nevertheless, protocol required him to report to his superiors in the Office of Immigration and Customs on Capitol Hill, along with calls to the Northern Marianas police and Micronesian Bureau of Investigation.

At last, late in mid-afternoon, George completed his tour of the island. If we missed a bar along the way, it could only be attributed to the fact he did not know it existed. Driving down Middle Road in the direction of what I assumed to be the dock, George suggested we meet for dinner at a place called Hamilton's, a steakhouse located somewhere in the hills off to the right, which he indicated with the wave of his hand, as we drove along.

"Just tell Hiroki to take you to Hamilton's. He knows the way. I'll get a party together. We'll be there a little after seven. Don't worry if you're late. They have a good bar."

It was obvious to me that George had a never-ending capacity for recreational drugs and alcohol. Little wonder he lived on an island far away from the restrictions of an enforced life. My thoughts returned to the vision of Beth leaning forward into the refrigerator. Just how much satisfaction could a woman like that get from a man who was clearly a lush? Possibly I was going to see more of Beth than I'd been led to believe. I wondered how George would take being cuckolded. Surely it wasn't a new experience for him.

I have heard it said that there are four main drives in

a man: food, sleep, sex, and religion. I intended to satisfy three of the four that night, but religion had nothing to do with my plans.

Chapter Four

It was nearing five when we returned to the *Monique*. I was surprised to see the orange Charger parked beside the boat, clearly visible from a quarter-mile distance as we drove down the road approaching the dock. I felt certain the boy had been snooping around the boat. As we turned left at the entrance to Charlie Dock, Hiroki saw us and quickly leapt from the deck of the boat onto the dock, losing his balance as he did so, landing roughly on his hands and knees. Rising, embarrassed, he walked toward us as I got out of the car. Without waiting, George turned the Nissan around and drove away down Beach Road.

"What are you doing?" I demanded.

"I was down this way and thought I'd take a look at your boat. I've never seen one as nice as this," he said, nervous, eyes avoiding me, making a feeble attempt to cover up the fact that he had been on the boat.

"I don't want you on the boat if I'm not here," I responded, a tone of malice creeping into my voice through clenched teeth, knowing he had not seen anything since I had locked the hatch leading to the cabin.

Still, I did not want him poking around things he did not understand or should not see. Accidents happened at sea when people who did not know what they were doing got to messing around with a boat. "People have been known to get hurt, seriously hurt, snooping around where they don't belong," I concluded.

I paused to allow my words to sink in. It may be I waited too long, for then, in a complete change of attitude from what he had exhibited only a few hours earlier, he looked me in the eye, understanding my verbal reprimand was all he would get. He replied, smiling, "Hey, it's okay, I understand. I didn't mean any harm. It is just a great boat."

What a fool I was. The sudden change in attitude so disarmed me I answered in a calm voice, without malice and no longer threatening, "You're right there. It is my home, and you know what they say about a man's home being his castle. A man has the right to defend his castle. Some folks would even say he has the right to shoot a trespasser."

"You don't have to worry about me. I was just looking."

"Yeah, I know." Then changing the subject I said, "Come back for me at seven. I'm meeting people at a place called Hamilton's for dinner. Do you know where it's located?"

"Sure, everyone on Saipan knows Hamilton's."

"How long will it take to get there from here?" I asked knowing that it could not be more than a few minutes. After all, the driving time completely around the island would not have taken much more than a half hour if we had gone nonstop.

"Not long, maybe ten minutes. It depends on traffic." He was grinning in an ingratiating manner, shoulders relaxed now, body released from the tension as he talked his way out of the discomfort of being caught.

"Good, be back at seven."

I looked forward to seeing Beth again. Following a wash-up and nap, I changed from my sea attire into white trousers and Tamarisk shirt open to the second button showing my well-tanned chest set off by an expensive gold chain. I changed dirty deck shoes to expensive brown alligator loafers but without socks. Taking a straight razor, I trimmed my hair for the first time in over two months and brushed it. A look in the mirror pleased me. Pleased by my appearance and the scent of expensive cologne, I felt confident that, if not tonight, soon I would in fact see much more of Beth Rowley.

Promptly at seven twenty, for on an island all time is relative, Hiroki arrived. He offered no explanation for being late. Experience told me there was no point in pressing him. Whatever he said would just be an excuse when the truth was he had no reason other than indolence. We drove away, and just as he said, the trip from Charlie Dock to Hamilton's Restaurant took less than ten minutes. Along the way down Beach Road, we met two cars near the entrance to the Continental Hotel, but no other traffic was encountered until we turned off Middle Road. According to Hiroki, traffic was light. We followed the narrow road to the very edge of the foothills. Finally, as we neared the end of the driveway, I saw ten or eleven cars drawn up around a wooden building that looked more like a large house than a working restaurant. It was half past seven.

"Wait here. If I don't need you anymore tonight, I'll send someone to tell you." With that abrupt comment, I walked up the three broad steps that led to the doorway and entered the building. The dining room was crowded, and as I looked around, I could not see either George or Beth.

"There you are, Henri Gener, over here," George called. "I called a few people and thought we'd make a party out of your arrival on the island. You know island life, any excuse for a party. We had just about given up on you; thought maybe you'd changed your mind."

"Oh no, my driver, Hiroki, was fashionably late."

"Well, after all your time at sea and stopping at small islands, I'm sure you didn't believe he would be on time."

I wondered, *Have I told him I stopped on small islands or is he fishing?* I answered, "Not really, but when you are paying someone to drive you, they should be on time."

The group of four couples was seated at a long table along the rear wall of the room, a room devoid of luxury, with steel and Formica tables, chairs covered with a cheap dark red plastic, and original cowboy oils by someone named Knife hanging on the walls. Ceiling fans gently moved the humid air. Lighting was intentionally low, more for the purpose of reducing heat than atmosphere. Cowboy art aside it reminded me of a dozen places I had visited on a dozen different islands.

George spoke first, "Don't be put off by the décor. The food is great. They serve the best steak on the island."

The men were from the poker party of the night before, all with their wives, except for a young woman Beth introduced as Sydna. "Sydna works as a secretary in the AG's office. She's one of the few secretaries on island who still takes dictation." The discrete wink said, *Not me; her. I'd hate to see you deprived.*

I smiled, turning my attention to Sydna. Her white cotton peasant blouse had a scoop neckline so that, as I leaned forward to greet her, I was greeted with a pleasant view. "Tu as de beaux seins," I commented.

Without a moment's thought and much to my surprise, Sydna replied in halting French, "Tu es completement grossier."

In English I responded, "Nevertheless, a most pleasant view."

"Possibly I've not understood," she answered playfully. "After all, my French isn't very good."

"No, no, you were quite correct. Nevertheless, you were no more correct than I was. It is a compliment, is it not?"

The man sitting next to Sydna rose with a jerk. He was an imposing man standing more than six and a half feet tall. He was agitated. "I'm Mark Meriday. Sydna is with me." The thought occurred to me that by stating the obvious he must have doubts.

A second man rose from his chair. "My name is Ferd, Ferd Meier, and this is my wife." The fact that plump, pasty Ferd did not tell me his wife's name amused me. Like Ferd, she had not missed many meals.

"So where'd you come from?" the heavyset man named Ferd asked.

"The sea. I'm from the sea."

"Yeah, we all figured that, but where from, Henri?"

"Oh, here and there, I've been sailing for months.

What about you, Ferd? I don't think I've ever met anyone named Ferd before."

He answered, "It makes even less sense when you know my full name, Ferdinand Meier. Now what kind of name is that for someone with German blood," oblivious to the fact that many Germans were named Ferdinand.

His wife answered, "Well, they could have named you Sue like that song 'A boy named Sue.'"

Ferd frowned.

Sydna enjoined, "Don't be so stuffy, Ferd. It's better than Ferd, Ferd the Nerd."

They all laughed. Ferd's neck reddened with the appearance of hackles, but he said nothing.

Drinks were ordered, and moments later a man the others called "Ham," undoubtedly Hamilton, appeared from the back. "The rib eyes are good, fresh from Australia. They came in on the barge from Guam yesterday. I think you'll like them, grain-fed and marbled, not the grass-fed dairy steers we get from Tinian."

My companions exchanged glances and nodded in approval. "Oletta," the man named Ham called out, "take these people's orders."

Orders were placed. Everyone followed Ham's advice. I ordered three bottles of the best Bordeaux they had in stock to be followed after dinner by a bottle of Delord Freres Armagnac, 1974, surprised at the sophistication of Ham's bar.

Conversation was lively at dinner, George and the man named Mark regaling the group with stories of their exploits years before as members of the Los Angeles police and sheriff's department, during the days leading up to and during the Watts Riots. They referred to it as "when we were in the cops." The two men had been friends from that time, forging a bond that led them both to the storefront law schools that existed in Los Angeles and finally to the islands where their indolence, vices, and passion for sailing, novice though it was, could be indulged.

The third member of the poker party was the man I knew as Ferd, who gave the impression of being a perpetual victim, a short, soft, puffy accountant in the Treasury Department, a man whose pasty complexion seemed completely out of place on a tropical island. After his initial attempt to be engaging, he had withdrawn, sullen and hurt.

Dinner concluded; Jonathan Cartwright, the fourth member of the poker party, lit a Tobacalara cigar and, breathing in the aroma of the cognac, said, "This is an excellent choice, Henri. We thank you for your hospitality and your company. It has been a most enjoyable evening." Until that moment Cartwright had been the quietest member of our group, a man like me content to sit back and observe others.

"And so, Jonathan," I began, "what is it you do on Saipan?"

"I have a dual position here. I work on the transition team helping the Northern Marianas government move from the Trust Territory into their status as a U.S. commonwealth. The people of the Northern Marianas voted to break away from the TT and adopt an independent relationship with the United States. It is quite a lengthy process, and there is a good deal of detail necessary to separate functions from one government to another. I also work for Ambassador Williamson on the status talks with the other districts."

"And what might that entail?"

"Many things," he added vaguely. "Technically I'm an employee of the Interior Department in Washington but am TDY to 'State.' Setting up the government here and having the proper liaison with Washington is a little tricky. We want to be certain we have it right."

He is as coy about his answers as I am, I thought to myself. "And what is it you do for the ambassador?"

"Oh, it is much the same only in a more preliminary way. The relationship with the other districts is in an embryonic state. Each district will make decisions, and then they will undoubtedly make some joint or unified decisions. I'm just here to help the ambassador ana-lyze the situation. You could say I'm a sort of glorified 'go-fer.'"

"I am not familiar with your word 'go-fer.' What does it mean? I was under the belief a gopher was a small rodent of some kind."

"Right you are. But in this context, a 'go-fer' is a per-son who runs errands, gets things, you know, go-fer this, go-fer that, does whatever his boss needs. You see, he goes 'fer' things. That pretty well describes my position." I caught the light snap in his eyes as he gave me the answer.

He believes he has taken me off the thread of my question, I reasoned. He could not be more wrong. "It must be a most interesting job, this being a 'go-fer.' I imagine you are involved in virtually every aspect of the discussions. Your ambassador must trust you implicitly."

"In a way I suppose he does. He's my uncle. He and

my mother are brother and sister. I don't suppose I would have the job otherwise." With that piece of personal explanation, he seemed to be saying, *Enough is enough. I do not intend to answer any more of your questions on this topic.*

I eyed my four male companions. They were certainly all very different, not just physically but emotionally, intellectually, professionally. George and Mark had the air of men who were content to be perceived as big fish in small waters, too weak, lacking in ambition to succeed on a large scale. I had already seen enough of George to know he had respect for the law only to the extent he was able to stay above it. Both he and Mark were men who used their positions in law enforcement to promote themselves while continuing to indulge their secret attraction for the seedier side of life. From their conversation, it was obvious they had acquaintances, business dealings, with every level of island culture from the American-dominated government officials to the local leaders.

As for Ferd, I wondered what he had in common with George and Mark and, for that matter, especially Jonathan Cartwright. Was it just that his name, Ferd, rhymed with the slang word in American vernacular that described his personality, his relationship to the others? Did they tolerate him just for comic relief? Was he merely someone so starved for attention he could be humiliated any time someone chose? I would be willing to wager he was routinely the big loser in the poker games.

Finally, there was Jonathan Cartwright. He was the truly odd one in the group. A man like that was out of place on an island such as this, in this crowd especially.

Jonathan was a man with substance, clearly educated, probably in a prestigious university. There was no mistaking the physical carriage, the confidence, the sophisticated wife. There was something about him that spoke of old money and big houses with servants. In his late twenties or early thirties, he reminded me of the people in my past.

As I looked at him, it occurred to me he resembled a younger version of my father as I now remembered him, only not bowed by the stress of open conflict. Given another ten years, I wondered if I could tell them apart, both dedicated to a cause they deeply believed right, willing to make great sacrifice to see it to the end. How like him, them, I once was. How unlike them both I had become!

Suddenly conscious of Sydna's warm hand on the inside of my thigh, I thought to myself, *So, Sydna is here with Mark Meriday but has no intention of staying with him. Why should she? The man is a buffoon, a loud-mouth buffoon at that. It shouldn't be too difficult to get rid of him, leaving Sydna all to me. Tonight there will be fresh bread. Not Beth tonight, but younger, fresh bread.*

Chapter Five

By the time I awoke the following morning, the sun had been above the mountain for a half hour casting the kind of soft light you only see on land in the early morning. Three things were apparent that morning: the coolness of the day, something you did not experience at sea where the sun seemed to jump into the sky with its heat searing down on you; the smell of the earth, an olio of scents, flowers, trees, moldy soil, fungi all mixed with the damp decay of fallen foliage, an aroma not missed during weeks and months at sea yet one you never failed to notice as you approached land, a smell both alien and comforting; and finally, the smell of a woman, clean and erotic. The feeling of contentment soon lulled me back to sleep. I dreamed the woman next to me was my wife, but I knew that could not be, or could it? I was dreaming, just that. The woman Sydna lay beside me, the tension in my body gone for the moment. Her back was turned toward me, her body curled into the hook of my own.

As she woke and rolled over toward me, the tension returned, and we copulated once more. I do not say we made love, for there was nothing of love in the act. It was for me the same desire for pleasure, a primal instinct to mate, that any animal had when the female of the species came into heat. This was an act I would repeat as often as I could while I stayed on any island, not knowing after I set sail when I would be able to experience the complete yet transitory fulfillment the act gave me. It was the enthusiasm, the intensity, of my performance that women found satisfying rather than in any fulfillment I gave them.

Finished, I rose from the bed and with my back turned to the woman pulled on my shorts. She rolled across the bed and touched my left shoulder at the place where the insect had been tattooed years before with its stinger poised over its back ready to strike. "Well, isn't that pretty, poised to strike too. I've never seen anything like it; is there a reason for it?" She laughed.

I dressed quickly before answering. When I did, I ignored her comment reflecting privately on the black scorpion that now identified me. I had considered removing it or at least altering it, but my ego would not permit it. The mark, I felt, was one of distinction given many years earlier. "I'm going on deck to meditate. I suppose you will be going soon."

At the same time, on the other side of the island, barely four miles as a bird flies but farther by road, Hiroki turned down the lane leading to the Xarkus house. After he dropped me at the dock the night before, he had proceeded to meet friends and spent the night drinking. The sound of the approaching Dodge roused his father, who met him as the car came to a stop.

"Where have you been all night? What did you learn?"

"That man, the Frenchman, his name is Henry something-or-the-other. It sounds kind of funny. He had me take him to Hamilton's where he met up with some friends of George Rowley. There were three other men, but I didn't know two of them. Mark Meriday was there and some women. The Frenchman cut me loose at about eleven thirty. He wanted me to get out of there as soon as we got back to the boat. I think maybe he'd picked up the woman with Meriday and was spending the night with her, so I met up with friends and we had some beers and then slept on the beach."

"And that's all. You didn't learn anything else?"

"Well, yeah, I did. I waited until Hamilton's closed, and then I went back and picked up Oleta, you know, the waitress. She told me the other two men were some guy named Ferd who works in the TT Finance office and the other guy is some big shot working on the transition and with the ambassador. His name is Cartwright."

Xarkus let his son talk and did not tell him he already knew who Cartwright was. "Did you find out what they talked about?"

"The Frenchman is real particular about where I spend my time. He doesn't want me hanging around where I can hear what he is saying. But Oleta said they just talked about a lot of nothing until the Frenchman and Cartwright got into a conversation. She said it looked like those two were kind of feeling each other out, you know, trying to figure out who—"

"Is that all?"

"Yeah."

"What about the boat; did you get on it?"

"I tried, like you said, but the hatch was locked. I looked around on deck but didn't see anything there. It is a fancy boat though. It has a wooden hull, teak, I think, with lots of brass fittings. It looks sturdy enough for our waters, but I wouldn't want to sit out a typhoon in it. It's not that big! From the condition of the varnish and the tarnish on the brass, I'd say she had been at sea for a long time."

"Anything else?"

"Uh-huh, the Frenchman came back to the boat while I was on deck and got scary mad."

"What did you do?"

"I covered it up pretty well, I think. I told him I thought the boat was really nice and I wanted to get a close look, like I'd never seen one like it before."

"Did he buy it?"

"I think so. He told me to pick him up today at about ten. I'm going to have Mother fix me some breakfast. Then I'll go down there and get him."

Xarkus looked at Hiroki with a mixed look, satisfaction that he had done what he was told and dismay that he had not been able to learn more. "Stick close to him today. You know what we want, but I don't want to risk anything if there isn't going to be a good payday at the end."

Now I see Mark Meriday rise from the queen-size waterbed in Unit 8 of the Pink Apartments at the foot of Navy Hill on the floor above and at the far end of the building from Sydna's apartment. Mark felt betrayed by his friends. George and Beth knew he had a thing for Sydna, and they set up the dinner at Hamilton's for the sole purpose of getting Sydna and that Frenchman together.

Mark had invested three months in his courtship of Sydna since she arrived on the island from Eureka, California, fresh from a divorce. Recruited by the TT liaison office in San Francisco, she worked as a secretary in the office of the attorney general. Mark felt it inappropriate for him to move in on her rapidly, not so much out of concern for her as worry that he would be accused of sexual harassment if he showed too much interest too soon. As an attorney in the office, having any form of sexual relationship with her until a reasonable time had elapsed could prove costly. Now he understood he had waited too long. The Frenchman had not waited. He had moved in the moment he laid eyes on her.

Mark did not rise from the bed to check whether her car was still parked in the lot below. He knew it would be gone. Sparks were flying between her and the Frenchman when they had all left Hamilton's. She had dumped Mark as soon as they got back to the Pink Apartments. Minutes later he heard her car leave the parking lot. George and Beth had arranged for her to go with the Frenchman. At least he would not have to be humiliated by facing her at the office. He felt an "I" problem coming on.

Chapter Six

Of the four poker players, only Jonathan Cartwright and Ferd Meier went to work that Friday. Jonathan went in early to get the cables from the State Department as well as those sent in the name of the State Department. All three looked routine enough to the machine operator who always read them, for that matter read everything, especially when it was sent by or to someone the bureaucracy designated as important whether he agreed or not.

These three addressed to Jonathan appeared to the machine operator to be the usual diplomatic drivel. *That Cartwright guy must be incredibly lucky to be born into a privileged family,* he thought as he placed the documents in the slot marked for Ambassador Williamson. *Preppy college boy, thinks he's better than everyone else. Talks funny too. If it was not for the fact he was related to the ambassador, I doubt he would even have a job.* The only messages he got were boring housekeeping crap.

To anyone with even a modicum of sophistication, something lacking in the operator, the message and its recipient would have set off an alarm. The messages provided a background to the casual observer, against which the one disguised important message lost its significance.

As Jonathan entered the cable office, he inquired, "Anything for me?"

"It's in the box," the operator replied without looking at Jonathan, thinking, *Good grief, who cares? He is the only person on the island who insists on wearing a suit, white shirt, and tie to his office. Not even the high commissioner or the ambassador, when he is on island, does that.* If he had looked, he would have seen that that day Jonathan Cartwright was wearing khaki chinos and a powder-blue knit shirt.

Jonathan walked to the box without saying anything more and removed the three one-page documents from their slot. As he retreated to the door leading into the main hallway of the headquarters building, he tossed off, "Thanks." He continued with a deliberate pace up the stairs to his second-floor State Department liaison office, next door to that of the high commissioner, where he unlocked his desk, removed a code book, and, tossing aside two of the sheets of paper, proceeded to read the only real message he received. Once he had finished, he took out a blank cable form from his desk and referring to the codebook wrote his response. This message he placed in the "urgent" outbox to be sent the same day. Since there was an eight-hour time lapse between Saipan and Washington, there was no hurry for routine messages, but this message was one requiring an immediate response. He then returned to his office.

When the operator sent the message minutes later, he once more thought, *Urgent—yeah right! As if anyone cares. Good grief, he can't even write a message that makes sense, and he wants it sent out with the important communications.* However, at the other end someone would care.

Unknown to Jonathan Cartwright, there was another man working that morning on the second floor of the headquarters building. In the Attorney General's wing, the Director of the Micronesian Bureau of Investigation was following up on a phone call he had received from Immigration the previous afternoon concerning a Frenchman who had arrived on the island the previous day. The name Henri Gener sounded familiar, and when he looked through his files from Interpol, he found a man using that name. He also found that the man had last been seen on a sailing vessel, a ketch, with the name "Monique" painted on the stern.

He studied the flier for a few moments and then prepared a cable message to the FBI. Though not directly in his chain of command, it was the director's policy to coordinate closely. The lessons learned as an army intelligence officer and embassy military liaison were never wasted, though his thick body and jovial demeanor were sometimes mistaken for good-natured incompetence.

"Man identified, Henri Gener, carrying French passport arrived by private sailing yacht, *Monique*, on Saipan Island. Ushered through immigration and customs by assistant attorney general for the TTPI. Connection unknown at this time. Advise."

Leaving the cable office, MBI Director Leroy Harkins walked down the hall, turned the corner at the lobby, and walked into the high commissioner's wing, where he found Jonathan Cartwright.

Entering the office, he closed the door. "Something's

up, and I thought you should know about it." Director Harkins' experience led him to recognize there was more to Cartwright than met the eye. It would not hurt to keep him informed. Who knew, if Harkins was right, keeping Cartwright up to speed might even help get Harkins the job he really wanted in Manila. "I suppose you've heard about this Frenchman who arrived on island yesterday, the one sailing the boat in the harbor. I was checking my files, and it seems the name Henri Gener and the sailboat *Monique* appear on some fliers out of Europe. I've sent a cable to the FBI and thought I'd pass along the info. You never know when someone like this might be of interest to 'State.'" Only Harkins did not really believe State would be the least bit interested.

On the ground floor of headquarters, Ferdinand Meier was the first one to arrive at the TT Finance office that Friday morning. In fact, he was only one of the four employees in a department with a staff of eighty-three who came to work that day. Even eight of the eleven Americans, all high-ranking accountants, had called in with an "I" problem.

The Director of Finance had scheduled a meeting knowing, under holiday conditions, their conversation would not be overheard. He wanted to discuss the latest efforts to reconcile the hopelessly jumbled financial accounts he had inherited when he accepted the appointment by the Secretary of Interior in Washington. He knew tax receipts were virtually nonexistent in the Trust Territory and that the revenue to run the government came directly from the U.S. Treasury. The trouble was the money that came had only the scantest controls attached. To make matters worse, whenever the TT government needed money, all they had to do was write a check. It did not matter whether there was money in the TT treasury. If there was not, Uncle Sam simply paid the overdraft.

On his arrival, the new director designated Ferd Meier, as the longest-tenured employee, to head up an ad hoc committee to bring some semblance of order and figure out exactly where the money came from and where it went. In the event of an audit on his watch, he knew he would be the designated felon when it was discovered the accounts could not be reconciled. He had been a fool to accept the position even for a two-year term without first having a completed audit before his arrival and assumption of duties. Money was gone, unaccountably gone, and no one either could or would say where. Now it was impossible to go back, and all the sins of his predecessors were his to atone. At the very least, beginning a review now would mitigate in his favor and cover him for any future misappropriations.

His appointment of Ferd seemed logical at the time. Who could know more about the TT's finances than him? Yet something was wrong. As the review dragged on without any resolution or meaningful conclusions, the director began to suspect something else was amiss; just possibly, the long-standing employee, the one he had appointed to oversee the review, the one whose tenure outdated the other ten *haoles*, was the biggest thief.

Virtually everyone on island knew that Ferd drank too much, gambled too much, and traveled off-island more often than most. He looked continually for an excuse to go back to the states or to some Pacific Rim conference. What they did not know was the extent of his vices or the seemingly limitless appetite he had for not only those but also a whole list of others he only indulged when he was off the island.

Ferd was now nearing the end of his eighth two-year contract with the Trust Territory, and although he desperately wanted to return home to Nebraska, he knew he was trapped. If he left, his theft would be discovered. If he stayed and the Trust Territory ultimately dissolved according to the timetable he understood from Jonathan, he would be discovered and ruined anyway. For Ferd the answer was easy: steal more, faster, and hide the money in some numbered account, and when the time came, run. The problem was there was no numbered account. There was no money. What he got went through his hands like water through a leaky cup.

Dissolution was still over a decade away, and at the rate of thirty thousand dollars a year, he would have enough to disappear, maybe not in style but disappear. The problem was that Ferd's appetites never allowed him to hide away the thirty thousand a year he thought would do the trick. Every year he embezzled more and, like the U.S. national debt, each year saw more and more used to hide the excess of the preceding year.

Why did the Secretary of Interior appoint this Honest John, a seemingly competent one, to be Director of Finance now? Ferd wondered, *What do I do?* Who could he trust? Certainly not anyone on the island. Well, maybe, just maybe this Frenchman could be of some help, but he would have to play his cards carefully.

The meeting droned on. Resolution of the audit

problem lie a long way off so long as Ferd was in control, and he believed he could control the study, but headway had to be shown or else he would be removed from this critical job. If only he could stop the inquiry altogether. Ferd knew that was impossible short of some accident to the director, but could he do that? All he had to do was keep making certain the director did not do anything foolish like initiate meaningful controls from now on. Ferd's main objective was not to make any mistakes and be certain everything continued to work just as it had since he got here. Theft had been a time-honored precedent among his predecessors before he got here. The only person who seemed to care was the new guy at the top. Ferd knew he had to have time but feared time was already running out.

At last the meeting ended. The director and assistant director stayed behind after Ferd had gone. The director spoke first. "Do you think he's on to us? Do you think he has even a hint that we suspect him of being the culprit?"

"Not a chance," the other responded. "Ferd is really a pretty arrogant guy beneath that nerdy exterior. He thinks he is smarter than everyone else is and is out to prove it. Why else would he be taking the chances he is? Good grief, there are only fourteen thousand of us on this rock. Surely we're not alone in noticing his gambling. I really believe the guy thinks running the investigation out, bringing us phony reports of what he is investigating, will give him time to cover his tracks."

The director added, "Yeah, that makes sense. It makes our real work even easier. We just let him eliminate the ways he is not stealing. It leaves us with fewer trails to follow and gives him less time to plan on running, if that is what he tries."

"Thankfully we can tick off three more trails with the report today. He is going to run out of phony leads soon." With that, the assistant director left the room. Smiling as he left, he called back, "See you next time for chapter twenty of the continuing saga of Ferd Meier."

When George Rowley awoke on that second morning, the main things on his mind were vodka, pot, and the poker party he planned to attend with Ferd and the Frenchman at the home of a Palauan senator, Yasoru Nakamura, that evening. George was delighted the Frenchman agreed to play. He liked Gener and was curious to see him in action at the table. Besides, it would give them an excuse to leave Mark Meriday out of the game.

Mark had been clearly upset at the end of the evening. The attention Sydna paid to the Frenchman had caused a reaction George had not seen for several years, not since the incident with that girl in California, what was her name? Nakamura had asked George to invite two more players. Gener would be one, but who else? Jonathan Cartwright would never agree to interact on that informal basis with any of his counterparts in status negotiations. Besides, he hardly ever played two nights in a week. His wife would not stand for it. Maybe he should give him a call anyway, though. He then turned his thoughts to the Frenchman. No one knew anything about the way he played cards, but even if he were good, the winnings would undoubtedly be split, and Ferd could always be counted on to drop a couple hundred in a bad night, in a good night up to a grand. George wondered, *Where'd he get the money anyway? Certainly not on his salary as a contract employee of the government, not on twenty-two thousand a year.*

At Charlie Dock, it promised to be another beautiful day in paradise. The woman Sydna had left three hours earlier, going first to the Pink Apartments to dress then up Capitol Hill to the office of the Attorney General. The sky was a pale blue with wispy cirrus clouds pointing a gentle breeze from the direction of the Philippine Sea. If I had been at sea, I would have gauged the wind on the Beaufort scale, the way seafaring men had for decades, at force two. A light breeze caressed my face, and as I looked toward the lagoon, small wavelets moved lazily toward the beach. I went below. There I retrieved a passport and letter of credit from the Swiss bank where I had a numbered account and checked my barometer. It was holding steady, no storm, at least for now.

I reveled in days such as this at sea aboard *Monique*. There was little to do, and the surface of the water allowed for time on deck air-drying bedding and clothes washed in seawater. These I left hanging on the spars while the wind freshened and the salt clinging to the cloth dried and blew away. On the days when wind registered force zero or force one, when *Monique* and I were moving slowly, I would strip off my clothes and lie on deck enjoying the gentle undulation as my boat rose and fell with the swells, nearly imperceptible, always mindful that if I went overboard I might not be able to swim back to the boat as she drifted along. Therefore, on those occasions, I tied two hundred feet of line around my waist and would exercise by dropping into the water and swimming until the line drew taut then swam back to the boat. I would repeat the movement for sometimes as long as an hour. The thought of my lifeline comforted me. If *Monique* suddenly moved beyond my ability to swim back, all I had to do was tow myself to her safety.

I thought of other days when the sea was still. Lying for days on a becalmed sailboat carries with it a kind of peace, the sun warm, the sky cloudless, utter stillness. The water was not just still; it appeared to be liquid carpeting inviting me to step out onto its shiny blue surface, not a ripple disturbing it. Of course, to do so would be testing Poseidon, and so I resisted. Not even sharks that inhabit these latitudes far from land, endlessly searching for the chain of food on which they are dependent, could disquiet my reverie on days like that.

On this day, I began with yoga exercise on deck and then spent a couple of hours diving to caress *Monique* by scraping barnacles from her hull. At ten o'clock, when Hiroki arrived, I had dressed. Not seeing my money clip, I shoved two twenties from the bulkhead safe into my pocket. I told him to drive me to the Bank of America branch office in Susupe. He drove away from the dock, turned right onto Beach Road, then proceeded past the Continental and Inter-Continental hotels and the ruins of the old church at Garapan with its skeleton bell tower standing starkly against the palm trees, a reminder of the war that had been fought on this island three decades earlier. As we approached the commercial part of the island, a part I had heretofore not seen, an old DC-3 airplane passed overhead.

"What was that?" I asked.

Hiroki answered, "That is the Trust Territory plane. The high commissioner uses it to fly between the districts sometimes, but mostly he just uses it to go to Guam. He's been off the island for a few days down to Truk, and he must be coming back."

We continued in silence for another minute before I asked, "Truk must be an interesting place. How long have you lived here on Saipan?" I wanted to ask about Truk but decided to go at it in an indirect manner.

"We've lived here since I was eleven."

"Ah, then I don't suppose you have many memories of Truk and its famous lagoon."

"Not too many. We go there about once a year, but the trips are taken up with family celebrations."

"Have you ever done any diving while you were there?" I asked. My curiosity for the place piqued.

"No, we fish some but not much. There are too many sharks in the water. Here we are." Hiroki turned the car across the road coming to a stop at a row of single-story businesses. The center business in the building had the name "Bank of America, Saipan Branch" stenciled on the window and a small painted sign announcing the same information fixed to the wall above the glass front.

"Wait here," I said. "I won't be long."

Walking into the bank, the mean appearance of the place struck me. One large room with teller windows toward the rear and two desks on either side of the main door for officers dominated my view.

"You must be Henri Gener, the Frenchman I heard

arrived yesterday." With that greeting, a thirty-some-thing American moved toward me, hand extended.

"Yes, but how did you know?"

"On an island this small the banker knows and hears about everything. You've been here over twenty-four hours. I heard last night."

I did not smile. With a serious expression, I answered, "I trust my business will remain my business. It certainly isn't for anyone else, just you and me."

"Well, of course. I didn't mean—"

"Is there somewhere we can talk out of the hearing of others?"

"We have a small conference room behind the teller's counter. Come this way."

The conference room, if it could be called that, was small, little more than an expanded closet containing a desk and three chairs, one behind the desk and the others facing it. The branch manager closed the door as we entered, sat behind the desk, and asked, "What is it that we can do for you, M. Gener?"

Handing over the letter of credit and the passport I was carrying, I answered, "I am low on funds and need to make a draw against this."

I noticed the widening of his eyes as he opened the envelope and saw the credit line was for $100,000. "And just how much of a draw did you have in mind?"

"Don't worry," I answered. "I only want five thousand dollars."

The branch manager sat for a while before responding. "I'll have to make arrangements for this with my home office on Guam. It will be Monday before the funds will be available I am afraid."

"You don't keep five thousand on hand?" I asked incredulously.

"Of course, but the paperwork, verification, you understand."

"That's fine," I replied, knowing that unless the weekend activities went especially bad for me I would not need it at all. Moreover, if the weekend went well, I certainly would not need it.

As we walked out of the room, I saw that Hiroki had ignored my instructions. He stood near the door engaged in conversation with a Chamorro girl who worked as teller and secretary for the bank officers.

The branch manager spoke first, "You shouldn't be back here. Customers are to wait at the front of the teller counter unless they are accompanied by an officer."

With eyes cast downward, Hiroki said, "I am very sorry."

I see it all clearly now; Jonathan Cartwright was still in his office when I left the branch bank office. He reflected on both the efficiency of the U.S. government and at the same time marveled at just how compartmentalized it truly had become. The Director of the Micronesia Bureau of Investigation had just left his office after delivering a copy of the message he sent to the FBI headquarters in Washington, D.C. The director apparently wanted him informed, as a nominal employee of the State Department, or possibly the director merely wanted him to know just how clever he had been. Cartwright noticed the heavy set director certainly did not suffer from lack of ego.

Reaching for the black telephone on his desk, he dialed 203. Beth answered.

"Hi, Beth, Jonathan Cartwright here. Is George there?"

"Just a minute, and I'll get him. He's momentarily indisposed."

While he waited, Jonathan reflected his wife was not going to like it if he played cards again tonight. She did not like many things about his activities. Since they were posted to these islands, she believed he had gotten lax in his habits and exercised poor judgment in his choice of companions. It bothered him that the wives did not know what their husbands were doing, but it made sense to keep that information compartmentalized. Too much information in the wrong hands simply led to complications and difficulty. More than one man had been recalled and his career damaged on that account.

"Cartwright, is that you?" It was George Rowley, his voice already thick.

"Right, I got to thinking, is there any chance I can get in the game tonight?"

"Yeah, I'm sure there is. I thought about calling you, but I didn't think your wife would like it, especially knowing where it is we are playing and who with."

"I'll take care of that. Count me in." With that, he hung up the phone and thought, *George is right, I will pay for this.* Caroline's Philadelphia blue blood had run cold ever since the posting to Micronesia. She did not like the climate. She did not like the people. She did not like the isolation. She hated the lack of culture. The smell of Asian markets repulsed and disgusted her. Moreover, she would not tolerate insects and rodents at home, but here they were simply part of life. *Playing cards in the home of a Micronesian politician regardless of the circumstances, which I cannot tell her, is bound to lead to problems.*

Chapter Seven

My first stop after leaving the bank was to deliver gasoline to *Monique*. Even though I preferred to sail only by wind power, there were times when safety dictated use of the engine. Approaching reefs and maneuvering in close proximity to large ships was far too dangerous otherwise. In the event a large ship came between my tiny boat and the wind, I was powerless in the lee of the four or five hundred feet long monster. On more than one occasion, sailing boats had been de-masted, or worse, by just such an accident. Even my arrival on Saipan had been delayed because of a lack of fuel, and so I had Hiroki stop at the Joe Ten store where I purchased the last jerry cans in their inventory.

The Mobil Oil facility located at Charlie Dock had opened late that Friday because of the holiday, and it was half past eleven by the time my onboard tank was topped off, and my four new five-and-a-half-gallon jerry cans were filled. Hiroki helped me carry the cans below where we stowed them aft in the engine room. As he did so, I could not help but notice his interest in everything below deck, moving slowly, much slower than necessary as his eyes darted here and there.

"Can I look around?" he asked.

"What for?" I replied. "You seem to have taken it in already." Then in a moment of carelessness and pride in *Monique*, I continued, "Oh, all right, go ahead."

Impressive as *Monique* is topside, those who see only comfort instead of safety appreciate her below most of all. In Hiroki's case, the outward appearance of the boat overwhelmed his senses, being accustomed to the small craft he had seen on Saipan and at his parents' home at Truk Lagoon. He was completely unprepared for what he saw once we came down the ladder into the passageway leading to the engine room.

Being watertight in a storm, *Monique* was carpeted throughout. Her passageway was paneled in dark teak, hand polished to a deep luster. Her brass fittings below, I kept polished using the activity during the hours at sea to pass the time.

He went all the way aft to begin his exploration, entering my quarters first. When I saw he had gone into my cabin, I quickly ejected him from the large berth. As I followed him from my personal quarters, I noticed I had failed to secure the small bulkhead panel disguising a sort of priest's hole for valuables when I removed the letter of credit, leaving the door ever so slightly ajar. Had he noticed? Possibly. Though, if so, his impassive countenance revealed nothing.

I see now that the instant he entered the cabin he saw both the bulkhead door and my money holder embossed with the fleur-de-lis containing fifty dollars American, all I had left from my expenses of the night before. Knowing he did not have time to explore the hideaway, he picked up the money clip and slipped it into his pocket. Then, almost as an afterthought, he picked up a scrap of paper on which I had handwritten some notes.

As he proceeded along the passageway, he saw the impressive navigation station with the chart rack full of records necessary for my passage, wherever I chose to go. Adjacent to the nav station, there was the second ladder for access to the cockpit where I could steer in relative safety and comfort even during a violent storm, having only to drop below should *Monique* be topped by a rogue wave. Beyond that, I allowed him to poke about a bit in the mid-ships berths, a small single berth to port and a larger one to starboard. When he came to the galley and main salon, he stopped and gasped. The teak bulk-heads were lined with custom-built wine racks, still very nearly full with each expensive bottle carefully secured cork down against even the possibility of my lovely lady being knocked down. I doubt Hiroki had ever tasted any of the wines I had stocked or for that matter any wine at all. The sheer extravagance caused his breath to escape audibly.

After a few moments, he smiled. "Thanks, this is really a great boat. I've never seen one like it up close. How does she handle at sea?"

"There is no problem for one man so long as that man knows what he is doing. Let's get some lunch. It is nearly noon and I'm hungry. You must be too. How about you show me a place you like that captures the island's culture and taste? I'm buying."

Hiroki drove away from Tanapag Harbor, turned left, and followed the winding tree-shaded road I had first traversed with George yesterday morning up Mt. Topachau. We passed the Trust Territory Health Department, housed in the old CIA gymnasium building, then the headquarters building with its blue flag with six stars arranged in a circle in the middle representing the six districts of Palau, Yap, Northern Marianas, Truk, Ponape, and the Marshalls. The flag flew from a ship's mast that served fittingly as a flagpole. Going on we passed the small concrete block building operated as a family-owned grocery.

Hiroki drove on, passing the road that led to the clearing and house with its noisy children playing half-nude in the rising heat, twisting and turning, rising and falling, but always descending ever lower toward the Pacific coast. At last we seemed to level out on a road that roughly followed the coast some fifty feet above the water heading toward what I understood from the preceding day to be San Vicente, a cluster of buildings near the south end of the island.

Just before we reached the village, Hiroki turned right onto a road, no more than a path, and continued for two or three minutes into the foothills of the mountain until he came to a clearing with a half dozen rusting pickup trucks and one expensive American sedan parked around a large typhoon shack. Here he stopped without regard to either the other vehicles or the shack and announced, "This is it. They have the best fruit bat soup on the island here. It is a Palauan bar run by people named Rechucher." As we got out of the Dodge, I heard the sound of music playing and men's voices talking loudly.

We entered the dark building lit only by a single low wattage bulb hanging from a cord in the center of the room. As my eyes grew accustomed to the dim light, I saw we were in a room roughly twenty-five feet square with a bar running part way along one wall. A man who appeared to be about my height but, judging by his large belly, considerably heavier wearing an old-fashioned cotton wale undershirt, once white now gray, the kind having straps over the shoulders, stood behind the bar. His stance and heavily muscled dark brown arms and shoulders asserted, *You are welcome here so long as you do not cause any trouble.* Standing next to him was an attractive dark-skinned woman wearing a cotton dress that had once borne a brilliant color now faded by the sun, age, and laundering.

The room contained five tables, each having four chairs. Six men crowded around two tables shoved together. Of the six men around the joined tables, one man stood out from the others. The other five were listening, hanging on each word as he spoke in a language I did not understand. As we moved into the room, the music stopped. The only sound I could now hear other than the man speaking was the rhythmic hum of a gasoline engine electric generator running somewhere outside. The man behind the bar spoke first. "Hiroki, I suppose you came to eat your favorite soup today."

"Yes," Hiroki said. "I've come for the soup and brought a newcomer to the island with me. He just got here. He came by the big sailboat down at Charlie Dock. He sailed it by himself. We want two bowls of your soup and two bottles of beer."

The men at the table stopped and looked, their eyes settling on me. One of the men said something to the others I did not understand. They all laughed and once more diverted their attention to the better-dressed man who was the center of their attention.

The man at the bar did not move, but the woman by his side went to the end of the bar, where she proceeded to fill two bowls and bring them to our table. I could smell the aroma of onion and ginger well before the bowls were placed before us. The bowls contained a liquid I learned was coconut cream with chunks of flesh and what appeared to be both flesh and viscera, the remains of a bat that fed only on the island's vegetation. Instinctively I reached for the bottled beer placed on the table by the man in the undershirt. The beer was cool but not cold. *No matter*, I thought and took a long drink, then picked up my spoon and tasted the warm liquid and chewed the meat. "Not bad," I announced, trying not to show too much expression.

At that, one of the men at the other table spoke, in hesitant English. "He said not bad!" and they laughed again, all except the man who was clearly their leader. "I don't suppose you ever saw a fruit bat," the man continued. "Lupie, you've got another one, don't you? Show it to him."

The woman did not move. The man behind the bar said, "Go ahead; show him."

The woman left the room and seconds later returned with a cage. Inside a small manlike creature covered with a hairy hide and folded wings hung upside down from a perch. The man at the table said, "If she needs to make more, that one will do. She just throws him, hair and all, in a pot of boiling water, and when he looks done, she rips the hide off him and tears up the meat and insides—"

Kent Weatherby

I interrupted, "I said 'not bad,' and that is precisely what I meant. It isn't bad. In fact, it is quite good. Where I came from, we often ate rats. Cats and dogs were considered a delicacy. So if you don't mind, I'll enjoy my soup without your inane conversation." I moved my chair slightly away from the table leg as if to make myself more comfortable.

"You calling me insane?" The man rose with indignation. I could see he was just shorter than I was but had a build much like the man behind the bar.

"I'm telling you I don't want to hear any more out of you; inane or insane, it is all the same to me."

The other men at the table said nothing but looked from one to another. The leader of the group appeared amused and said something in the language I did not understand. With what must have been some form of instruction, the tough-looking man moved toward me in a menacing manner. I sat perfectly still with my hands quiet on the table in front of me.

Hiroki also sat quietly neither moving nor speaking.

The man advanced with slow, deliberate, and powerful movements. "I don't like the way you talk. You're not American. I don't know who you are, but you need to learn our ways if you plan to stay on this island."

I waited patiently for my opportunity, which an instant later came when he shifted his weight heavily on his approach. With a forceful sweep of my right leg, I cut under his weight-bearing leg, and he fell backward. By the time he hit the floor, I was on my feet preparing for the battle that had to come, weighing my chances and not liking them.

"Stop!" the leader of the group of six called out. "My

84

friend did not mean to appear rude. Perhaps it is a misunderstanding. English is not his native language. Much is often misunderstood."

Only two men remained seated at the table; the other three had leaped to their feet when their companion landed on the floor. The man who had cried out to me spoke in the foreign language, and they sat back down. The man on the floor relaxed. He said nothing but rose from his back, looked embarrassed, and walked out of the room. The two men who had remained seated throughout the encounter exchanged a glance, muttered something in a low voice, then all five men stood and without saying more followed out the door.

Turning to Hiroki I thought, *Little rat brought me here to set me up*, but said instead, "Our soup will get cold. Who were those men?"

"They are men from my home. They are from Truk Lagoon. The man who was boss is my uncle. He is my mother's brother from Dublon. He is Senator Tobias Bili. He is a very important man in Micronesia."

Minutes later, as we prepared to leave, I reached in my pocket for my money holder, a soft leather case with an embossed fleur-de-lis on the front and back cover. It was not there. Forgetting I had not found it that morning, I thought, *I left it on the boat*. Fumbling in my other pocket, I found a stray twenty, all that was left from what I had shoved in my pocket earlier in the morning, and paid the bill, $7.50.

George Rowley picked me up at my boat that evening just as the sun set. We drove to the home of Palauan

Senator Yasoru Nakamura at the edge of a clearing on Capitol Hill, though it was not part of the TT head-quarters complex. A flat roof concrete structure stained by streaks of mold, it could have passed for a rectangular WWII bunker. The three-bedroom house had originally been home for senior agents of the CIA and was capable of withstanding the two-hundred-mile-an-hour devil wind that struck the island from time to time.

George pulled the old Nissan off the road and stopped the car on the grass in front of the house where Jonathan Cartwright and Ferd Meier sat outside on molded-plastic patio chairs sipping lemonade with the senator. They watched as the sun set into the ocean eight hundred feet below, casting an orange and pink glow that spread across the entire sky. Ever mindful of the traps George had set randomly on the floor and seats of his mobile home for shrews, I carefully removed myself from their tiny but painful jaws.

Jonathan Cartwright spoke first. "Gener, good to see you."

"I didn't think you were planning to play cards tonight," I responded.

"Well, life on the island can get pretty boring. The idea of taking a little of your cash was just too inviting."

I smiled at the challenge. "Of course you can try, but it may be more difficult than you think."

Turning then to Senator Nakamura, noticing George had drifted into the house looking for the Pilipino houseboy to add something with a kick to the lemonade he had picked up from a tray on the metal patio table, Jonathan said, "I'd like for you to meet our host. Senator

Nakamura, this is Henri Gener, the man we've all been hearing about since he arrived yesterday."

Nakamura was a small well-built man who I would pass for being under forty, with dark black hair neatly trimmed. He wore dark slacks and off-white barong tagalog. The black-rimmed eyeglasses he wore completed a transformation that belied his ancestry as a Pacific Islander. Sophisticated and educated at the University of California's Boalt Hall, he could have been a successful lawyer anywhere in the world. In fact he was just that, having returned home abandoning a promising future with a prestigious admiralty and maritime firm in San Francisco, a man now climbing the political, economic, and social ladder all at the same time. For Senator Nakamura, the card parties had little to do with gambling. They were about the never-ending rounds of networking he knew would pay dividends in the future.

"Thank you for having me, Senator. I have been looking forward to this all day."

"I'm glad to have you. We are short one for the game. Oh, here comes his car now."

Turning around I saw a familiar car approaching from the direction of the government buildings. As it drew nearer, I saw distinctly the face of the man driving. It was the man I had had the altercation with at the Palauan restaurant earlier in the day.

"You'll have to watch out for Senator Bili," my host warned. "He has a reputation for cheating at cards, for that matter, any game of chance."

The car stopped, and Bili got out from the backseat. He looked in my direction and smiled, although I was not quite certain whether it was a smile of greeting or something else.

"We meet again, Mr. Gener. My brother-in-law told me you would be playing cards tonight. I could not resist the temptation. Hello, Nakamura." Senator Bili did not acknowledge Ferd but did nod to Jonathan, casting a glance that conveyed some meaning, though at the time I did not understand. I do not believe any of the others noticed.

"Shall we get started?" Senator Nakamura asked. "It is almost eight. Pleasant as it is, we gathered to play cards."

"Won't this be a little awkward?" Ferd asked. "There are seven of us. Seven at the table are too many. I don't see how it can work."

George had rejoined us, drink in hand. "Aw, we can play draw poker. We'll just have to limit the draw to three cards each."

"I don't know," Ferd commented. "I don't get it. Seven times five is thirty-five, and seven times three is twenty-one. That makes fifty-six."

"Oh, all right," George conceded, "we just leave the two jokers in the deck as wild cards. There will always be someone who won't draw three cards." Exasperated by Ferd's endless whining he continued, "Whatta I care? If you don't want to play, we can just call off the game and—" George had started to add *you can go home* but then thought better of it. If Ferd left, who would feed the pot?

"No, no," Ferd interrupted. "It's just that I don't know that I can figure the odds in a game like that."

"So what? You never get it right anyway. Add it up,

man; you're an accountant. Seven times seven is only forty-nine. We can always play seven-card stud too. There are some pretty wild and fun games that come out of stud." What George wanted to say but did not was that with Ferd odds had nothing to do with his losing. The man was simply a bad card player.

"What about stakes?" I asked.

George spoke up again. "Ten-dollar ante and twenty-dollar limit on openers, thirty-dollar limit on raises, around the table twice. We don't want to make it too easy to buy a hand. Besides, it's a friendly game, right?"

We entered the house; that is six of us entered the house. Bili's driver was not playing. It seemed everyone knew that except for Ferd and me. For the others it was one more opportunity to ridicule Ferd. George, never wanting to miss an opportunity, left in the jokers just to irritate Ferd.

I want to make one thing perfectly clear—I cheat at cards. Of course I cheat at cards, but I do not do so for the money. I told you I cheat for the thrill of cheating and not being caught, and I cheat when something important is at stake. This night I cheated when Senator Tobias Bili cheated, only I was better at it.

Bili for the most part made a clumsy effort to stack the deck and deal from the bottom. The others had not seen the joker I palmed in the early hands waiting until it would be of real advantage. That time came on the last hand of the game after Ferd was already the biggest loser at the table. The hand was five-card draw.

I looked at my cards, nothing paired, no possibility of a straight or flush, just an ace high and the joker I got on the deal. That gave me a pair of aces and a third counting the joker no one had seen for over an hour. Bili opened after the other players checked their bet. Under our rules, jacks or better were required for openers, so I knew he had at least a pair of jacks. Ferd raised, as did Jonathan. I followed suit, and as the betting proceeded, the pot grew to over four hundred dollars. Ferd was desperate to recoup some of his early losses.

On the draw, Ferd took one card. I doubted he had two pair, so he must be drawing to a straight or flush. His aggressive betting during the evening suggested he was going for the long odds chance to fill a flush. His hands were sweating. The back of his shirt was stained. The closed house had no air-conditioning, and the temperature hovered in the high eighties. His eyes were drawn and squinting in anticipation, hope.

Bili drew two cards. He had three of a kind unless he was trying to bluff Ferd into believing his imaginary three of a kind would beat two pair. I also drew two cards keeping the king against the possibility Bili held three natural aces. The king would be my kicker.

Ferd wasted no time in beginning the betting with the pot limit. Jonathan and George soon dropped from the game, as did Senator Nakamura. The pot now exceeded six hundred dollars, with two hundred of that from Ferd.

When the hand was laid down, Ferd had a flush. Just as I thought, he had bet with nothing on the deal, hoping to draw to the flush. Bili, who had a full house, eights over tens, beat him. I had drawn another ace and so won with a pair of aces in the game and a pair of jokers in my hand. Four aces.

I am certain the others knew Bili had cheated drawing a pair of tens from the bottom of the deck, but no one had seen my sleight of hand as I switched the second joker for a lowly four.

The audible groan escaping Ferd's body was exquisite. I could not help looking at George, who seemed puzzled by my good luck, knowing it was not luck at all but something he could not prove. I nodded knowing he would recall our conversation the day before at Old Man by the Sea.

"Tough luck, Ferd. Third high never wins." I raked in my winnings from the hand that covered my evening's entertainment still leaving Bili as the big winner.

"I have a marker for that last stack of chips. I'll get to the bank for the cash as soon as I can," Ferd called out, his voice quivering.

"That's fine, but don't take your time. I'll only be here a few days, you know." I intended to pressure him for the money, not for the sake of the money but for another reason. I wanted to break him as I had described to George on the day before. I had listened and watched. I believed with all my being that Ferd was a desperate man. You may say I am not a nice person to take such a personal interest in a man I had only met the evening before. You would be right. I intended to break someone, anyone, just for the fun of doing it, and Ferd Meier was simply the first opportunity I had to do so.

As we left, Senator Bili took me by the arm. Turning to George, he said, "I'll give Gener a ride." Then to me he continued, "I'll give you a ride to Charlie Dock or wherever you want to go. Maybe we'll run into one another again before you leave. There will be gambling on Monday night at the Inter-Con Hotel. See you there?"

"If I'm still here, you definitely will." I dropped the four spot on the concrete pad just outside the door knowing it would be found and word of my deception would spread among the other players.

Chapter Eight

Saturday morning came for me before the sun had risen above the mountain. Darkness in my aft cabin gave way slowly to the morning light as if a thousand veils were being raised one at a time. I am at peace in the coolness of the predawn. Recollection of the card game the night before caused a smile to flicker across my lips. I rose from bed, put on my shorts, and, going on deck with my face to the sea, assumed the Lotus position. My mind went to that inner place where I no longer thought. I existed only. In that trance I observed myself, now, then.

We are a family, my father, mother, and older sister. My memories are shadowy recollections of the lovely tree-lined boulevards of our home in Hanoi. I see lakes and, on our trips outside the city, green forests. It is an idyllic place and time. We lived here before the Japanese invasion and returned following the war, though this memory is before the war. It is the first home I can remember. My father is an important man, but as a boy, I do not understand what he does. He dresses for work in crisp linen/silk suits and leaves home in a chauffeured car.

Our home is a two-story white building with balconies. My parents tell me it reminds them of home, Toulon, but it is much nicer than the pictures of that home.

My sister attends a school run by nuns while I am left in the care of Vietnamese nannies. I run and play with the children of our servants. We are in a garden surrounded by a wall with trees and benches and flowers.

I speak to them in their language, Vietnamese, and they answer. Our games are simple ones we make up. Since I am younger than the other boys are, I do as they say. Rank and status mean nothing to boys at play. We have our own order, and as the smallest, I am at the bottom. My nanny yells out to the other boys to play nice with me. It is a comforting feeling just to play. No fear. No responsibility. No worry.

I experience the place, the love, the joy of an existence long past, a feeling, a recollection I could not go on without, though I know it can never be recaptured in life, not this life, my life now.

The sun was above the mountain now, and I felt its warmth against my back. The spell was broken. *What happened to that happy boy?* I wondered. *Was it the war? Why have I changed so much?* I no longer just played. Now there was always a purpose, one might even say an evil purpose, to my actions. I was no longer at the bottom of any game. I was the dominate male in every game, or so I strove to be.

I opened my eyes and looked at the lagoon, the tiny island, and the reef. I slowly rose to my feet. Let the game, my game, begin.

Today Hiroki was taking me around the island to places I had not seen. We would go to Bird Island, Banzai and Suicide cliffs, where Japanese civilians and soldiers leapt to their death rather than be taken prisoner and eaten by the cannibal Americans, so they were told. Most of all I looked toward seeing the grotto, to swim and enjoy the cool water lit from beneath by a great light shining through the rock.

We drove north from Charlie Dock, and Hiroki began what sounded like the chatter of a tour guide. He pointed out the place where the Japanese soldiers made a final assault on U.S. Marines overrunning their position for a short while, using whatever weapons they had, some no more than spears cut from bamboo. He pointed out where bulldozers had been used to push the bodies of the Japanese soldiers into trenches cut into the side of the hill, buried in mass graves, following the battle.

A short distance beyond we came to a memorial beside the ocean. Banzai cliff stood at the edge of the water with a peace memorial across the road. I showed little interest, and so we drove on, again a short drive, to the base of a high cliff. We were at the northernmost point on the island. A collection of rusting anti-aircraft and artillery field pieces marked a place known as The Last Command Post. Hiroki told me a trail led up from there to the top of the cliff, the place where the Japanese soldiers walked off choosing death over surrender. I noted the place thinking I would make the climb if I had the time, but now I was more interested in getting to the grotto.

We left after a few minutes and continued. We parked the Charger and walked down the hill to the place Hiroki indicated. We were alone. No one else was about. As we entered the cave I glanced at Hiroki; he was watching me. I stripped my shirt off and prepared to dive into the water.

"It is dangerous to swim here," Hiroki tells me.

"What can be so dangerous? The water is clear, and the light coming from the tunnel makes it easy to see."

"But there have been people bitten by sharks here. Not big sharks. Little ones that sometimes venture into the grotto."

"Are you so frightened of a little shark?" I ask.

He did not answer but looked away as I dove into the water.

"Come on in. There is nothing to fear."

He looked at me and shook his head.

I swam back and forth across the open water, a distance of only a hundred feet, then dove and swam toward the light, toward the hole in the rock, toward the open ocean. The hole was large and not far through to the sea. When I surfaced hardly aware of having been under water, I felt the surge of the ocean throw me against the cliff rising over a hundred feet above. I was just able to steady myself for the blow and manage to propel myself backwards into the water and swim with the outward tow away from the rocks. Because there was no reef at this end of the island, the ocean rose against the cliff, not breaking in waves, but pushing me as if by a giant hand.

What a fool thing to do, I thought and dove down to

swim back into the grotto. *Where is the hole?* I could not see the hole. There was nothing but rock, jagged rock, volcanic rock, jutting out in huge sharp bulges leading me inward only to discover more rock. I dove again, and again, and again. I could not find the way back inside. I could not find the way to safety.

I was not a man who panics easily, but the repeated dives against the ragged rocks began to take their toll. Time after time, I dove down working against the rocks and press of an ocean trying to crush me. Each time the exertion caused me to run out of air before I believed I should, forcing me to surface. The ocean surge crushed me against the island twice as I mistimed my ascent for another breath. After what seemed like an eternity, I gave up and began looking for a way to climb the rock cliff.

Now, in my altered state of existence, I see Hiroki sitting on the ledge inside. At first he was calm, but when I did not resurface, he began to call out.

"Frenchman, Frenchman! Where are you?" Nevertheless, he still did not come into the water, afraid of the grotto, afraid of sharks, afraid of what else?

When I did not answer, he walked out of the cave to the edge of the cliff and looked into the water. Panic was in his voice now as he continued to call out.

I read his thoughts. He feared Xarkus. What would his father do to him? He was to watch me, to learn my secrets, to find a fortune that could be stolen. What if I was dead? What would Xarkus do?

The truth of my situation sunk in. If I stayed outside, in the open ocean, I would die. If I continued battling the island and the ocean, I would die. The entrance to the grotto, bright and inviting from the inside, beckoning to me with the promise of light and warm sun, had become a trap. Once more, I had been attracted to the light only to find that in that light there was darkness. The way back in was so well concealed, my sense of location so distorted, the minutes dragging on in a futile effort to regain safety, that I finally acknowledged that truth.

I swam away from the point of the cliff looking for a spot where the swell was gentler, a place where it might be possible to climb up to the top. I was thankful for the days, months at sea, hardened by work and calmed by yoga; at last I found a protected place where the rock wall appeared to be a little lower. I swam away from the cliff outside the swell of the ocean and counted the seconds between the thrust of water against the island, then timed my approach and rode the swell. At the last moment, I reached out and grabbed the sharp rock for a handhold. I struggled to hold on as the water receded then finding a foothold as well began to climb slowly above the returning surge working carefully upward on the hard, sharp volcanic rock.

I was in a zone of mental and emotional acceptance. Fear had come and gone when I could not find the opening. If I was going to survive, I had to keep climbing and dare not fall. I climbed, and as I approached the top, the sense of desperation left and fear returned. Looking down, I once again saw only death. If I fell from this height, I would surely die.

Exhausted from the mental and physical strain, I pulled myself at last over the top and lie still for a few minutes before looking around to get my bearings. In the distance, a hundred yards away and thirty feet below me, I saw the orange Charger. Hiroki was still here. I would not have to walk home after all.

Chapter Nine

On every small island I had visited, there was one day, night that islanders anticipated. That day may be related to church, Catholic Mass, on some islands; on others it may be a cultural event. On Saipan, Saturday night was party night, the high social event every week. It was an occasion for the island elite to dress for dinner at the Continental Hotel. I have alluded to the hotel in the past, but you have never seen it.

The building itself consisted of two wings, forming an obtuse angle outward toward the ocean, each six stories tall constructed of concrete tinted off-white toward beige. The parking lot on Beach Road led directly to an open-air lobby at the point of the "V," furnished with huge overstuffed chairs located to catch the sea breeze created by the open shape. That in turn opened on the large end into landscaped gardens. Here the war-ravaged island, only partially healed, vanished, and a fairy tale existence became reality. Palm trees, carefully placed to provide shade along the meandering sidewalks through the lush grass, led to the cabana, fresh water pool, sand volleyball court, and beach with its umbrellas and varnished wood lounge chairs looking outward to the reef, but before the reef to Managaha Island. On those days when ships slipped through the channel to Charlie Dock, they passed in direct view of the Continental Hotel beach.

This was the world of the foreign dignitaries, the wealthy business leaders, the social mavens of the island, for them to see but more importantly to be seen entering and leaving but never observed at leisure. Noticeably absent from the scene were the Micronesian politicians and business executives. The Continental Hotel provided an open-air barrier between the classes, *haole* and native. The gift shop provided expensive jewelry and trinkets for the wealthy, things not available anywhere else on the island with the sole exception of the duty-free shop at the airport. The liquor and wine available in the dining room and bar far exceeded even that. The hotel was five-star only because no rating service awarded a higher classification.

The uniformed staff dressed in white trousers topped by blue-and-white-flowered shirts. The female staff wore the same blue-and-white-floral pattern in provocative dresses. There were no ugly staff members here. You were either one of the pretty people or you worked elsewhere.

The dining room, located to the left of the lobby on the garden side, provided dining in air-conditioned comfort for those who did not prefer the atmosphere of the garden and terrace, for those who took their pleasure from the idyllic surroundings with its subdued sights and sounds. The aroma of the salt ocean air and the Canada geese that roamed freely over the grounds completed the scene.

I had Hiroki drop me off early so that I could enjoy the ambiance for a few minutes alone before my dinner partners arrived, the Cartwrights and Sydna. The warm and humid evening reminded me of weather I recalled as a boy in Indochina. Our movements then had been languid, relaxed, everyone conscious of the heat in the days before air-conditioning. They were merely thought of as the warm slow-paced days of summer. I welcomed this evening as a reminder of better times, times when I was truly free to go where I wanted, only restricted by my parents.

I stopped for a few minutes talking to the **maitre d'** to make certain they had the wines and cognac in stock I preferred. Then, indulging myself uncharacteristically in a bamboo cocktail, a mixture of rum, peach schnapps, lemonade, pineapple and cranberry juices, I strolled out to the chairs arranged in the garden where I could close my eyes and enjoy the sounds, the feel and smell of the tropics.

A half hour later, I was greeted by the soft, warm, cultured voice of Caroline Cartwright.

"M. Gener, so here you are. As we were entering the hotel, we saw the young lady, Sydna, driving into the parking lot. My husband is waiting to escort her."

Rising to greet her, I replied, "Madame Cartwright, it is a pleasure to see you this evening. You look enchanting." I inquired, "Could I order you something from the bar?"

"Thank you, but I believe I'll wait for the others. Then you can order me one of what you are having."

She sat down opposite me dressed in a cool white

and yellow polished cotton halter dress, the low neck-line exposing her pale skin. Moments later Jonathan Cartwright and Sydna appeared, and I beckoned one of the waiters, a boy dressed in the blue-and-white-flowered shirt.

"We'll have four bamboo cocktails," I announced, looking at my companions for their approval. They nodded in appreciation.

Jonathan sat across the table from me in a high-backed rattan chair. "So," he began, "what have you been up to today?"

"I had Hiroki take me out to the grotto; it is a lovely place."

"I agree, but it has been known to be dangerous. A while back, a tourist swam out of the hole and could not find his way back in. They sent a boat out for him, but they brought him back dead. He'd been banged against the rocks and drowned."

"Understandable. I swam out and had a difficult time before finding a place where I could climb the cliff." I intentionally left out the detail of fear. "The rocks are sharp," I added, holding out my sea-toughened, scraped hands for inspection. "My feet are much the same."

"I hope you didn't get any cuts. Infection sets in easily in this climate."

"No. The scrapes are all I got."

"Where was Hiroki?"

"Outside looking over the cliff when I got to the top. I was a ways off and just watched for a minute while I got my breath. He seemed to be worried. Guess he didn't want to answer any questions about what had happened to me."

"Probably not. In case you are unaware, his father is a bit of a nasty character. The family is related to Senator Bili. Word has it the entire family is involved in all sorts of shady dealings."

"Hiroki actually told me his mother was a sister of Bili's. You would never guess it by her appearance and the way Xarkus treats her."

"I think it's just a cultural thing. Women are expected to be nurturers and workers."

"She certainly appears to qualify in that regard, but what about the family? What sort of shady dealings are you talking about?"

"Oh, it's all just rumor, but the rumor is they are involved in illegal fishing, dynamiting, and other criminal activity at Truk. It's no big secret. They are running a risk of damaging the coral reef. That would spell environmental disaster for the whole lagoon. Problem is they don't seem to care. In fact, I think the senator gets a kick out of acting the part of a gangster when he is not busy pretending to be interested in his constituents. He always has a retinue of heavies with him, at least most of the time he does."

"Well, no one is perfect," I said, dismissing the rumor as fact, but unimportant fact.

"Xarkus isn't any better. He is trying to get a job where he will have access to high explosives."

"So?"

"I guess what I'm trying to say is I like you. Watch your back, and as we like to say, 'Keep your powder dry.' Your association with these Trukese people can lead to trouble."

The sun had slid low on the horizon when we decided

to go in for dinner. We had talked for over a half hour as we enjoyed our drinks watching while the sky changed color from yellow/orange to red and finally pink as the gigantic orb slipped into the ocean. The twilight that followed was warm and humid with streaks of darkening light running across the sky highlighted and colored by the wisps of clouds that lingered, waiters moving silently lighting the tiki lanterns.

The effect of alcohol relaxed us all and heightened our anticipation of the dinner that waited. The chef at the Continental Hotel, a countryman of mine, had for years worked for the international hotel chain and had applied for this position, not because it was a choice location but because it was a stepping stone for the grand hotels in Hong Kong, the Philippines, and Japan. He had a reputation for having mastered oriental cuisine but tonight had laid-on a table filled with French food, *Mignons de filet de boeuf, sautés Madere, Pain francais, Petits pains-galettes, Artichauts al la Barigoule, Asperges etuvees a la crème, Tarte au citron, La Pitchoune* using local fruit. For the more plebian, taste chicken with a butter milk/flour coating, sautéed in butter.

My new friends and I, seated on the veranda, having chosen our meal, were awaiting the waiters to carry it to our table. The wine I ordered was a pinot noir from the Côte d'Or. The table was set with white linen and fine cutlery while the gentle movement of Casablanca fans overhead stirred the air, the outdoor table lit by candle and the soft glow of light from inside the hotel.

An eclectic group of lawyers, judges, government functionaries, and clergy occupied all but one of the eight tables on the veranda. The latter, an aging monsignor, wearing a French-cut Soutane with an antiquated black zucchetto bearing the red piping of his station, and two priests sat at a table centrally located where they enjoyed the attention lavished on them by the Catholic hotel staff.

At another table, a small party appeared to be celebrating some special event. Jonathan explained it was a bon voyage party for the tall man, an assistant attorney general named Layton Hayes, whose contract term had reached its conclusion. He, the strawberry-blond woman with him, who Jonathan identified as his wife, and their two daughters were leaving the following week to return stateside.

The evening wore on, and conversation became lively with one or more persons from a table exchanging places with those at another table. Jonathan excused himself and went to the table where Hayes sat enjoying his farewell party to the island and had a few words before motioning for me to join them. He made the introduction, stating that I was the mysterious Frenchman who had raised something of a stir since arriving. He spent a few minutes in friendly conversation with members of the party inquiring about my past. As always on such occasions, I chose my words carefully. It was my intention to appear companionable without revealing too much about my past. Jonathan, on the other hand, seemed adept at using virtually any excuse to learn more about me. Hayes and his party provided just one more vehicle.

We had just returned to our table when we were approached by a man and wife of middle age. At once Jonathan stood. He called the man and woman by name, Mr. and Mrs. I Didn't Catch Your Name. "I would like to present M. Henri Gener. Of course you know Sydna and my wife, Caroline."

Turning to me, Jonathan announced, "Mr. Idcyn is the Trust Territory of the Pacific Islands Deputy High Commissioner."

"Nice to meet you, Jenner. Nice to see you ladies again. So, Mr. Jenner, where are you from and where are you bound?" The clumsy oaf could not pronounce my name.

"I am from France, and I am bound for those places where wind and current take me," I responded, then turned my attention to his wife hoping to deflect any more question. "And what of you, Madame? What has brought you to this place?"

"Politics and my husband's work. We're from Arizona. My husband was County Executive for Yuma County until the last election. He was defeated, and a congressman friend got him this job."

Mr. Idcyn glared at his wife then said, "Why don't you shut up." She did. He continued, "I was hoping to run into you. You've been all the talk since you arrived. We don't get many visitors sailing in by themselves. In fact, since we've been here, you are the first." He paused, waiting for me to respond.

I said nothing reflecting that he had been unnecessarily rude to his wife, something I would never do in public, though once, in private, had been severely rude to my own wife. Of course, his wife's comment about his failure at elective office was uncalled for, but she gave every appearance of having had too much to drink, just as he did.

Jonathan broke the awkward silence. "I haven't seen

much of you while the hi-com has been off island. I guess you've been pretty busy running the shop."

"Well yes, as a matter of fact, I have been. Someone has to do it, and that is my job as the number-two man in the Trust Territory. For the most part it's a lot like being ..."

He stopped short of saying vice president, the job FDR's VP said was not worth a bucket of warm spit. It might have been what he thought, but his ego would not allow him to say it.

It seems odd to see things so clearly now, know the things people thought but did not say. Death has given me extraordinary talents, knowing things, things that might have made a difference now seen clearly for what they were. In that momentary pause as Mr. Idcyn recovered from his near embarrassing gaff, he thought, *I've seen this Frenchman someplace before, but where?* His mind was spinning with his personal history. *It couldn't have been in the U.S., and I've never been to Europe. In fact, the only time I was out of the country other than to go to Canada or Mexico before now was ten years ago, to Vietnam. Could it be I ran into him there?*

Aloud he said, "Well, you know, there is always something going on in the Pacific Rim. A cable came through today concerning the Vietnamese boat people. It seems like they will try anything to escape from the North Vietnamese. Every day we seem to find a few derelict and dying souls, their boat abandoned, adrift, or worse. The stories make you sick."

Jonathan answered, "We didn't do those people any favors when we abandoned them to the North Vietnamese. I suppose, as a Frenchman, you have some opinions on that whole conflict and how it ended, Henri."

All eyes were turned on me. I calculated my answer. "I doubt it could have ended any other way. At least when 'we' left, there was a partition of the country and not everyone was subjected to Communist rule."

"What is that supposed to mean?" Mr. Idcyn demanded.

"Just this, when we left, there was honor. We lost an army that endured a death march like the one your soldiers endured on the Bataan peninsula in the Philippines. The Vietnamese people who wanted something other than a Communist government had a place to go. They may have been displaced to the south, but they still had some hope. When you Americans pulled out, you abandoned them to the North Vietnamese and didn't care what happened. You lost your political nerve and just wanted out. The decades of hatred built up spilled out on those people you now call 'boat people.'"

"You don't know anything about America or its foreign policy," Mr. Idcyn challenged, his voice shaking. "We were trying to help those people."

"That, my 'friend,' is so much ordure! J'ai besoin de gerber. I imagine that is what you told yourself every time you installed a different puppet government. The hope you raised in the people led hundreds of thousands of them to believe in you, and you betrayed them. You betrayed them all because your politicians did not have the courage to live up to their commitments. You caused thousands of deaths. You signed their death warrants just so a few politicians could be reelected. If you truly wanted to help, you would not have cut and run."

The words *cut* and *run* were no more out of my mouth than I thought back. What had it been, two months, ten weeks? Certainly no more than that. Even in these latitudes, *Monique* made at least four knots. I had passed through the Strait of Malacca, past Kuala Lumpur and Singapore, choosing that route over the longer and more dangerous passage through Selat Sunda separating Sumatra from Java, and proceeding into the South China Sea.

My plan had been to sail north along the east coast of Malaysia toward the Gulf of Thailand then turn east toward the southern tip of my old home, Vietnam. If everything worked out, I would make a short call. If conditions were hostile, I would sail past, as near as possible, before continuing on to the Northern Mariana Islands.

The passage through the strait had been a bit dicey. Because it is a heavily traveled shipping lane dotted with small islands and trafficked by everything from tankers, container ships, freighters, fishing trawlers, tugs, and the thousands of other small boats, I had to stay awake for several days only allowing myself sleep for minutes at a time during the daylight hours while tending the wheel. A small boat such as mine was nearly invisible in the hours of darkness, and large ocean vessels do not turn on a pivot. True, I had my gasoline engine at the ready, but even that might not be enough to avoid colliding with one of those leviathans. As it turned out, I had needed the engine when I dozed only to see one bearing down on *Monique* like a gigantic sea monster intent on our destruction. It had been a narrow escape, but we had survived.

The alternative to continuing my non-stop passage through the strait was to anchor near shore, close to one of the islands in water too shallow for the big ships to navigate. The problem with that was the threat of piracy. The strait is notorious for piracy and had been for as long as I could recall. The prospect of encountering pirates kept me on my guard. If they successfully boarded *Monique*, my life would not have been worth a sou. I only had a pistol to ward off attacks, and my chances of survival were not great in the event they suddenly set upon me. Therefore, when I departed the strait and the danger passed, I felt a sense of relief.

A week later, with favorable wind and current, I found myself off the southeast coast of Vietnam. The waters were familiar to me having served for a year aboard a junk-rigged coastal freighter working the trade route between Saigon, Tra Vinh, Rach Gia, and Ha Tien, a sort of apprenticeship for my uncle who a few years later took me into his import business. Those were the days before the American Central Intelligence Agency recruited me into their undeclared and largely ignored war with the Viet Cong.

I recognized some of the small islands as *Monique* drew closer to my childhood home. However, my hopes of reuniting myself with my adopted homeland were dashed shortly afterwards when coastal patrol boats intercepted *Monique*, warning shots were fired dangerously close to us, and I was turned away.

I did so knowing that to invite the wrath of these people would result in my being imprisoned or killed.

The year I had spent in a camp following the death march from Diem Biem Phu, the disease, filth, and neglect were more than I wanted to endure a second time at their hands.

The day after turning away, I encountered the flotsam, both structural and human, floating on the calm surface. Some horrible force had torn the boat apart, yet there had not been a storm for over a week and even then it had been little more than a squall. Certainly whatever had destroyed this boat was more than that. When I pulled near the bodies, I could see the cause of the wreckage. Large caliber bullet holes riddled many of the bodies.

The wreckage had to be the result of an attack by a patrol boat like the one that had warned me away. They had used their big gun to destroy the boat and then machine-gunned the survivors once they were in the water.

I had yelled at Mr. Idcyn about these boat people. They were the survivors, only they were not survivors, of the failed American foreign policy, a policy borne out of misguided idealism and popular public defeatism, the foreign policy that led them to take impossible risks to reach the Philippines on little more than waterlogged and sinking wrecks, wrecks even before they were attacked.

I reefed my sails and motored along slowly among the bodies looking for any person still alive, no matter how tenuous that life might be. Just when I decided that no one had survived the attack, I saw a child not more than ten years of age half-lying across some boards that once must have been a crude deck shelter. The child looked to be alive, and so I approached, stopped, and went over the side with a line tied around my waist, the water being too deep for my anchor to be of any use. As I swam to the waif, it raised its head and tried to speak, but dehydration, sun, and shock prevented it.

Gathering it in my arms, I realized it was the body of a small girl and swimming on my back carried her back to my boat. I pulled the girl on board *Monique* and at once began giving her small amounts of fresh water in the shade of the cabin. I tried my best to reassure her that she was now safe. I had rescued her from the sea, from the men who tried to kill her and had undoubtedly killed her family. She looked small, frail, and helpless. She looked to be about the same age as my sister who had been lost when the Japanese invaded Vietnam during the war. I had been too young to help her, to protect her, but now that I was a man, it would be different.

I hoisted my sails and began moving away from the grisly scene hoping to be well out of sight before the girl was conscious of the carnage around us. I then took her below and placed her on the cushions in the salon. I could do nothing to help the others; they were all dead, but I could at least take this small one to some place of safety. *Monique*'s engine carried us outside the national waters of Vietnam along the east coast of that country heading in a northeasterly direction until we were, I thought, well away from the scene of the attack.

We then sailed, drifted more correctly, in the calm sea all the rest of that day and throughout the night. The girl slept fitfully, tossing and turning, muttering in her sleep. Most of what she said was garbled, and I did not understand. Late the following morning, she awoke, sat up in bed, and with a look of fear shrank back against the bulkhead drawing her knees up as if to protect herself.

"Don't be afraid, little one," I spoke softly and soothingly in Vietnamese. "I am your friend and will help you."

She did not answer.

"Do you remember what happened?"

She shook her head from side to side but still did not answer, her body still drawn up tightly in a defensive position.

"You will be all right. I will take you to someone who can take care of you."

She blurted out in Vietnamese, "Mama, Papa. I want my mama and papa."

"I know. I don't know where they are." I did not lie. I had no idea whether they had been part of the wreckage or if they were somewhere else.

"Take me to them," she pleaded.

It pained me to answer. "Were they with you on the boat?"

"Yes."

"Then they are lost. You don't remember anything at all about what happened on the boat?"

"Only that we were being shot at."

"And that is all?"

"Yes."

"It is just as well. Your parents are dead, but I will take care of you."

She did not cry. She just looked straight ahead, and I saw her body relax. She turned her face away from me and lay there with her face to the bulkhead.

All that day the girl stayed below deck in the cabin.

Slowly she began to take a little food, and, as children do, she seemed to recover rapidly. During this time, we had sailed only a short distance. My sextant readings and calculations showed we had traveled only sixty-one miles on the calm, windless sea from noon the day before until noon that day.

For me this was normally a rare treat. It provided an opportunity to go on deck without worrying about being knocked overboard by a wave or wind or some other rogue event. Nothing is as frightening to a lone sailor as being alone in the water as his boat sails away leaving him to struggle, only finally to give up in despair and take that final breath, not of air, water, deep into his lungs and feel the darkness close around him.

On days like this, I would lie naked on deck letting the sun warm my body, but today, with the girl on board, I wore a swimming suit. I had been on deck about an hour when she stuck her head out of the hatch and asked in Vietnamese if she could come out.

"Of course, only be careful. You don't want to fall back into the water."

She moved out tentatively until she sat close beside me. Then she began to talk, the words pouring out of her like a river rushing toward the sea.

"We were trying to get away," she began. "There were many of us. I do not even know how many there were. There was not room for everyone on the boat, and it sat so low in the water that even small waves came over the top. The boat went lower into the water. We didn't know how to get it out, and everyone was afraid the boat would sink."

She paused to take in air. I asked, "Who was with you?"

"Mama, Papa, Grandpapa, Grandmama, and others I didn't know." Without waiting, she continued. "We were gone a long time. A week I think. The engine stopped working and the boat drifted. Some of the men were worried that the boat would go back to Vietnam. They were afraid that if we were captured they would kill us."

"Where were you trying to go?" I asked.

"Papa said we would go to the Philippines, that someone would help us there."

"How did you get away?"

She did not answer, continuing on with her thought instead. "My papa knew them. They had all been important people before the North Vietnamese came. One of the others got the boat. We left suddenly, so we didn't have anything with us but our clothes."

"What happened?"

"I don't know. It was night and I was asleep. When I woke, there was noise and screaming. Everyone was afraid. I heard something blow up, and the boat fell apart. I heard more explosions and knew someone was shooting at us. People were hurt. The boat was sinking. People were throwing things in the water and jumping in. Someone yelled at me, 'Can you swim?' and when I said yes, they threw me in the water."

She began to sob uncontrollably, her shoulders heaving, her tiny body going into convulsions.

"You are safe now," I assured her. "You are with me and *Monique*. We will look after you."

A few minutes later she began again. "I did not know where my family went. They were not with me in the water. It was horrible. The boat was burning and then it

sank. Only junk and pieces of the boat remained, floating all around me. I crawled up on some boards and
lay still. I was afraid to do anything. My family was all
gone."

I did not know what to say so I repeated myself.
"You are safe now. You are with *Monique* and me. We
will look after you."

"Once the boat sank, it got really dark. I heard
people yelling. They were fighting over pieces of the
boat floating in the water. They were fighting over who
stays on top of those pieces. So I stayed very, very quiet.
Then they came! I heard the sound of a motor and saw
the boat with a spotlight shining on the water. Then
I heard the guns. I never heard anyone cry out. I only
heard the sound of the gun and sometimes a strange
noise, a sort of thud. I was afraid the spotlight would
shine on me and then they would shoot at me too, but
they never saw me. When they left, I was alone."

The girl soon grew weary of talking. The effort of
telling the story appeared to drain the spark of life
out of her, and she retreated once more into silence.
I contemplated my options during that silence. It was
important to get as far away from the coast, the scene
of the attack, as soon as possible. It was also important
for me to remember our position at sea, where nature
could be every bit as unforgiving and cruel as men. I did
not have sufficient fuel to motor away from the coast
and still have a reserve for some emergency later, and so
I did what any experienced seaman would have done.
I used only a portion of my fuel to take us some thirty
miles off shore, well beyond the twelve-mile territorial limit, even six miles beyond the additional twelve-

mile security zone claimed by that government. There the engine was shut down and we continued our drift, catching what small wind existed to put a margin of safety between the girl's attackers and us. When evening came, we watched the sunset and then went below where I prepared the fish I had caught as we talked on deck. The girl ate very little. She no longer talked at all but sat with her legs drawn under her, looking sad and lost.

Looking at her reminded me of the sorrow in my life. There had been joy and privilege once we had moved back to Indochina following the Japanese defeat, but that had also been the source of much sadness. This small girl represented all that I knew had gone wrong with our colonial policy. I was just a small boy, in the years before the war with Japan, when we had gone there, yet even at that young age, I understood everything that was done had to enrich France and the planters who owned huge plantations.

We were free people, so why had we not wanted the Vietnamese people to enjoy the same freedom, the same good life we had. Why did we take all the wealth of the country and keep it for ourselves? As a boy, I understood that if you were French you lived very well. If you were not French, you worked for someone who was French. It was good to be tall and white. It was bad to be small and brown. Now, looking at the girl withdrawing somewhere safe, a place where she did not have to accept her life as it now was, I saw the reality of French/American colonialism. This girl's suffering had resulted directly from our misguided and selfish policies.

The following morning, as the sun rose higher in the sky, I again took the girl on deck with me. The sea remained calm and we continued to drift. I reckoned we were somewhere southwest of the island of Cu Lau Thu. A fresh wind continued to be my fondest hope; I wanted to leave these waters. However, it was not to be. During the night our drift had been toward the mainland, not away, and in fact we were now within the security limit claimed by the newly unified Vietnamese government.

Chapter Ten

The events of the past two days made me wonder why I wanted to return. Too much had happened to me, to these people, to the country during the six years since I left. It had been folly to plan on returning. You cannot go back, and I was not a person who normally spent time looking back or thinking about things I could not change.

This small orphan affected me in a way I did not understand. I felt an obligation to care for her instead of just looking out for myself, and I resented it.

My thoughts and my position with my back to *Monique*'s cabin prevented me from hearing the patrol boat engine until it was a scant few meters away. Suddenly, there it was with its red flag and five-pointed yellow star, nearly on top of us before I saw it. I stood so the men on the approaching boat could see me waving my right arm in the air as a greeting and acknowledgment of their presence. I had no intention of running. Using my left arm, I shooed the girl below hoping I could talk them away.

I felt certain they not had seen either of us as they

were approaching from the stern where the aft cabin shielded us from their view. *No*, I thought, *what is a patrol boat doing this far from shore?* Then aloud in Vietnamese, I cried out, "Ahoy, what can I do for you?"

The captain of the twelve-meter boat came alongside with her crew of six armed and ready. "What are you doing here?" he shouted, the tone aggressive, challenging, the men ready for a fight. This was another of the boats, this one smaller perhaps, but a boat like the one that had warned me away from land, like the one that had attacked the girl and her family. The small man who shouted to me appeared to be serious and businesslike in manner.

"I am French, sailing around the world alone for pleasure. I am becalmed by the weather and have drifted toward your country. I am still in international waters I believe, I hope."

"You are not. The Republic of Vietnam has a two hundred-mile limit, and you are well within it. I believe you know that."

"My charts are old," I lied, "and I did not know you had such an extensive territorial claim," knowing the two hundred-mile limit pertained only to the country's economic zone of protection.

The word *claim* riled the captain. "It is not a 'claim.' It is our legal right, and it is the law of our country."

"My apology, I did not intend any offense. You are correct. It is what I meant to say."

Our boats were now only a few feet apart, theirs smaller than *Monique* but obviously much faster. I had no thought nor hope of escape beyond the limits of my wits and charm.

"You speak very good Vietnamese. How do I know you are not an imperialist spy trying to find a place to come ashore?"

"Alone, and on such a large boat, I would be very foolish to try such a thing. I know nothing of such matters, but my boat *Monique* would certainly draw considerable attention wherever I docked."

He nodded in agreement. "You say you are alone?"

My heart sank. What now; if I lied and he boarded me, they would find the girl. Then what would I do? Anything could and probably would happen. On the other hand, maybe he did not intend to board me. If he did, they would already be aboard. "I am French. I sailed from the Mediterranean port of Toulon six months ago. I passed around the cape at the tip of Africa and crossed the Indian Ocean through the Strait of Malacca and had planned to go north around the Philippines."

Everything I said was true, but I wondered if it would satisfy him. Did I dare lie and tell him I was alone on my boat? I continued, half lying, "Of course I am not alone. Any good seaman would tell you I am accompanied everywhere I go by *Monique*. When we are sailing, she is in charge; her nature is to follow the wind and the course I have set for her. Only now, I do not believe she is very happy with the lack of wind. After all, she is a sailboat, and sailboats depend upon the wind."

My attempt at levity did not work. The captain became wary. "Why do you treat me like a child? You do not answer my question. Are you alone?"

I had tried. "There is a child with me. That is all."

"Why didn't you just say so? We have no interest in a French child. Now we will have to board and search for ourselves." My clumsy answer had backed the captain into a corner. If he did not board, the men under his command, and who knew who might be a political operative placed there to watch and report his every move, would think him weak. He had to take action.

I too now felt my back against a wall. "The girl is not French. She is Vietnamese. I found her a couple of days ago in the sea. She was shipwrecked and all alone. I would have taken her to the nearest port only I was warned off by one of your patrol boats." I lied.

"We will throw you a line. Tie it off so we can bring our two boats together."

I prepared to receive the line.

The girl had, all during this time, not bothered to hide below, knowing such action would be useless if they boarded. Instead, she had remained at the foot of the ladder leading from the deck to the passageway below where she could hear but not see what happened above.

Only now in my altered state can I see her as she stood. The terror she had felt mere hours before was gone; she accepted her fate.

Just as the captain finished shouting the command to board *Monique*, the girl, small but no longer huddled with fear and uncertainty, rushed on deck with something in her hand. With a quick savage slashing movement across her throat, she severed the large artery. She went over the side away from the patrol boat into the water, blood surging from the wound in strong spurts.

I started to go over the side after her, but the captain of the patrol boat cautioned, "Leave her. She is dead anyway. It is better this way. You will come with us and explain yourself. Now! We will have nothing but the truth, no lies, no evasion."

Two men came aboard my boat and tied my hands behind my back, roughly, tightly, shutting off circulation. They went below and searched the cabin but finding nothing belonging to the girl soon lost interest in everything except the wine and some cash they found in a chart table drawer together with my French passport in the name of Henri Gener. They brought back a case of wine, a bottle for every member of their crew and more. They also carried the cash, two thousand American dollars about the equivalent of twenty-two million dong, a few hundred in French francs, and lesser amounts from my ports of call along the way.

They secured a line from the patrol boat to the bow of *Monique* and began towing her back the direction we had come, making the stop I had planned but not the way I had planned it.

The captain now became polite though clearly suspicious. Courtesy, I knew, was a trait for these people. After all, it cost nothing to be polite, even while you tortured someone, the threat made even more terrifying when you realized your tormenters had no need to hate in order to torture or kill.

He questioned me about my travel, where I had come from, when, where I had stopped, how long at each stop, what I did while there, where I was going, when I intended to return to France, making careful notes of my answers. At length he turned to the fact that I spoke fluent Vietnamese. "It is not uncommon for a Frenchman to speak our language, but what is your connection to Vietnam?" he asked in an off-hand manner.

I had anticipated the question and decided to tell him the truth, though not all of it, planning to leave out my military and paramilitary experience. "My father was an employee of the government before the war with Japan, and we returned after the war. We lived near the south end of Hoan Kiem Lake. My Vietnamese playmates and I often swam in the lake and even in the river when we could escape from our parents."

He looked at me with interest knowing that if we lived near Hoan Kiem Lake, my father was not a minor government functionary. In addition, if I had Vietnamese playmates, they had to be the children of servants in our house. He betrayed nothing. "And what is it that has now caused you to sail into our waters?"

"Nostalgia. I wanted to get a glimpse of a place that is more my home than France can ever be," I answered. "Now that the imperialist American war is finished, I thought it would be safe to do so. Depending on my reception, I planned to continue on to Haiphong and maybe visit Hanoi."

All he said was, "I see."

At last he turned to the girl and the circumstances of my finding her.

"Where did you find the girl?" he asked.

"It was two days ago. I cannot give you the exact position. It was at sea. I have entered my positions in my log and made entries in my diary. That is the best I can tell you."

I realized it was important to hold back nothing. The interrogation now would be child's play compared to what would come if the level of suspicion remained high. Being French was now positive compared with being American or any nationality closely identified with America and its war. After all, the presence of French merchant ships in the port of Haiphong bringing supplies to the beleaguered regime in Hanoi had played a significant role in limiting the American attacks on the harbor.

I knew my boat would be searched by men more skilled than these sailors once we reached port. The compartment in the bulkhead might be discovered. If so, they would find my other passports, and then they would know the one I carried with the name Henri Gener might be a forgery. It would bolster their suspicion that I was a spy. In that event, they would undoubtedly hand me over to the secret police for the kind of interrogation that often led to beating, broken bones, and worse.

"If you will permit," I continued, "I will retrieve my log book and diary. They will verify what I have already told you."

"We have already found them," the captain announced. "Unfortunately for you, none of us can read French. So we can neither confirm nor disprove what you say."

"I would be willing to interpret for you, and you can make notes in Vietnamese. Then when the documents are interpreted by your language experts, they can see that I have given you accurate equivalents."

"That would be good for you if what you tell me matches the interpretation made then. If not, it will be very unpleasant for you."

My hands were untied. I rubbed my wrists and hands trying to get the circulation started once again. My naked chest glistened with sweat, and my ears were ringing, no doubt from stress. I could only hope the captain wrote down everything I said. Whatever he added or deleted would no doubt be taken as an attempt at obfuscation.

To my relief the captain continued, "When we have finished I will let you read what I have written. I want it to be accurate. It will be good for my career to have been judged thorough in this affair."

With that, we began. For a man untrained, or so I believed, he was surprisingly efficient and capable in the art of interrogation. He did not take me immediately to the entries relating to the past few days but instead jumped around from place to place in the log and diary testing my current memory against those things that had been important enough to inspire notation in the more distant past. My responses were noted in his book along with notations he seemed to be marking against my official entries. I knew the slightest discrepancy would receive additional attention when we arrived at our destination.

Several hours passed as he slowly and methodically continued his questioning. Then with a sudden change in demeanor, he said, "My men brought aboard several bottles of your wine. Perhaps you would join me in sharing one of them." He intended to see if the effect of alcohol would loosen my tongue and put my mind off guard.

Since I had been completely forthright in answering his questions about my activities, I did not hesitate. "Of course. You are most kind."

A bottle appeared with porcelain cups. I was surprised when the captain did not open the bottle and pour but allowed the wine to decant for several minutes. He poured into both cups, although the amount he poured into his own was noticeably less than what he poured into mine. We chatted amiably for a while drinking the wine, he refilling my cup more frequently than his own but never giving any overt indication or word that he wanted me to become intoxicated, which I did not, though I did allow my words to intentionally slur just a little.

When we finished the wine, he continued in the less formal, amiable tone but now turned the conversation back to my log and diary. This process of questioning and drinking continued throughout our entire passage, although at the time I did not know our destination.

When we arrived at our destination, the captain delivered me to soldiers immediately on docking. I recognized their uniforms; they were officers in the military intelligence apparatus. To my surprise, they did not immediately subject me to additional questioning or any form of physical, emotional, or mental discomfort. I was taken to a room, a cell if you prefer, where I had a cot, chair, and chamber pot. There I was abandoned for several hours.

Hours later one of the officers who had placed me in the cell came with two large men, wearing the uniform of enlisted rank, men who took orders and executed them without question or emotion. These men bound my hands and took me along a hallway stained with the greenish/black mold that grows on the walls of all tropical buildings not air-conditioned.

Near the end of the hallway, we entered a door into another cell, larger than the first, this one equipped forceps, battery terminals, hoods stained with what appeared to be dried blood, and a table with straps for holding a man down. At first my hands and feet were tied to a wooden straight-back chair. The officer looked at me impassively, without expression of any kind. Then the interrogation began. This time it had no air of subtlety. No reference was made to my forthright answers given to the ship's captain or even acknowledgment that such an interrogation had taken place.

The officer nodded to the two enlisted men, and they immediately began to beat me, each man standing slightly behind me on either side, striking me in the back and side of the head, the officer standing in front watching. Suddenly, the chair overturned and the beating continued, now with feet in the stomach and groin. The beating continued until I lost consciousness. I cannot say how long I was unconscious, but when I revived, I was once more sitting upright in the chair.

Following the beating, the interrogation began as if nothing had happened. A stenographer had entered the room while I was unconscious, and she now recorded my answers verbatim. My answers were consistent with those I had given earlier, since they were true and there was, therefore, no need to attempt to remember a lie.

Even now, in my altered state, I cannot tell you just how long the beating and interrogation lasted. When it ended, the two thugs who had been the instrument of my discomfort took me back down the mold-stained hallway to a small room, no more than four feet wide and six feet long. There they bound me with my hands pulled back above my head tied to my feet. This left me with my back arched, cramping. I lay in that position on the concrete floor the entire night with the sound of rats scurrying around the room—coming close though in the darkness I could not see them—waiting for them to attack, an attack that did not come.

Not even my skill in yoga could save me from the agony of that night bound, stripped to my shorts. The next morning the two enlisted men came to get me. They dragged me along the same moldy corridor to the same room where they had beaten me the day before. They placed me on my back below a large drum-like reservoir that had been placed above the table and tied my head and body securely to the table covering my face with one of the hoods. The intelligence officer entered the room and once more gave an abrupt order to the men who opened a valve, and water rushed directly onto my head and face. I held my breath as long as I could but in the end made a futile attempt to breathe, breathe the putrid water that cascaded into my mouth and nose. Slowly drowning, I lost consciousness.

I now see the two men working to revive me, but at the time, I was only aware of coughing, feeling sick, awakening to be subjected to interrogation once more by the officer who remained calm throughout. They repeated the procedure twice more until at last I gave up the only information that had not been true, my name. Then they once more dragged me down the corridor to the cell where they again bound me hand and foot leaving me to spend a second night of misery. The long intervals between interrogation sessions were being used to break my will to resist, leaving me to imagine torture that surely must come.

I awoke on day three filled with terror that some other, worse, ordeal awaited me. The light of morning passed, and the temperature rose in the tiny cell until it must have been mid-afternoon. Finally the two men once more entered my cell and unbound me, dragged me once more down the moldy hallway, this time in the opposite direction of the place of my torture until at last they put me once again in the cell I'd occupied the first night. That day they brought me some food for the first time since my capture.

During this period, the intelligence officers studied my log and diary, comparing it to the notes made by my captor and the answers I had given under extreme torture. Some time later, a higher-ranking officer entered the room and announced in Vietnamese, "Take this man back to his boat." Turning then to me, he said, "You are free to go. We know who you are. We know your name is not Gener, and to us your name means trouble. We know you are trouble and have been trouble much of your life. We know about your double life. We know you worked for the Americans during the war, and we know you betrayed them. We know you are not to be trusted. You are to leave our waters immediately and not return. You will be watched. The tide is in your favor, but if you are not beyond our territorial waters by this time tomorrow, you will be brought back and imprisoned. Do you understand?"

Shocked, I could only answer, "đúng."

When I reached *Monique*, I found her tied to the dock. I wasted no time in setting off using both engine and sail. I checked the priest's hole. It did not appear my tormentors had found it. A small amount of cash, several hundred dollars, was still on board along with my passports and letter of credit. *Monique,* traveling with the aid of both tide and a following wind, carried me as far away, as fast, as she could—I too had cut and run!

Chapter Eleven

"What is it?" Sydna asked. "You seem to be so far away."

"Oh, it is nothing. I was just lost in thought. How do you Americans say it, 'wool gathering'?"

I glanced at my watch. Nearly ten minutes had passed since Mr. Idcyn had stalked away indignantly, his wife trailing behind as they went out of the restaurant into the lobby. *Why,* I wondered, *do Americans always assume they are right, that their way is the only way? Why did he have to come over and ruin our, my, evening by prompting memories best forgotten?* My silence had created an awkward moment at the table, and I wanted to make up for it.

"How about some cognac and cigars? I have some excellent Havanas." I pulled the trim case from my pocket and offered one of the panatelas to Jonathan.

"Wonderful! I don't suppose you'll be telling anyone I stooped to smoking a Communist cigar, will you?"

The ice was broken. The women laughed as I extracted the bullet-shaped cutter from my pocket and, with a quick practiced twist of my fingers, extracted a piece of the tip so the cigar could breathe. I handed the cutter to Jonathan, who looked at it.

"Interesting, I don't believe I've ever seen one exactly like this. They are mostly fat little scissors." With that, he followed my maneuver exactly.

"Very nice," I teased, "not bad for a novice. I picked it up years ago, looks like a real nine-millimeter bullet. After having a few drinks, it is less likely to take off the end of your finger than your scissors."

As we lit the cigars, the ladies excused themselves to go to the powder room. Once they had walked away from the table, Jonathan said, "You were pretty tough on the old boy, don't you think?"

"Yes, I do. He just struck too close to home. I came on some of the boat people as I passed by Vietnam a few weeks ago. It was ugly. You don't forget something like that for a long time."

"Want to talk about it?" Jonathan was a considerate man, if not forthright.

"Not really; there was a little girl. She is dead now. I don't know, maybe I could have done more. I wanted to help, but…"

"I'm sure you did all anyone could have done." Jonathan wanted more information, but my pause indicated a cessation of the story. "Were you far off the coast when it happened?"

"No, not far; in fact, I was quite close. It was at the south end of the peninsula."

"Were there many of them?"

"Not alive; their boat had been attacked and sunk. There were bodies all around. I don't know why they didn't kill her too. I guess they just didn't see her. At least that is what she thought."

"So you found her alive?"

"Yes, but a patrol boat caught up with us, and she killed herself."

"How awful for you. I understand. It must be terribly distressing."

"It is. So many times in my life I have set out to do the right thing only to have it end in death or tragedy. I suppose it is that way with many people."

"Possibly, I don't know. I guess I've just never been placed in that position, at least not so I ever saw the ending in the way you describe."

I must tell you, I liked Jonathan Cartwright. He was a decent man. I now know he was not being honest with me when he made that statement. Of course, he made decisions every day that ultimately led to tragedy for someone. It only mattered that the interests of America were not compromised.

"So, M. Henri Gener, I find you to have a most interesting name." Jonathan opened up in a more direct manner. "You know I speak a little French. Your name is a playful way of describing yourself. Gener means 'trouble,' does it not? Moreover, Henri sounds amazingly close to our word 'ornery,' so then your name translates to 'Ornery Trouble.' Is it a coincidence?"

I smiled, then replied, "No, but you are the first person to tumble on to my little joke. After all my travels, no one else has noticed it. Well, almost no one else."

"I imagine the Vietnamese saw through it. They are, after all, a very clever people."

I chuckled. "I don't believe they did. The ones I saw didn't appear to speak fluent French."

"So, what is your name?"

At that moment, the women returned to the table, and

I was spared the sparring. "Gener, of course," I answered playfully nevertheless. The two women sat down.

"What was that about?" Caroline wanted to know.

"Your husband noticed my name means 'trouble' and wanted to know if it was really my name."

"And is it?"

"Why yes, of course it is. The origin of names is a fascinating subject. I once knew some German people; their name was Zumwalt. Loosely translated that means 'to the woods.' Your own name 'Cartwright' refers to someone who makes repairs to carts and wagons. Why shouldn't my name mean trouble? After all, it would certainly seem to apply tonight."

"Touché," Caroline replied.

Dinner ended with the announcement the movie would start in fifteen minutes. We adjourned to a comfortable room furnished with plush leather chairs where the movie, *The Way We Were* with Robert Redford and Barbra Streisand, was to be shown as part of the entertainment for those dining at the restaurant. The movie stopped at the end of each reel while the projectionist made the change. This provided a break for the spectators and gave the hotel an opportunity to offer refreshments; waiters circulated throughout the room taking drink orders.

During one of those intermissions, when there was a lull in the conversation, I was approached by a fellow citizen who introduced himself to me as Monsignor Boulanger from Mount Carmel Cathedral.

"I have been hoping for an opportunity to say hello. It is not often I have the opportunity to speak my native tongue. Have you been enjoying your stay on our island?"

"Hello, Monsignor, yes, I have. I've found the people and activities most interesting, especially after spending so much time at sea."

"Ah yes, it is a most beautiful boat you have. One of my parishioners gave me a ride down to the dock to see it. I'd hoped to run into you there, but alas you were away enjoying yourself."

"I am sorry to have missed you. It would have been my pleasure to give you a tour of the lovely *Monique*. You can imagine though it is a great joy to have the feel of solid land under my feet. Since arriving I have slept on the boat but otherwise have been occupied all over the island."

"And tomorrow, what are your plans?"

"I thought I would take in the beach festivities. I hear the boat races will be exciting."

"No doubt! I too may walk up the road to watch a little. Earlier in the day we will celebrate Mass. Being French, I thought perhaps you were Catholic and would want to know the time. We begin at nine, before the sun gets too high and the building is hot. I am certain you have noticed as you drove down the road that we have no glass in our windows. Ours is an open-air church. It allows us to be close to our creator and at the same time enjoy the natural wonders of his creation."

"It is kind of you to extend the invitation, but no, I don't believe I will attend."

"That is too bad. A man at sea, alone, never knows what will befall him. We must all be prepared for the end, must we not?"

"And so I am, in my own way."

"And what way might that be?"

"It is the way of seamen from the earliest time. I prepare myself for the rigors of ocean travel, the solitude, the dangers, storms, calms; the possibility of going aground on shoals; of falling overboard. One never knows what awaits him, and so one never acts imprudently to anger the god of the sea."

"But surely the god of the sea is the God of all creation?"

"So you believe and teach your flock, only I am no longer a member of that flock. You see, I go my own way."

"I understand, maybe better than you think. It is a dangerous course you have set for yourself. Remember the holy Word says there is a way that seems right to a man but in the end it leads to death."

"I presume you are talking about spiritual death, Monsignor."

"But of course. We are taught; we believe; we have faith; and we put our trust in Jesus Christ who overcame physical death to show us he had the power to overcome spiritual death as well."

"So what would you have me say, that I believe in God? Of course, your Book says even the devils do and they shudder. However, do I believe in God with a passion, a longing, without uncertainty? No. My reason tells me he exists, but I have no strong belief he considers me individually. So what is the point of my belief, faith you would call it? If he exists but does not care about me, what is the point of my abasement before men, before the image of such an uncaring God? I am sorry, Father, but I do not share your kind of faith. Events in my life have shown me that God, if he exists at all, does not care for us. If he did, so much of my life that has ended in pain and suffering would not have happened."

"Suffering is part of life, my son. It was through the agony, the passion of our savior, that he was exalted to the right hand of God. St. Paul teaches us that no temptation has overtaken us but that which is common to all mankind. He says that with the temptation, the suffering, the agony, the disappointment, God has given us the way of escape. He has given us Jesus Christ."

"No, Father, I simply don't buy it anymore. What you say is for your own good. The Church has prospered throughout the ages on the sweat and blood of simple people. I personally see very little difference between what you say and do and what the scribes and Pharisees said and did in the time of Jesus."

"Ah then, you acknowledge the life and teaching of Jesus, do you not?"

"I did not say that. I was merely using your text to refute your argument. For my part, I renounce your Jesus. He has never personally done anything for me. I have nothing against you, Father, but I have no part in your so-called savior. Where was he, where was your God when my wife was murdered while in bed with her lover?"

The priest recoiled at my words. To this point, our exchange had been a pleasant if not challenging discourse. Now he heard the words of blasphemy that would subject the soul of the unrepentant to the tortures of unrelenting suffering.

"I am sorry for you, my son. I urge you to repent of those words and seek comfort in the confessional. The word teaches us in Hebrews, 'It is impossible for those who have once been enlightened, who have tasted the heavenly gift, who have shared in the Holy Spirit, who have tasted the goodness of the word of God and the powers of the coming age, if they fall away, to be brought back to repentance, because to their loss they are crucifying the Son of God all over again and subjecting him to public disgrace.' Do not put our Lord to the test in this matter; repent before it is too late."

"No, Father. It is you who are wrong. You live a good life on the money of others and in return give only false hope. For my part, it matters not at all whether your hell is a place of fire and brimstone or a place of darkness. I don't believe in it any more than I believe in your heaven and your God."

At that moment, the projectionist turned out the lights, and the third reel of the movie began.

Not willing to let the conversation end on such a negative note, the priest had one more rejoinder. "It is never too late to come to repentance. I believe you are speaking in the heat of discussion, nothing more. Be careful with your immortal soul. So long as there remains in you any vestige of life, it is not too late. I will pray for you, my son. I will pray that God will grant you time to see and understand the nature of what you have done, where you have been in error, and give you the opportunity to set matters right. I know that in your heart you do believe in God, in heaven and hell, and as St. Chrysostom reminds us: 'We must not ask where hell is, but how we are to escape it.' And so, my prayer for you will be that God will provide a way for you to escape the hell that would seem to await you."

The opportunity for further discussion gone, the priest walked back to his seat. Sydna stared at me for a moment then said, "Do you really believe what you said to him?"

"Your French is much better than I imagined. Did you understand all that we said?"

"Not every word, but I certainly got the gist of what you said."

"Well then, if you got the gist of the meaning, you understand what I meant to say."

The movie ended at last. Catholic Robert Redford and Jewish Barbra Streisand continued their strange dance of conflicting faith and belief until in the end they separated, finally, wistfully, yet irreconcilably.

We said goodnight to the Cartwrights, and I went with Sydna back to my boat. That night Sydna seemed confused, reserved, while I looked toward moving on.

Chapter Twelve

Much of what I now want to relate I only know because of the miraculous gift of understanding I have been given, a gift even more profound than I first realized, to know things before they happen. Had I taken heed of my dreams of Mark Meriday, I would undoubtedly have seen him as someone dangerous, not merely a buffoon.

Meriday rose early on Sunday morning, his thoughts filled with anticipation for the sailing races. He would certainly win. The glory would boost his mercurial ego, and he could always use the money he would win by betting on himself. He was after all the best catamaran sailor in the islands. He had proved that last Christmas in the winter regatta, although the strong trade winds that prevailed in the winter months were now only a faint memory. The race today would be much different with less wind, temperature in the nineties, and the air heavy with humidity.

The boats will all be more sluggish, he reflected. *With light wind, there will be no need to have a crew, even a crew of one. Today it will be just me, on my own, sailing the bright green and yellow boat, recently renamed* Sydna. *The course* once more passed around marker buoys anchored two miles apart in the lagoon. The southern buoy had been placed just beyond the derelict Sherman tanks rusting in the clear green water where they had been dumped during the invasion thirty years earlier with only their turrets and big guns showing.

Leaving his cluttered third-floor rooms in the Pink Apartments, he drove down Beach Road to Tank Beach at the Royal Taga Hotel, all the while his anger rising at the humiliation he'd felt after the incident Thursday night at Hamilton's. He wanted to let go of these feelings, but that had never been possible. It was his anger, his temper that had caused him to come to the islands.

Tall, clumsy in appearance with a huge head crowned by a shock of red hair, he looked more like Raggedy Andy in his sailing whites than the respected lawyer he wanted to be. His whole life had been one humiliation after another. As a boy, the other kids made fun of his hair calling him carrot top and laughing at him as he tried to participate in sports, always falling, always failing.

The three years in the L.A. Sheriff's Patrol after graduation from the academy had been no better. It was always Mark who got the worst detail. He had left the Sheriff's Patrol for a job as lifeguard at Laguna Beach. It was no different. Girls laughed at him behind his back when they did not think he could hear. He knew they did not laugh because they thought he was cool. His well-muscled shoulders did not tan; he turned lobster red, a lobster red redhead.

He believed attending the storefront law school on Figuroa Street would change things. Not so. Now he was not just an overly tall, clumsy, gauche carrot top, he was a pseudo-intellectual as well. The only job he could get was prosecuting traffic tickets in municipal court, a position not likely to impress anyone.

It was there he met Dorothy. She had been ticketed for driving too slow, impeding traffic on the San Diego Freeway, and it had been his day to prosecute. He had liked her from the moment he saw her. Here was a girl he would have a chance with. Sure, she was a little on the pudgy side and her nickname was Chub, but she seemed to like him too and so he showed mercy and dismissed the ticket when it came up on the docket. After that, they went out a few times, but his clumsy approach in the end made her laugh too. He had not meant to hurt her, but she was just like all the rest looking down on him even though he stood six feet eight inches. Thank God, no one had connected him with what happened to her. Thank God even more for the job here in the AG's office. From so far away, he knew no one would ever connect him with that horrible incident.

Now, once again Mark felt the growing anger, hatred, and jealousy, the feeling of loneliness and rejection that had haunted him all his life. As he turned off the road at the Royal Taga Hotel and parked under the palm trees, he no longer felt the exhilaration that came from knowing he was a winner. He was a loser, and he knew it.

Getting out of the car and unfolding his long legs around the steering column, leaning forward to get his massive head out the door first, he heard a familiar voice.

"Mr. Mark, you're the first one here, just like last time. No one else even been by; the racing don't start for hours."

"Yeah, I know, just thought I'd launch the boat a little early and get a feel for the water, the wind, you know, get a little advantage." Talking to the Chamorro beach boy for the Royal Taga lifted his spirits. This boy recognized Mark. He remembered Mark had won the races in December.

"Here, I'll give you a hand pushing your boat into the water."

They were a comical pair, the gangly carrot top man and the short, brown, stocky Micronesian boy struggling to move the boat that had sat on the beach for weeks, her pontoons sinking into the coral sand with the rain that had stopped in the middle of last month. After several attempts to inch the cat toward the water rising with the incoming tide, Mark said, "Come on around on this side. We'll have to walk her out of the ruts until we can push her into the water."

"Sure, Mr. Mark." The boy moved around the boat, and with both man and boy on the same side, they lifted the cat and managed to move her at an oblique angle.

"Now then, let's get on to the other side. If we can move her out of that rut, we can push her into the water." Again, both man and boy lifted and strained to free the right pontoon. "Got it," Mark exclaimed. "Let's give her the old heave ho!"

It was easier said than done. The grit of coral sand scraped against the bottom of the pontoons, removing microscopic bits of the slick marine paint that allowed the *Sydna* to ride effortlessly on and through the water. At last free of the alien environment, she began the slow bobbing motion of a ship in her natural element. Mark quickly hoisted the sail while the boy held against the ebb and flow of the tide.

"You sure do know how to do that fast," the boy commented. "I'll bet you're going to be the big winner again this time."

"Yeah, I wouldn't be surprised," Mark responded, his confidence and mood swinging once again like a pendulum toward the manic side of his rapid-fire personality. "I brought a couple grand with me to bet on the races," exaggerating not to impress the boy so much as to inflate his own ego. "You just put out the word that Ol' Mark is here and he came to win. That ought to get some action started."

"Sure enough."

Mark slipped the boy five for the help. "Here, you might want to put some money on me too." Then, feeling generous, he said, "Here's a ten spot."

Mark caught the gentle breeze, took the *Sydna* out into the deeper water of the lagoon, and glided with the wind at his back on a reach toward the buoy two miles away.

I don't need anyone to help me sail, Mark thought. *In December, everyone talked about how I wouldn't have won without the expert crew help from George Rowley. What do they know; it wasn't that scrawny Rowley that got me to the finish line first in all of the races except one. Rowley had to have weights added to his life vest so he could hold the windward pontoon down leaning flat out working the trapeze, suspended by the harness, his head nearly touching the water as it rushed by. It was the way I came about, the way I tacked into the gale that made the difference. George slipped and fell into the water allowing the boat to capsize in the one race we lost.* Well, this time there would not be any doubt. George would be watching from the beach.

In these wind conditions, I'm on my own. This time they'll all know it is because I'm the best. Then, in a moment of doubt, his mood and confidence slipping, he thought, *Those pontoons sure took a lot of abuse in getting the boat to the water. Maybe I should have done some sailing before now. The other boats don't seem to be stuck like* Sydna. *Their hulls look clear and shiny, no scratches there. I suppose the others have all been out practicing. Oh well, let 'em. It won't make any difference.*

The wind changed direction after three circuits around the buoys. Now it was at his back as he returned to the starting point, the Hobie-Cat seeming to fly even in the gentle breeze. He had to beat in that breeze now from the start, but that would work to his advantage in the races. *Sydna* was faster on the reach than the other cats. After his fourth lap, testing the new wind direction, Mark came back to shore and, jumping into the ankle-deep water, pulled the boat onto the edge of the beach and dropped the anchor onto the sand, holding her in place.

The boy was still working setting up the umbrellas and chairs as he walked toward the car. "You sure looked fast out there, Mr. Mark. I'm going to bet on you today."

Feeling a rise in confidence coming from the words of this boy who knew nothing about sailing, Mark's shoulders came back, and his stride took on a long swagger. Calling back without diverting his eye from the beach ahead, he said, "You do that on every race, and you'll turn that ten into nearly a hundred dollars. But don't you go betting on any other races. You don't know if they can win or not."

"I won't."

"If you're going to be out here for an hour or so, I'll give you another five to watch the boat. I'd hate to have anything happen with the races just a couple of hours away." Feeling hungry for the first time that day, he added, "I'm going to get something to eat."

As he drove back up Beach Road, the knot in his stomach returned. Turning up Navy Hill Road, he drove into the parking lot of the Pink Apartments. Sydna's car was not there. His jealousy returned. *Where is she? Who is she with?* Turning as he accelerated, his tires spun on the coral slick pavement, and he drove toward Charlie Dock. Even before he turned off the road onto the dock area, he saw her car parked beside the *Monique*.

They, they, they… They can't do that to me. I'll… Mark stopped, his brain incapable of continuing. At best, he had always been a man of action. With no more than average intelligence, he had more than once been reduced to action, to violence, when his ability to express himself had failed. Animal instinct took over. There was nothing else, not then, not now. He did not know when, how, or where he would take his revenge, but take it he would.

Turning the car, he drove without regard for anyone or anything, a hot, searing heat burning through his head, his heart beating fast, eyes not really focusing on the road ahead. He did not see the Chamorro boy on the road until it was nearly too late.

Both he and the boy reacted at the same time with the two unaccountably taking the right action. The boy walked head down in the center of the coral pavement not expecting to see any traffic on the road then looked up to see the approaching car hurtling toward him. It must have been fate, or a guardian angel, that caused him to look up in time to see the car just feet ahead giving him time to throw his body to the right at the same time Mark swerved to his right. The two avoided the killing blow by inches with the boy nevertheless thrown to the pavement by the suddenness of the event and the rushing wind as the car crashed off the pavement onto the dirt, rock, and sand that made up the shoulder. The car came to a stop a hundred feet down the road from where the boy, shaken but otherwise unhurt, rose with a bewildered expression thankful to be alive.

Mark slammed the automatic shift into reverse and, tires spinning in the loose material that doubled as dirt at this point on the island, managed to back onto the pavement. Only then did he look back to see the boy standing looking back at him. "You stupid Micron, watch where you're going!" he shouted. The boy stood still for an instant too frightened to speak or run, then turned and ran cross country toward Middle Road not knowing where he was going but too scared to stay where he was. Mark thought, *Why don't the Micronesians keep their kids under control? I could have killed him. He had no business being out here walking down the middle of the road.*

No longer hungry, he drove back to Tank Beach, arriving thirty minutes after he had left. Early picnickers were busily staking claim to the choicest spots under the shade of the trees, building their rock fire pits over which they laid the flat diamond-mesh material that doubled as a security screen on the Samoan houses and cooking grill for their pit fires. Small Micronesian boys and girls ran naked along the beach, looking for the shells that no longer existed on this stretch of beach, under

the watchful eye their mothers wearing bright multicol-
ored dresses made even more brilliant by their dark skin.
The women talked in groups of two or three while the
fathers, drinking beer, throwing the cans on the beach
for the Royal Taga boy to pick up later, or not, once the
festivities were over, paid little or no attention.

An old rusted pickup truck had parked at the place
where he had stopped earlier, and so he now had to
park in the sun. The Royal Taga boy ran toward him. "I
watched your boat like you said."

"Well, I was only gone a few minutes. Whata you
want?"

"You said you'd pay me."

"Get lost. I was only gone a couple of minutes, and
I'm not giving you another dime."

Dejectedly, head and eyes cast downward, the boy
walked away, embarrassed by the outburst that seemed
uncalled for especially in the presence of the women
who heard yet pretended to not notice. He thought the
Americans, not just the Americans, but more often than
not them, certainly more them than the New Zealanders
or British on the island, but maybe less than the Aussies,
would be nice when they wanted something. Otherwise,
the *haoles* were rude and bullies. Only the Japanese,
who treated all Asian people on the island as inferior,
having once virtually enslaved them all, were worse, or
so he thought. The Royal Taga boy had not included
Frenchmen in his thoughts because he had not yet met
Henri Gener who disguised with civility could match
the worst.

Skulking toward the beach a scant hundred feet away,
Mark, with a mixture of shame and remorse for the way
he spoke to the boy, yet still in the clutches of jealousy,

pulled a pocketknife from his front pocket. Extracting the sharpest blade as he approached the *Sydna*, he instantly set to work scraping away the offending name from the boat, possibly the only thing he could still love, now defaced by the name of the traitor.

The other yachtsmen began arriving minutes later, setting to work preparing their boats for the coming races. The man designated by the racers to serve as commodore, the principal race officer and protest judge, the sole member and arbiter of any disputes that might arise during the course of the races, soon called them together where, by lots, the individual pairings were established for the double elimination regatta.

Of those entered in the event, Mark knew he had beaten them all in the December race, all that is except for the sole new entry, a friend of sorts, Jonathan Cartwright, but there was no reason to take him that seriously. His boat, a Sunfish, recently delivered by the Enna G from Oakland, surely could not compete against the cats with their double hulls, shallow draught, and larger sails. The yachtsmen and spectators watched with interest as the pairings were written on the small chalkboard, considering their bets.

Saipan as I have already told you is not a large island, and, with only fourteen thousand people, there is not a lot to do. Each person made his own entertainment, compartmentalizing his life against the sense of isolation that otherwise overwhelmed them all. For that reason, the races and festivities surrounding Liberation Day and the American Fourth were times of excitement, the kind of excitement repeated only at Christmas, New Year's Eve, and first birthday parties.

The men drew lots to pair off for the races and then

moved to launch their boats. The last boat in the water was Cartwright's Sunfish. He backed the trailer into the water, and two men struggled for several minutes before getting the small boat launched. The lagoon filled with a rainbow of color. Boats of red and purple, blue and gold, pink and green tacked back and forth in the wind, each watching to stay clear of the others.

The children of American families ran along the beach throwing firecrackers at one another, some of the older boys tossing them in the direction of the naked Micronesian toddlers who shrieked before retreating to the protection of their mothers' bright skirts.

As this scene of mayhem continued, the orange Dodge Charger stopped at the edge of the pavement. I stepped out, pausing to look around before entering into the festivities. Hiroki turned left and parked in front of one of the buildings on the other side of the road where he joined several other Micronesian young men who were all of an age that resented rather than feared the rich foreigners who dominated the beach scene across the road. They were men who wanted what the foreigners had without wanting to be like them. Hiroki identified himself as one of the leaders of this group or any group of young men his age.

Casting my eyes around the crowd, I spied several people I had met. The wives of several men racing beckoned me to join them. I acknowledged each in turn then moved away toward a beautiful Ponapean woman, bare breasted in the custom of her island, wearing only a long skirt wrapped around her broad hips and legs, tucked in at the waist. Her raven hair fell to its full length down her sculpted back.

Stopping before her, confident of my own physical appeal, I said, "Mademoiselle, you are the loveliest woman on this beach. No. I am sadly mistaken. You are the most exquisite creature in the entire Pacific."

Unlike most women from her island, she did not avoid my eyes but looked directly into them. "You are very kind."

Her manner and speech identified her as different from most of the other island women. She was educated, not merely intelligent, poised, confident, experienced.

"I cannot tell you how much I hope you are here alone."

"No, I am with my husband. He is over there under the tree."

She looked in the direction of an aging, bald white man whose eyes, even from that distance, were obviously sightless. "Such an old man for such a young and vibrant young woman!"

"In many ways, yes. He has been very good to me though. He took me in as a child when my parents were killed by a typhoon that struck Ponape. He provided for my education, and now I take care of him. Thankfully he is blind, for he is otherwise very jealous of me now that I am a woman."

"I can see why. He is a most fortunate man to enjoy the intimacy of someone so rare, so young, delicate, yet strong. Has he reason to be jealous?"

"Of course, I'm talking with you, aren't I?"

"And nothing more?"

"Perhaps."

"What is your name?"

"He calls me Tanya."

"I shall call you Monique. That is the name of my boat, and she is the most graceful ketch in the Pacific."

She smiled catching the compliment. "I will look forward to visiting your boat."

"Tanya, Tanya, where are you?" the blind man sitting under the tree called out.

"I am here, Papa."

"Come here."

Obediently, Tanya led the way to where the old man sat. "What do you want?"

"I didn't know where you were. Is someone with you?"

"Yes, he is the stranger on the island, the one who came on the sailboat. You know, we heard about him the other day."

"Of course I remember; I'm blind not stupid." Extending his right hand in my direction, more an act of formality than friendship, he added, "My name is Ned Simons. Once upon a time, it was Colonel Ned Simons, but that was before I lost my sight in a vehicle accident a few years ago. It's nice to see you."

The expression "see" struck me as just a little strange, but then I was surprised that he knew where I was standing. I took his hand. "It's equally nice to meet you as well," I answered noncommittally.

Just then, the boats returned from their preliminary lap around the course giving the crowd a chance to see how each of the contestants handled the wind and water. Mark Meriday was the first to beach his boat. I waved a greeting to him, but he did not return the gesture, walking instead down the beach the other direction toward George and Beth Rowley, where he stood feet apart, shoulders back for a few moments, his great shock of red hair bobbing as he talked. His demeanor was one of anger spilling over before he stalked off to join a group of single men.

The two boats in the first heat were in place maneuvering in the lagoon then making an orchestrated turn as they approached the imaginary starting line. The two boats seemed to continue as if tied together tacking back and forth down the course until it was no longer possible to see who was in the lead.

The wind had freshened since early in the morning, unusual for the time of year, and a half hour later the red and purple boat returned just a little more than three boat lengths ahead of the other. At last it was time for the last pairing: Mark Meriday and a man I did not know.

Mark walked to his boat. He appeared to look in my direction as if to say, *Now you'll see some real sailing.* Just under an hour later, true to the look he had given me, Mark returned well ahead of his rival. He puffed up with pride as a group of his supporters shouted out their approval and delight that he had won so handily. His step seemed more of a swagger as he passed by me again without comment, his feet flipping the coral sand backwards as he walked.

The next two races were between the losers of the first round. It was then that one of Mark's friends approached me to ask if I had ever sailed in a Hobie-Cat.

"Not that I recall," I lied. "Since I became a man, I've stopped sailing toys."

The man was either incredibly stupid or devoid of pride. My barb had gone past him without as much as a flinch. "Well, maybe you can give it a try today. I am sure someone here will loan you his boat. Your appearance on the island has created quite a stir, and I'm certain we'd all like to see you handle a boat."

"No, I don't believe I'd care to do that."

The first race in the winner's bracket was well under-way when the man returned to the group including Mark. I noticed Mark casting long side-glances in my direction as the men continued to talk. From their posture and gesture, it was clear they were all excited by something more than the alcohol they had consumed.

Three hours had elapsed by the time Mark's turn came up to race again. The sun was now high in the sky, and the heat coupled with the beer had taken their toll on his coordination. Nevertheless, when the commodore called for the two boats to launch, Mark was on board and, although shaky, prepared to sail. His opponent was the newcomer Jonathan Cartwright.

Mark moved over the start line just ahead of Jonathan but soon fell behind as the more maneuverable Sunfish tacked into the wind. At the turn buoy, Jonathan had what appeared to be an impressive lead, what looked to be at least a quarter of a mile. Once around the two-mile buoy, Mark's cat caught the wind. His boat appeared to leap forward as the precious lead built up by Jonathan with so much effort vanished in just a few minutes as the two crafts raced on a broad reach toward the finish-ing buoy. From somewhere off to my right, I heard one of the men who had been sitting with Mark comment, "Would you look at Mark go; that baby can really fly."

The two boats neared the finish buoy when Jonathan's Sunfish altered course, nearly causing the two boats to collide. Mark spilled the wind from his sail to avoid the collision and again fell off the pace. At the finish, he was clearly beaten. Even before the boats reached the beach, Mark screamed Jonathan had interfered and should be disqualified. The commodore, now acting as protest judge, called out that all bets should be held while he considered the circumstances. A driver was dispatched to bring the two-mile buoy judge back for consultation. All the while Jonathan protested that being in the lead he had every right to maneuver about as he did.

Mark's face flushed; his pale legs covered with red hair trembled. His twitching shoulders and incoherent speech caused the crowd to wonder at his mental state. Sure, he had bet on himself, but only now that I can see everything clearly, with my ability to know the past without impediment, do I realize that he had bet more on himself than he could afford to lose. He would be humiliated when he could not pay. Worse yet to be beaten by an "east coast pansy" after the bragging he had done would be unbearable. On a small island and with more than a year on his current contract with the government, the shame would make life unbearable.

Fifteen minutes later, the protest judge completed his review and in a loud voice announced his decision. "Mr. Cartwright has been disqualified. Mr. Meriday is the winner."

Mark fell to his knees sobbing for joy as the assembled crowd stood in horror at the behavior, his former appearance being, on the surface, reduced to a mere trifle by comparison.

I found the scene amusing, disgusting, and encouraging. I reconsidered my decision to not race and now

determined to race if Mark should prove to be the ultimate winner of the regatta. I planned to insist on a race
of two laps around the course instead of one. That would
give me the opportunity to familiarize myself with the
feel of the toy boats. Not knowing the financial position
of Mark at the time, I nevertheless resolved to goad as
large a wager as I could.

An hour later the finalists were determined, and once
again Jonathan Cartwright and Mark Meriday would
be paired against each other. Betting was now spirited
since many on the beach believed Jonathan had truly
won the first race between the two, suggesting he would
easily triumph in the rematch. His skill with the Sunfish
would more than offset the cat's intrinsic speed on the
reach. Others insisted Mark had the advantage by vir-
tue of the fact that Jonathan had been racing without a
break for the last hour and a half and would no doubt
be mentally fatigued by the effort in finding the wind
that could carry him to victory. Still others contended
that very fact made him the favorite. The wind, though
not strong, had been shifting throughout the day, and
Jonathan's experience with the prevailing wind would be
the difference.

I noticed Mark had not bet on himself in the race. He
stood aloof from the process contending his seamanship
would speak for him. This time he would race for prestige
not money. It occurred to me Mark Meriday could not
stand the thought of losing both prestige and the money
he had won on the earlier races. When the two men
launched their boats for the finals, Mark was composed
but without the swagger he had exhibited earlier. In the
first race, Jonathan had clearly out-sailed Mark and the

judged foul aside may have won the race by a narrow margin anyway, a fact ignored by the commodore.

In anticipation of the outcome, I slipped away from the crowd going down the beach to a point where I could see the two-mile buoy, intent on seeing how the two men handled their boats as they made the turn. The effects of the alcohol had seemingly worn off, and Mark sailed at his best, though it astonished me to see that neither man was more than a weekend sailor. Both men reached the buoy and simply came about, a maneuver both clumsy and slow. It was all I needed to know. If Mark won, I would goad him into a large wager and pick his pocket.

Mark did win. He won by the smallest of margins, but he won. I insinuated myself in the midst of the congratulatory slaps and offers to buy drinks at the bar of the Royal Taga, barely able to conceal my delight at the opportunity afforded me. Extending my hand to Mark, I said, "Well done. You've proved yourself to be the best seaman on this small island, at least."

His mercurial confidence took the bait.

In a malevolent voice, he responded, "I haven't beaten you yet. But unless you are afraid to race, I will."

"Why should I race you on your toy boats?" I answered. "I sail only the open ocean boats, going where you would be afraid to venture." I counted on the humiliation he felt, cuckolded and goaded, to push him over the edge.

"French coward," he shouted. "You're the one who's afraid. If you're so good, then place your money where your mouth is."

"Big boats or small boats, it's all the same to me. You, sir, are all mouth. Maybe I will teach you something about sailing. But if I am to risk my reputation on something as childish as racing these pond boats, you and your friends will have to make it worth my while."

Now, not just the bait, the hook too was firmly set in his brain. "I've got five grand in the bank. That says I can beat you."

"Well, if you have five, maybe your friends will put up another five with it. If so, I will be more than happy to accommodate you. If not, then I guess your friends do not have much faith in you. I race only on my own terms."

He turned, his eyes pleading with his companions. They hesitated. "It's just a loan. I'll pay you back. Don't you see; I've got to have it. I've got to beat him."

First one then another stepped forward, agreeing to put up a small wager on their own and loaning him the balance to cover the bet. In the end, he was still a thousand dollars short.

"If you are so confident," I continued, "then maybe you'd be willing to put your boat up for the balance of the wager. One race, two laps. If you win, I pay you ten thousand dollars. When I win, I take all your money and your boat."

His voice quaking in rage, he said, "Done."

I had him. Now I'd show George Rowley what I meant by breaking someone, break him until his humiliation would cause him to act irrationally, even kill himself, or try to kill his antagonist. At the time, I did not know Mark Meriday lacked the courage to commit suicide. Being backed into a corner, he would become a truly dangerous man.

"Who'll let me use his boat?"

Silence, then from the back of the group I heard, "I will." It was Jonathan Cartwright.

"Thanks, Jonathan. I like the way your boat responds."

Once again, Mark's Hobie-Cat with its green and yellow sails was paired against the white and gold of Jonathan Cartwright. Only this time, it would be my own sensitive touch on the tiller, feeling the lines, talking to the wind. It would be my considerable skill on the water, not some casual sailor. As I strode to the boat, I saw for the first time that Sydna had arrived, no doubt while I had been occupied down the beach on my reconnaissance. She looked directly at me and smiled. I walked by without acknowledging her presence.

Once on board Jonathan's boat, named for his wife, Caroline, I made a couple of tacks to get the feel of her without giving away my skill in small boats. Then we made a broad turn approaching the starting line on the fly, the wind now crossing from seaward.

On the first attempt to begin, Mark crossed the line so far ahead that the race starter declared a false start. On the second attempt, he once again crossed ahead, but when the starter again appeared to be prepared to declare a false start, I waived him off—the race underway.

The crowd solidly backed Mark shouting encouragement for him to beat the arrogant Frenchman. I lagged behind allowing the Hobie-Cat to tack back and forth ahead of the Sunfish as I followed Mark to the first buoy, trailing slightly when he came about. With his sail flapping harmlessly, he looked across to see how much of a lead he had. Only a few feet separated us though he was now around the buoy and I was still approaching it. I looked directly into his eyes and smiled. Outraged at my apparent arrogance, he looked straight ahead and tended to the business of now handling the sails of the cat to catch a mostly following wind.

Now was the time I would let them see my skill in small boats. I set the tiller, clutched it from behind by my thighs, dropped the line, flattened myself on the deck, and as the boom flew over my head completing the gybe, the white and gold boat lurched ahead. By the time Mark had found the wind, I had already made up half the lead he had taken into his clumsy turn.

Now was his time to shine. The twin pontoon boat barely drew any water, and she flew down toward the starting point building a sizable lead. By the time we passed the rusting tanks and approached the finish line buoy for the first time, I looked at the faces in the crowd. This was not going to be a race after all. At the point where Jonathan Cartwright had been bowsprit to bowsprit with Mark Meriday as they had approached the finish, I now trailed by well over fifty yards. If the race had been only one lap around the buoys, it would have been over, but this was more than just a race; it continued to be about humiliation, to bring Mark all the way down.

I followed Mark as he came about. I called to Mark to do his best. I watched as his boat slowly completed the turn in a slow crawl, with the wind crossing a little to his bow, toward the far end of the course began again. This time my skill caused *Caroline* to move forward, first catching and then passing Mark, leaving him a hundred yards behind at the buoy. Shocked at the turn of events, Mark calculated his chances, knowing how well *Caroline* handled as I had gybed into the crossing wind. He had to try something to keep me from running so far in front on the turn he would not have a chance to catch me even with the faster boat.

He had watched me gybe and had read the books, and so he tried his best, though his best simply was not good enough. A man his size on such a small boat had no chance. The humiliation was complete. As the boom swung across, it struck him in the back, and although the wind was not strong, he was hurled headlong into the lagoon, the boat with no name drifting harmlessly out toward the reef. He stood in the waist-deep water. I looked back and waved.

Twenty minutes later, I was back at the finish line. The crowd began packing up; only a few stragglers remained. I collected my bets from those who bet against me, all except for Mark, who had been picked up by a motor launch and returned to the starting point. Telling Mark I would settle up the next day, I turned to leave. He stood in shock, no longer shaking or crying. He stood as a man turned to stone. His eyes were the eyes of a man who had ceased to be a rational thinking being.

Sydna took a tentative step in my direction, but I walked past her and, brushing against my ebony Monique, whispered, "Come to my boat tonight after the old man goes to sleep."

She nodded; she would come.

Chapter Thirteen

Back on my boat, I showered and lay down, thinking about the excitement the day had brought. The sights and sounds of boisterous *haoles* and Micronesians mingling together, children playing without regard to race or status, the smell of tangen-tangen charcoal in the grill pits, the aroma of the marinade chicken and flank steak being seared over the open fire, and most of all the beautiful Ponapean woman who would soon be coming to my boat after dark, after her old husband/papa had gone to sleep, filled my thoughts. Without intending, I too fell asleep.

I hear a knocking at the door, and my mother tells the Vietnamese houseboy to see who it is. The Bougainvillea is in bloom, and its scent fills the room through the open double doors leading to the garden. The room is an odd mixture of styles; country refectory table and chairs from our home in France, a sideboard and chairs that do not match the table, also from home, are interspersed with the things my mother bought once we arrived in Hanoi.

The day is unusually pleasant for the time of year, and I wonder why I cannot go to the river and swim. After all, it is safe in Hanoi. There is nothing to worry about here. The Viet Minh are in the countryside. They are not here, in the city. I want to swim with my classmates from the French school, the sons of other government officials. All the other boys my age get to go to the river. Nothing bad ever happens at the river. Sure, there was the incident last year when one of the boys nearly drowned, but he could not swim. I am a good swimmer.

Mother is in the next room with three of her friends, also wives of government officials. They are all dressed in their fine Chinese silk dresses and have lunched on fruit, cheese, and fresh bread. Now they are sitting at a table having tea while playing Mahjong, a Chinese game they learned the year we got here, not this time, the first time. I do not get it, something about the wind and dragons. It makes no sense, although I sometimes get out the tiles and look at the markings.

I see the houseboy scurry across from the open doorway into the hall heading for the room where my mother has been sitting at the table for the last hour. He says something I do not hear. "Very well," she says, "show the man into the dining room. I'll see him there."

She comes through the communicating door without going into the hall and shoos me out into the garden. From there I see the large black Citroen with its government license plates parked on the circular drive in front of our house. I hear voices now and go to a point beside the doors where I can see into the room, but I cannot see who it is that has come.

"Yes," it is my mother's voice. "What is it that I can do for you?"

I strain forward and can now just see the man. He is dressed in a dark suit, but his back is turned to me; I cannot see his face.

"Madame," he hesitates as if searching for the right words. He repeats, "Madame," pauses, then continues. "We have had news. There has been an attack on the river, on the boat from Saigon. It happened near Hanoi. It was the Viet Minh. I am afraid it is your husband; he has been killed."

My mind goes blank. I do not understand. I hear a muffled sound I cannot quite make out as if something dropped on the floor. Then there is the sound of a man's footsteps walking on the hardwood floor. *What's happened?* I think and rush into the room. *He's done something to my mother.*

"Come quickly." It is the visitor's voice.

I am in the room and my mother is lying on the floor. The houseboy runs from the hall as the women come from the sitting room. "She's fainted," I hear one of the women say as they begin to position her.

I stir, not quite awake yet not completely asleep, and I think, *I dreamed it before it happened, not exactly the way it happened, but yet I knew my father would die. Throughout my life I tried to avoid the details I recalled from my dreams but in the end just followed my own desires. What… Why…* then sleep once more came troubled as before.

The small house is surrounded by hedge; the house is in France. I see my sister, not the one who died in Vietnam, my younger sister, but I cannot make out whom the woman is. She has gray hair, but she does not look old enough to have gray hair. She is fussing with my sister's dress, a poor cotton dress. She ignores me. She does not seem to know I exist.

I look at her. It is my mother. She looks in my direction, not at me, through me. She does not see me. There is a mirror on the wall. I look in it, but I cannot see my reflection. She does not see me because she cannot see me. I do not exist.

My mother and sister are living in a cottage on her father's farm. They are poor. If it were not for her parents, we, they, would not have anything to eat or place to stay. It is the government's fault. It is the Viet Minh's fault. No, it is not, it is mine; everything that is, has been, is my fault. I could have stayed, should have stayed to help them, but I left and they are on their own.

Suddenly I am back in Indochina. I am in the army, a paratrooper.

"Why don't they attack, Sergeant?" one of the privates asks me. "They've had us surrounded, pinned down in this God-forsaken place for weeks. We can't get out, and now that the airstrip has been destroyed, no one can get in either."

"I don't know." I am weary from the strain of looking after men under my command. I am weary of trying to stay alive when those in authority make such horrific decisions and put all our lives in jeopardy. We are hot, dirty, and hopeless.

We are in an exposed position outside the perimeter defenses. It is the same month my father died. No, it cannot be. I was only thirteen years old, and now I am in the army. How old am I? When did my father die? It cannot have been this year; was it this month in another year? I do not know that either. Yes, I do. It is May 1954. Where am I? I am afraid. I am terrified. The young men in my squad, boys really but barely younger than I, tremble and cry at night when the mortar shells fall around our sandbag bunkers, exploding without killing, terrorizing us.

I am not in the bunker. I am outside the bunker. We are part of a skirmish line, an advanced position just outside our perimeter. We are the first line of defense, if we can be called that, to warn of an attack by our enemy. We are expendable. When they come, if they come, we will give the warning and fight our way back, if we can. We are expendable. We are paratroops. Why are we here in a jungle without roads, with tanks? This is crazy. We are expendable.

It is only two hours until dawn. Someone will relieve us, and it will be his turn to sit out here. They will sit and wait for the attack that never comes. "Can't we go back now, Sergeant?"

"No, that would be cowardice, but I can go back and see if they will send the relief squad forward a little early."

"Do it," they whimper.

I crawl away from the pit, away from the machine

gun, away from my men, away from my friends. We are expendable. I crawl away and do not return. From inside the perimeter, I hear the *thonk* of a mortar close by, an explosion, the sound made by a shell as it hits its target, but nothing else—then the screams. I crawl out toward the pit and see smoke rise from inside. They were expendable. The nightly shelling begins again. We are all driven crazy by the suspense, not knowing when we will die, or worse yet, mangled, hurt, and taken prisoner.

We quit and become prisoners of war. We are beaten, and some are dying. I should have died at Dien Bien Phu instead of being marched through the jungle.

I awaken, naked and drenched in sweat. It is the dreams that haunt me. *My dreams have always haunted me, leaving me uncertain whether they are dreams or reality, suppressed tragedy or prophetic foreboding.* This dream comes more often now after twenty odd years.

I heard the sound of tires on the pavement. It is dark. My watch tells me it is a quarter till twelve. I pulled on a pair of shorts, looked out of the hatch leading down from the center cockpit, and saw the old Jeep pull up next to the boat. Tanya, Monique, slid out of the vehicle and, seeing me, smiled, then walking with a provocative hip swaying motion, she came toward me.

"I knew you would come," I said.

"You are very sure of yourself. I thought the old man would never go to sleep. I cannot stay long. He has dreams and sometimes awakens during the night. If I'm gone, he will know something is wrong."

"Come on board. I'll open some wine."

"What for? Surely neither of us needs any alcohol."

She stepped from the dock onto the deck. I reached out with my hand to steady her, but agile she needed no help. I gathered her into my arms and kissed her hungrily, then led her below.

I am not certain of the time, perhaps only an hour later, when the angry sound of another car reached my ears. We dressed hurriedly and went on deck. The car parked beside the Jeep, and I could make out in the lights from the Coca-Cola building and the port facilities building nearby the figure of the old man and a young Micronesian boy who had driven him.

"I know you're here," the old man shouted. "Come on out." The man had a pistol in his hand and waved it around sightlessly. The Micronesian boy shrank away in fear. The old man fired a shot into the air for no one to hear but the four of us in this lonely place.

"I'm here, Papa," Tanya cried out. "It is all right. I am here. I will go home with you now." As she left, she stayed between the outraged old man and me.

I did not say a word. This was between them. I had no part in it.

Tanya stepped up from the deck onto the dock and walked confidently to the old man. When she got there, she took his hand, and then with the other hand, she lowered his gun hand. "It is all right. We can go now," she said again.

I stood still in the cockpit with my body partially shielded by the cabin, always shielded by Tanya, my Monique, shielded by both my Moniques. I said nothing as she turned him away and led him toward the Jeep. The Micronesian boy got in his car and drove away.

Tanya put her husband/father into the Jeep and walked around to the driver's side when suddenly and without any warning, the old man fired two shots in the general direction of my boat.

"You stay away from her! I may be blind, but I have my ways. If you come near her again, I'll kill you or I'll get someone to do it for me. There are people out here who would do it as a favor to me."

The Jeep turned away from the dock and drove off down Beach Road. Once she left the boat, the woman never looked back at me.

Chapter Fourteen

Monday morning marked the beginning of my fifth day on Saipan. I had already stayed here longer than anywhere since leaving Toulon and in a short time had made several acquaintances that bore watching. Events in my life had made me suspicious, distrustful, and the events of the past year had heightened that awareness.

I considered George Rowley and Jonathan Cartwright as warm acquaintances, but I was not very certain of Jonathan. There was something about him... Sure, he had warned me about Xarkus and Bili, but sometimes that is just a way of throwing a person off his guard. There was a lot more to the suave, sophisticated Jonathan Cartwright than met the eye.

The only person who seemed harmless was George. Even he could not be totally trusted. Anyone who drank as much as he did was likely to have violent mood swings. I knew that before I left the island, I would do everything I could to give him a reason to have one. Beth Rowley fascinated me; the long brown hair and sensuous body had become an obsession. I did not know when or how, but bed her I would.

I awakened that morning at first light. I had only one thing on my morning agenda. The bank had promised to have my draft ready, but that no longer seemed important now. My winnings from the races would cover any potential losses at the tables tonight. Nevertheless, I had gone to the trouble of arranging for the draft and would have Hiroki drive me to the bank. I could always put it in the safe hole secreted in the bulkhead. I told the boy to pick me up at nine thirty, so I had plenty of time.

I arose and went into the galley where the bananas and mango I purchased at the Flores Market on Saturday had ripened. As I prepared a plate contemplating the early morning sun and the promise of warmth on deck, I heard the noise of a ship approaching the dock. Looking out the galley porthole, I saw the Japanese cruise ship arriving, as they always do, early in the day so the tourists could have the visual pleasure of approaching land and docking during breakfast. It allowed them a full day of sightseeing before the evening gambling.

I went on deck and sat cross-legged atop the aft cabin as the ship maneuvered to its mooring. The disturbance in the water caused *Monique* to rock with the waves created by the large ship making me glad for the tires that hung over the side of the dock cushioning her collision with the concrete. I ate my fruit and drank my coffee as I watched the activity on the dock. The immigration and customs officials arrived first and went aboard, presumably to check registration and passports. An hour later, the crew began to prepare for the debarkation of the passengers. I had never traveled by cruise ship, and the bureaucracy associated with passengers coming ashore was a marvel. *Why*, I wondered, contrasting my arrival with theirs, *would anyone subject himself to the hassle of ordinary life while pretending to enjoy the freedom of the sea?*

At a quarter till nine, the gangway was in position and the passengers scurried out to the awaiting transportation. It seemed every taxi and private vehicle willing to carry the Nippon visitors around the island had crowded onto the dock. It occurred to me that in the crush of vehicles and people I would have trouble spotting Hiroki when he came to take me to the bank.

From my vantage point on *Monique*, I watched groups of three and four, sometimes as many as five, crowd into the waiting vehicles for tours of Banzai Cliff, Suicide Cliff, the Last Command Post, the Sugar King Statue, and other places of significance to the ship's passengers. By nine thirty, the dock was empty except for the crew who had business to attend around the ship.

I watched for Hiroki throughout this time.

I waited for Hiroki.

At ten, I became impatient for my ride. I did not intend to walk from Charlie Dock to Town Center—so I waited.

At eleven, my blood began to boil. I walked to the Coca-Cola plant where I asked to use the telephone.

"Hello." The voice on the telephone was warm and pleasant. It was the voice of Beth Rowley.

"Beth. This is Henri. Hiroki did not show up to take me downtown. I was wondering if you by any chance could give me a ride."

"Is this on the level?" she asked.

"Most assuredly, yes. That scoundrel was to be here at nine thirty, and he still hasn't arrived. I understand islanders don't pay strict attention to clocks, but this is ridiculous."

"We saw the cruise ship coming into dock early this morning. Rather, I saw it. George had a bad night, and he was moving slow this morning. George and booze don't mix very well anymore; they never did really." She paused then continued, "Hiroki is probably off carrying the tourists on sightseeing tours. I imagine he can make double per person what you are paying him per day, and he can take five or six people in that boat of a car. You probably won't see him again until the ship leaves. He'll make more today than what you pay him for the whole week."

"The little liar, I didn't see his car. One that ugly bright orange should be easy to spot. I was on deck most of the time but did go below for a few minutes when I brewed coffee. I really do need to get to the bank. Can you help?"

"Sure, I can pick you up. Give me a few minutes to get ready. You can buy my lunch at the Hafa Dai Hotel. They have the best sashimi on the island, but watch out for the wasabi sauce, it's really hot."

"It would be my great pleasure. Perhaps afterward you would like to see my boat." The glimmer of an idea, hope, crossed my mind. Just maybe Hiroki's misfeasance could be turned to my advantage.

"I'd like that. Give me about thirty minutes. Is that okay?"

"That would be splendid. Good-bye." I hung up the telephone and walked the hundred meters back to where *Monique* was berthed, passing the cruise ship along the way. I spent the next few minutes straightening up the galley and cleaning my private quarters in the anticipation of having a guest later. Being tidy by nature, there was not much to do, and I was finished well before I heard Beth's Toyota approaching.

Unlike the old Nissan George drove, Beth had a new gray Celica. I came on deck just as she stopped next to the boat and waved to her. She leaned out slightly from the window and said, "Come aboard."

I stepped onto the dock and with a walk some might consider a swagger reached the car. In a moment, Beth had turned and was driving down the road.

"I saw your friend as I came down Navy Hill road. He was going up to the old German Lighthouse. The Charger was literally crammed full of Japanese tourists. He must be making at least $125 this morning, maybe more. I would swear he had at least five, maybe six, people in there. At the going rate of $25 per person for half a day, he'll be cleaning up."

I looked at her gauging whether she was merely trying to irritate me. "Forget him. I have," I lied, thinking how I would get my revenge.

"So, are you planning on going to the Las Vegas Night tables this evening?"

"Well, I'd planned on it, but I may need a ride. Any hope?"

"Sure. They will be set up and ready for action at seven, but I doubt there will be much happening before seven thirty or eight. You have been on the island long enough to know no one is in a hurry here. Of course the Japanese tourists may be arriving early, depending on their rides. We'll pick you up around eight."

At that moment we were passing the Inter-Continental

Hotel. "They have the tables set up in the ballroom there. It is actually shameless the way the government made organized gambling illegal and then permits it when the cruise ship calls. I guess it's their way of getting back at the Japanese for the years of harsh treatment."

"What kind of tables do they have?" I asked.

"Normally there are two craps tables and two roulette tables. The biggest draw is always the slots, but there are only ten of them. Blackjack is popular too. I believe there are ten of them as well. It's crowded. The hottest action takes place at the craps tables obviously. There are always more people than places at the tables, so it makes for a lively evening, lots of jostling and lots of drinking. The hotel lets the Rotary Club have the room rent-free. They make enough on food and drink to more than pay for it."

"Sounds like it could be interesting. What's George's game?"

"George will gamble on anything, but the past few days what he's most interested in is drinking. He gets like that sometimes, and when he does, he is unpredictable. Here we are, the Bank of America. I'll wait in the car."

My business did not take long. I met the bank manager, and we retired once more to the closet-sized private office. He began making his excuse before the door completely closed. "I can't tell you how sorry I am, but I don't have the confirmation I expected. My home office on Guam called this morning and said they expect to have what they need early tomorrow."

I replied, "I am disappointed in the service your bank has provided in this matter, but it is of no great consequence. What time will you be prepared to complete the transaction tomorrow?"

"Why don't we make it tomorrow sometime after ten o'clock? If there is any further delay, I will send someone to your boat with a message so you will not be put out any further."

"That is acceptable; we'll just leave it at that."

I left the bank and got back in the car with Beth. "I hope some things are more efficient on your island than the banks. Let's get some lunch."

At half past ten, the courier delivered the diplomatic bag from the State Department liaison office on the first floor of the headquarters building to the high commissioner's second-floor wing of the building where Jonathan Cartwright had an office. The bag contained a message addressed to Jonathan in response to the inquiry sent to the FBI by the director of MBI.

Jonathan was fond of me, and I of him, but fondness would never stand in the way of either of us. We played a game of intellectual hounds and jackals both amusing and stimulating ourselves, each trying to outwit the other, cover our bases, and stop our opponent. For Jonathan the game was about to end—he would know much, if not all, the truth. I, in turn, had considerable respect for Jonathan, a man circumspect by habit and training while possessing the qualities of a forceful personality, without seeming to be overtly aggressive to anyone or anything. All the while appearing to be friendly and helpful, he used indirect persuasion to get others to act on his behalf, even when they did not know they were doing so.

Once the courier departed he rose, closed the door to his office, and turned the dead bolt. Opening the packet addressed to him by his superiors, not the ones in State, the ones in Langley, he removed the manila folder marked "Secret." He opened it to the first page.

The air-conditioning in the TT Headquarters building was on the fritz again, and the temperature on the second-floor office continued to rise. A small oscillating fan moved the warm, stagnant air providing some relief against the heat generated by the sun glaring on the flat concrete roof just a few feet above his head, penetrating into the room. Perspiration beaded on his forehead and upper lip and glistened in his eyes stinging them as he tried to focus on the page. His short-sleeve white shirt stuck to his back, the underarms already wet with sweat. Removing his eyeglasses, he wiped the sweat away; then adjusting them once again, he began to read.

SECRET SECRET SECRET
HENRI GENER

Assumed Identities

The man identified as Henri Gener is believed to be the same person known to us as Jacques Balagea, a/k/a Francois Fougeron, a/k/a Hans Zuelle, a/k/a Carlo Fosatti.

The true identity of this individual is unknown, but it is believed he may be the same person known as Charles Duvall, owner of an import/export business in Toulon, France. Duvall is known to have disappeared from Toulon on a sailboat bear-

ing the name Monique *seven months ago following the murder of his wife. Due to that disappearance, we cannot authenticate the identity of Gener
with that of Duvall who, though respected within
the community, led a reclusive life leaving the
public work of his firm to associates.*

*Gener has been known to use all of the names
listed above although he may be using additional
aliases at this time.*

Background
*He is known to have spent his early years in French
Indochina and speaks French, English, Italian,
Swiss, and Vietnamese fluently. During the early
years of the Vietnam War, he contracted as an
employee of the Agency, using the name Jacques
Balagea when recruited. He has had military and
paramilitary training in the past.*

*He has a known history of espionage. While a
contractor with the Agency working on Operation
Phoenix, he doubled to the Viet Cong and provided information that directly led to the deaths of
four RVN agents who infiltrated that organiza-
tion. One covert agent of the Agency working for
the government in Hanoi was compromised but
managed to escape capture.*

*Three years ago using the name Francois
Fougeron, he was identified as a person of inter-
est in the assassination of a French official to the
World Bank while on a business trip to the bank's
European headquarters in London. British immi-
gration records indicate "Fougeron" was in the*

U.K. at the time. Two weeks later he appeared at Alasio on the Italian Riviera.

Seven months ago, the wife of Charles Duvall was murdered along with her lover at a hotel in Toulon. The circumstances pointed to it being a drug-related crime inasmuch as autopsy showed both people were unconscious after ingesting large quantities of drugs at the time of their death. The deaths were execution-style murders with one bullet each to the temple. Both shots were fired with the small caliber handgun pressed against the victim's head.

The next sighting of this subject was four months ago following the attempted assassination of a French official on Saint-Denis, Reunion in the Mascarene Islands, a possession of France. Gener, Duvall, or Fougeron, as you will, was last seen on a sailboat bearing the name Monique *at Victoria on the island nation of Seychelles. The timing of this sighting coupled with the prevailing winds at the time make it possible he was near Reunion Island when the French official was attacked.*

He is believed to have connection to Algerian criminal and terror organizations along with others in both Western and Eastern Europe. The target of the assassination attempt at Reunion was last posted in Algiers.

Documentation

He is known to carry forged passports purporting to be French, Swiss, and Italian. All are of the highest quality and virtually undetectable by most immigration and customs officials.

Photograph
The last known photograph of Gener taken in 1969 *on the French Riviera is attached.*

Physical Description
Age:	*Exact age unknown—believed to be no older than* 45 *now*
Height:	5'11"
Weight:	175 *pounds*
Hair:	*Brown*
Eyes:	*Brown*

Action
Connecting his history of deceit and betrayal with these circumstances, the French government would like to question him. The Direction de la Protection et de la Securite de la Defense, DPSD, believe him to be the person they know as "The Scorpion" and may now be implicated in several other terror-related incidents in France and her possessions.

Because of his past involvement with the CIA and its clandestine efforts in Vietnam, the interests of the U.S. are not served by having Gener fall into the hands of the French intelligence services. It is, however, in our interest to inform them of his whereabouts. Discretion is advised.

Jonathan sat in stunned silence for several minutes. The man in the photograph was clearly the man he knew as Gener, though the man pictured could be as much as five to ten years younger. But where had Langley got wind of him; the MBI director of course, his cable to the

FBI had been passed along. Your "discretion is advised"; what were they saying? *My discretion; I am not authorized to conduct a wet operation, yet they want this Frenchman out of the way, away somewhere where the French cannot reach him. A man on a sailboat cannot get very far—certainly not very fast, though an ocean is an enormous place to hide. On the other hand, if they really did want me to have him killed, they would not likely put such an order in writing and then send it by diplomatic pouch.*

"The interests of the U.S. are not served by having Gener fall into the hands of the French intelligence services. It is, however, in our interest to inform them of his whereabouts. Discretion is advised." *Okay. What are my options? I can openly warn him to leave. No good. If the French catch up with him, he may implicate me. I can arrange for him to be kidnapped and killed. What then? There will be an investigation that I cannot control. An autopsy will be performed. A search of records will identify him, and that will eventually lead back to me.*

The MBI director is already on to this Frenchman. Maybe I can scare him off island using some of the shady characters he has been associating with. What will motivate them... money? He seems well heeled and the boat is a beauty, but they would have to get him away from here to take the boat. That alternative serves two courses of action.

Then, of course, there is his predilection for the ladies. Who knows how many he has bedded since he arrived. From the look in his eye, there have to be several, and some of them may be connected to jealous and possessive men. That can be used, but it is not terribly reliable. Last, what... That last one was the last one. There are no other options. Jonathan

Cartwright did not like any of the options. Why had they put this on him?

Jonathan sat for a few minutes more contemplating the alternatives. How had his life come to this? He possessed all the sophistication and charm that came from a life of privilege. Born in New York City just before the bombing of Hiroshima, he had been raised by foreign-born nannies. His first language was not English but Spanish, having been taught by his Costa Rican caretaker.

Educated at the prestigious New York Millbrook School, where his nickname "Arrow" referred to not only his physique but also his reputation for being a straight arrow, a boy who always played by the rules, he had been captain of the lacrosse team. He graduated from Yale and then the Wharton School of Economics at the University of Pennsylvania. By the time he passed his twenty-eighth birthday, he had been recruited by his older brother, a brother he had overpowered intellectually years before, into the clandestine world of the CIA.

As a small boy, the youngest of three each born a year apart, making Jonathan four when his oldest brother was nearing seven, he had been dominated by his siblings. Both the other boys were not only older, they were also physically larger, leaving Jonathan to fend for himself the best way he could. Until he reached the age of ten, that generally meant he took a subservient position. Then, gradually, he reasoned he had greater intelligence than his brothers had and began looking for ways to use that natural ability to his advantage. By the age of fifteen, he emerged as the alpha male, using his language skills and personality together with his persuasive talents to lead. His skills were honed by the fact the older boys attended schools nearby Millbrook, and the three young men spent one evening a week and weekends together.

By the time the boys split up, each attending a university that matched his intellectual ability, everyone who knew them thought Jonathan quite the brightest, though not one of them suspected that the mischief the others found themselves enmeshed in had originated in the fertile brain of their younger brother.

The pattern of quiet dominance continued when Jonathan went off to Yale. There he found himself embroiled in campus politics, always on the side of the establishment, always having considerable influence over the thoughts of the opposition whenever he could arrange those private midnight one-on-one meetings where he could bring his considerable powers of persuasion to bear. Never in those meetings did he propound the hard line establishment point of view, choosing instead to play the role of compromiser, conciliator, always willing to listen to the other point of view. All the while he remained true to his core beliefs in the establishment agenda.

The game of cat and mouse intrigued him, and though he sometimes walked close to the line between observer and participant, he carefully avoided crossing that line. Jonathan Cartwright knew he could play the game along with the best of them. He would outsmart the brainy ones, and he would manipulate the slow brawny ones.

Virtually everything he said and did now, he convinced himself, from his days at Millbrook was *"Non Sibi Sed Cunctis,"* yet the impact of his every move was calculated for self-promotion. Even the posting to

Micronesia carried a strict time limit. He would serve in that backwater hotbed of intrigue for only two years before returning to Langley. The experience gained in Micronesia, acting with only minimal direction, would, he knew, be used by his superiors to judge whether he possessed the qualities necessary for the next step in career advancement. His marriage to Caroline, daughter of the junior senator from Virginia, had brought him a step closer to his goal within the agency and the ultimate goal of a life in politics.

All this seemed threatened now by the appearance of a fugitive Frenchman and the cryptic message from above. *Why did I allow myself to get so involved with him?* Now, this one man could jeopardize what a week earlier had been a secure future.

In desperation, Jonathan Cartwright, before gambling his future, his career, reached out for advice from the one person he knew he could trust. One way or the other, he knew he had to rid himself of the Frenchman. For Jonathan it was time to stop being the preppy rich boy and become a survivor. It had become time for Jonathan Cartwright to acknowledge at last what he should have always known; the motto at Millbrook was just so much crap. Forget about the others, survive! Then, lifting the receiver on his Global Communications telephone, he dialed Guam 8830 and spoke to the man at the other end.

Ambassador Charles Williamson was a man who, as they say, had been around the block. When he heard the voice on the other end of the telephone line, he instantly knew something was up. At sixty-one years of age, he looked forward to the end of his career in government service.

"Johnnie, I was just thinking about you. With the talks later this month at Moen, I thought it would be a good idea to get together in the next few days. Caroline and you might want to catch the Air Mike flight down here so we can put our heads together. I am certain your aunt can find something suitable to occupy Caroline for a couple of days. After all, the opportunities on Saipan are, shall we say, limited."

Jonathan answered, "Sounds good to me. There are several developments here with all the Liberation Day festivities and dignitaries on island we should probably go over."

"Good. I will clear the decks for Thursday and Friday. You two can stay with us here on the naval base and go back on the Sunday afternoon plane." Ambassador Williamson had a strong fondness for his nephew. The two men had adopted similar career paths, and Williamson wanted to help his nephew advance. He knew of the dual role his nephew had in Micronesia and smiled to himself whenever he thought about it. He had been the person who set it up, not that his nephew knew that.

"Uh, Uncle Charles..." The manner Jonathan now took in the conversation, the hesitancy in his voice, the uncertainty, caused Williamson to wonder what was coming. "Uncle Charles, I have something I'd like to discuss with you. I can't wait until Thursday. It has very little to do with our work out here. I just need your personal advice."

"Sure, Johnnie, if I can help, I'd be glad to. Is everything okay with you and Caroline? Small island life can get pretty tedious for a girl used to living in the city."

"Oh yeah, everything is fine there. She's a real trouper, although I doubt she is terribly happy about being out here for another eighteen months. What is on my mind has nothing to do with that … Uncle Charles, when you worked for 'Wild Bill' Donovan in the OSS during the war, were your orders always clear? I mean, sure, you had to improvise all the time, but I mean, did you have to—"

Williamson interrupted, "Johnnie, I know what you mean. During the war, we had a plan, but it was just that, a plan, an outline; there were no day-to-day orders. There couldn't be. I was twelve thousand miles away and had almost no radio contact. What little I did had to go through India and took days to complete. Events moved fast, and we did the best we could. Sometimes it worked out well, sometimes not."

"Okay, but when you did get written instructions, were they always explicit? I mean, did you ever wonder what it was they wanted you to do?"

Ambassador Williamson did not like the direction this conversation had taken. Something must be terribly wrong. His nephew did not rattle easily, but clearly something had happened or he had received some directive from his other masters that troubled him. "Johnnie, there are times, as you are well aware, when not every detail can be conveyed in writing. In my early work, I had to make difficult decisions on occasions that were disturbing at the time. In every instance though, I can tell you hindsight vindicated the result of those decisions, but not always without a certain amount of pain at the time."

There was no such thing as a secure phone line with

Global Communications, and this conversation might very well be compromised. The ambassador felt certain his nephew would not say anything that would come home to haunt either of them directly. However, since he did not know what the problem was, he did not intend to speak any more directly than he already had.

"You have had some experience, especially since arriving here as my aide. We always do the best we can to provide clear direction in our correspondence. You will simply have to take the totality of that experience and your education along with special training and do the best you can." Then, pausing to choose his words carefully, he concluded, "Very few people are ever thrown under the train for an honest mistake. Sometimes it hurts your career for a while, but well, what can I say? Whatever it is that is bothering you, I'll always back you. Not because you are my nephew, but because you are a talented and level-headed diplomat. I hope I've helped you." With that dismissive comment, Ambassador Charles Williamson said, *The problem is yours. You will have to solve it. I have nothing more to add.*

Jonathan Cartwright sat for a few seconds pondering the words of his uncle, a man he knew must have had to be in the same situation he now found himself at some time in his long and successful career.

His uncle broke in on the reverie. "Johnnie, are you still there?"

"Yes, Uncle Charles, I am. I was just thinking. You have helped me. I will take care of my dilemma the best way I can and plan to see you on Thursday to go over materials I think will help us with the meeting at Truk. Thanks."

Chapter Fifteen

The Hafa Dai was not the newest hotel on the island. In fact, it was one of the older hotels surpassed in age perhaps only by the Marianas Hotel on Navy Hill. The Hafa Dai continued in business largely on the strength of its dining room and Teppan Yaki. Of the two restaurants, I preferred the Teppan Yaki because of its outdoor setting. I have never cared for air-conditioning. Having spent the greater part of my life outdoors, I found the artificially cooled air very nearly unbearable.

The outdoor setting for the Teppan Yaki was enhanced by its proximity to the lagoon. Guests seated on the sea side of the horseshoe table could dangle their feet in the warm green water, barely a foot below the pavement, when the tide was high, the atmosphere enhanced by colorful Japanese lanterns with muted light, dangling from low trees around the grill.

I had stopped there with a few of the beach crowd the night before, after the races, for a short celebration before hurrying to *Monique* and the unfortunate encounter with Colonel Simons, the pedophile husband of Tanya. I was certain the memory of that night would stay with me all my life. The moon had been full. Clouds drifted slowly by to obscure it, the soft classical Japanese music playing on a tape recorder. The chef had twirled the knives, launching a bit of steak into the mouth of an eagerly awaiting diner. We had drunk warm sake, the intoxicating rice wine traditionally served with the meal. As it turned out, it did stay with me for life, though not for all the years I had believed at the time.

Since the Teppan Yaki did not open until the sun set, providing the atmosphere I relished, Beth and I went to the restaurant inside, air conditioned but not chilling, my blood up and running in anticipation of the hunt. The restaurant was common, its furnishings similar to those at Hamilton's that I've already described to you, except there are two rooms instead of one large room.

As Beth Rowley and I entered just minutes after leaving the bank, a Chamorro woman dressed in a pink, white, and gray-flowered island dress who called Beth by name greeted us. Beth asked to be seated in the back, the smaller of the two dining rooms, where light from outside did not shine in brightly.

"Will there be two or three?" she asked. "Is George joining you?"

"It will just be the two of us," Beth answered.

A few moments later another Chamorro girl approached and asked if she could take our order. I asked Beth if she would like something to drink.

"Only water, with lemon please."

"I have noticed you do not indulge in alcoholic beverages."

"No. George drinks quite enough for both of us. It wasn't always the case, but since we've located here, he seems to drink and gamble more all the time." Her delicate chin quivered slightly. "Island life has been bad for us in many ways. When you are accustomed to the whirlwind life of L.A., what else is there? It's been much worse for George than me."

I looked intently into her face as she spoke. For the first time I noticed the mark on her left cheek covered by makeup on her well-tanned face. She had been struck. "Does he get rough with you when he is drunk?"

Her eyes widened. "Yes, but only when he's drunk, which means unless he has passed out, you never know what will set him off."

"I haven't seen that side of him. He seemed carefree to me. Has he always been like that?"

"No. When we first met, he was really nice, funny, thoughtful and kind, interesting, always on the go."

"How did you meet?" I really did not care but thought showing interest was likely to get me closer to her. My activities, my trysts, were clearly the topic of island gossip. Then too, my fleecing of Mark Meriday the day before had been shameless, only exceeded by my abandoning his boat to drift out to the reef with the ebbing tide before leaving the beach where it would surely be destroyed by the sharp coral. Showing a softer side could not do me any harm.

"We both worked at the courthouse. I worked in the county clerk's office, and he was on the floor above in the D.A.'s office. He started flirting around in the cafeteria and in the halls, wherever he saw me. I was in the middle of a nasty divorce at the time, and we started fooling around. At first I guess I was just using him; I thought he would be good protection from my ex. He was a jock at USC, and he could really get rough. Not like George, I mean really, really rough. Since George was an ex-cop and a prosecutor, I figured Dan would leave me alone. It worked."

"So when did you start getting serious about George?"

"It was actually before the divorce was final. You won't believe it, but he borrowed a pickup with a camper shell. We 'got it on' during our lunch break one day. We had the thing rocking so bad it drew a crowd and someone called security. I don't need to tell you our 'secret' was out and all over the courthouse before we got out of the camper. After that, we were the talk of county government."

"Sounds pretty wild. Have you ever made love on a sailboat?"

She smiled. "Well, what do you think? We came from L.A. There are lots of boats, and we had friends who sailed to Catalina for the weekends."

I changed my tack, beating into the wind, hoping to find the course that would bring me home. "I'd be willing to wager none was as nice as *Monique*." I then prodded, "Is George a jealous man?"

"He used to be. I don't know now. He drinks so much. I'm not sure he would even notice."

I had the wind behind me.

The Chamorro girl returned with our water and took our order. Beth ordered for both of us, sashimi, fresh yellow fin tuna, and sushi, a split plate for each. She laughed when I took too much wasabi and my eyes bulged, sweat pouring from my brow.

"I told you to watch out for that," she chided.

I retorted, "One hot thing at a time."

Our lunch concluded, we started to rise just as a tall, rather thick-set man entered, a man I had never thought I would see again. I recognized him in an instant despite the years that had passed since we last met. He no longer wore a uniform but now dressed in an island-print shirt and slacks.

He approached directly toward our table and greeted me. "Hello, Balagea, when I heard some mysterious Frenchman was on the island, I wondered if it might not be you. After all, you have always had a way of turning up in the strangest places under the oddest circumstances. The immigration folks got a picture of you out at the airport when you first came in. It wasn't very good and you've aged, but nevertheless I knew it was you."

"You can't possibly be more surprised than I. What are you doing here?" I answered, my voice icy, on edge.

"I'm the High Commissioner for the Trust Territory." The hi-com sat down at the table asking, "Do you mind if I join you for lunch? Afterward we can go to my office and talk." It sounded less like an invitation, more like an order—an order from a man I had once answered to but never expected to see again.

I did my best to disguise my anxiety. "Actually we have just finished lunch. So how is it you come to be here? It's a huge departure from your work in Saigon."

"Yes," he responded quietly. "I left the army after my tour in Vietnam and worked in politics. You know, behind the candidate. It led to my recommendation for this position by the Secretary of Interior. The appointment came from the president, of course. What about you?"

I gave him my usual story about traveling around

the world, leaving out all the details of my life from the time we'd both worked together in the early days of what eventually became the Phoenix Program, assassination of political opponents of the Republic of Vietnam puppet government.

At last acknowledging the presence of Beth, he spoke to her. "Mrs. Rowley, it's good to see you. So I see you know this disreputable fellow. Perhaps you would excuse us for a short while. I have some matters I'd like to discuss with my friend here." Then turning to me, he continued, "My car is outside. We can take it to my office where we won't be disturbed."

My initial reaction was to say no, but it was after all an order, not an invitation for private conversation. I did not like the tone the meeting had assumed. The hi-com seemed intent on resuming our former relationship of superior to subordinate. Always an officious, overbearing man, his newfound importance made him even more so.

Going along for the time being, I made my apology to Beth, asking her to meet me in about an hour at my boat, while I accompanied the hi-com to the government enclave on Mt. Topochau.

Immediately after being seated in his office, the hi-com got to the point, his point. "They tell me you've been here almost a week now. During that time you've been involved in more mischief than most folks get into during a two-year contract term." The reference to government contract workers' term of employment meant nothing to me at the time. "Now I hear you may be implicated in some political killings on the island a couple of nights ago. With the election for governor coming up, this sort of thing was bound to happen. Now, here you are. What a marvelous coincidence. I suppose we can now look forward to acts of reprisal from the other side?"

Comments, vague, little information, all accusatory, and they were all aimed at me. This news should not have come as any surprise, yet coming as it did from this man, it did. What, I wondered, did he have to do with it? Over a decade earlier, he had been intimately involved in the selection of high level Viet Cong sympathizers targeted for elimination. It had been my job to coordinate with the death squads in the execution of those orders. "Implicated in what?"

"Come now, Balagea, bodies were found this morning." I recognized the technique. No mention was made of how many or how they were killed, but why would this man be questioning me about them? That was a job for the police. He continued, "I must say you've lost none of your old skill."

I parried, "What makes you think I had anything to do with it—how many did you say were killed?"

"I didn't," he responded with only the vaguest smile crossing his countenance.

Wanting to gain control of the situation, I continued my own interrogation. "How and where were they killed?"

"I'm sure the police will go over all that with you when the time comes, if they are able to connect you to the murders. My interest is more of a personal, political really, nature. You cannot imagine how delighted I am the mysterious Frenchman turned out to be you."

I did not like the way he looked at me. There was

more of the former life of this man in the interview than one would expect from a purely political appointee.

"What do you want?" I asked.

"Well, my one-time friend, since you ask, there is someone else I'd like to see gone from this island. There is more than one, but one thing at a time. Let us just say that I have no doubt the police will be able to implicate you in these murders without my help in identifying you as a man with unique talents. Of course, if they have any difficulty, I could always tell them, indirectly of course through Washington or Langley, who you are. That would prove interesting. It would only take a phone call, if you get my meaning."

"Fine," I said. "I understand your threat. Now, what is it you want?"

"More of the same." His eyes squinted ever so slightly, hard and cold. "I want you to get rid of someone for me."

It seemed to me events were racing out of control. The last year had been a series of crises, beginning with the murder of my wife back in Toulon. Had I lost my edge? Why did I suddenly seem to be everyone's pawn? Why did I not see things coming at me as I had in the past? I looked him directly in the eyes and replied, "And why would I do that?"

"Balagea, didn't you listen to anything I just said? I can give you up to the police. These murders can be laid at your doorstep. Do what I tell you and then get off this island and stay off."

I considered my options, which consisted of doing what he said or going to jail for murders I had nothing to do with, or run, then responded, "All right, who do you want killed?"

"A man I understand is a friend of yours, anyway, a friend of sorts, Senator Tobias Bili."

Surprised by the request and the name, I answered, "I didn't think you Americans engaged in that sort of thing anymore."

"Well, let's just say this is a special circumstance and leave it at that. I don't care when or how you do it so long as you do it soon and then get out of here."

The high commissioner stood, indicating the interview had ended, and opened the door of his office. "I can't tell you how good it was to run into you like this. Enjoy your trip around the world. I don't suppose I'll see you again before you leave." The comment seemed more directed at his Chamorro secretary than me.

"No," I agreed, "I doubt you will. I'll be leaving in a day or so." Nodding to the woman, I left.

Walking out of the headquarters building to the car the high commissioner had arranged to take me back to my boat, I saw the orange Charger speeding past on the road going down the backside of Capitol Hill Road. I no longer saw my driver as just a sullen teenager prying into my private affairs. He now took on a more sinister appearance. Was he watching me for his father, reporting my every move to Senator Bili?

I did not want him driving me now, but just to dismiss him and then arrange for other transportation would not do at all either. No doubt someone else would follow me if they didn't already have someone backing up Hiroki. I got into the car and said, "Take me back to my boat."

Three miles away at Xarkus's house, Hiroki drove into the clearing and stopped next to the stoop just minutes after my meeting with the high commissioner ended. Xarkus heard the car engine as it approached. He met Hiroki as he entered the house. "What are you doing here? Why aren't you with that Frenchman?" he demanded.

Hiroki answered proudly, "I didn't get him today. The Japanese cruise ship came in, so I picked up a carload of them and took them to the usual tourist spots. See, I got paid a hundred and fifty dollars for three hours. I got them to pay thirty dollars apiece. I even got rid of them early. I had them back to their ship a little after noon. I didn't see anything of that Frenchman though."

He pulled the fleur-de-lis money holder from his pocket when the blow landed. "You did what!" Xarkus exploded. "Didn't I tell you to stay with him? You're off chasing chump change while there is big money to be had."

Hiroki dropped the money holder, fear once more in his eyes. Fear of his violent, dangerous father. As he bent to pick up the money holder, Xarkus grabbed it from his son. "What is this?" he demanded.

"It's something I picked up on the boat the other day." Fear still gripped the boy though he saw his father's face change expression, cunning now replacing anger.

"You been on that boat? You didn't tell me."

Hiroki backed away a step out of reach of his father fearing another blow was coming. "Uh, yeah," he remarked cautiously. "We put some gas cans on board. I was just there for a few minutes. He let me look around. You were right. The guy is loaded. There is a lot of expensive-looking wine on that boat. You should see the thing."

"Okay, but where'd the money holder come from?"

"It was lying out in his cabin. He wasn't looking, so I lifted it."

"Is that all? Did you take anything else?"

Fumbling in his pocket Hiroki answered, "Just this, it's a piece of paper with something written on it. I can't read it. It's in French, I think."

"Well, good for you, maybe you aren't so dumb after all. Give the paper to me. It may come in handy. And give me the money. You can keep the money holder."

"But it's ..." Hiroki stopped resisting, understanding it was the dumbest thing he could possibly have done at that moment. He was off the hook with Xarkus and belatedly knew it.

"Give me the keys to the car," Xarkus once more demanded. "I've got to go see Bili."

I now see that as I walked out of the hi-com's office Jonathan Cartwright put down his telephone. To a casual observer, had one been there, he appeared to be talking on the phone, although there was no one on the other end, at least not in the conventional sense. The telephone in Jonathan Cartwright's office, when properly adjusted, served as a listening device in several offices of the Trust Territory government, including that of the high commissioner. He sat idle for what seemed to be an eternity, thinking.

Events in the last two hours had drastically affected him. Now unsettled, unsure, he pondered not only the

strange communication he had received from Langley—
the word *action* had never before appeared on a message he received—but also the bizarre conversation he
had just listened in on between the high commissioner
and the Frenchman. Had the Frenchman descended into
the gray world of mist where right and wrong became
obscured by official orders in this manner? If he chose
the wrong course of action, would he become just like the
Frenchman, whatever his name was—a charming agent
who would kill when ordered to do so by his superiors?

It seemed to Jonathan events were spinning out
of control for him while remaining tightly in control
for others. There were many people interested in this
Frenchman, and there was no coordinated effort to bring
them together. In headquarters alone there were three
people, the director of MBI, the hi-com, and himself,
interested in the Frenchman for what could be loosely
called professional reasons.

Then, of course, there were George and Mark who
had reasons, no doubt, to want the Frenchman out of
the way.

At last, he concluded there might be a way out of the
dilemma. He picked up the telephone, dialed 980, and
spoke to the man who answered the phone. "Is Senator
Bili there? This is a friend calling."

No response. A short pause followed while the man
called Senator Bili to the phone.

"Senator, I thought you'd want to know the price of
yellow fin is out of sight."

Forty minutes later two cars pulled off onto a tangen-
tangen-chocked side road at the far north end of the
island, a place where a small fighter plane airfield had
been located during the war. Each vehicle had a single

passenger. The driver of the small Mazda got out first and greeted the other man.

"Bili," Jonathan Cartwright began, "I know this meeting carries with it a certain amount of risk, some that we agreed would only be breached in an extreme emergency, but I think you'll agree we needed to get together now."

The meeting time and place had been prearranged when either man called the other and spoke the words, "I thought you'd want to know the price of yellow fin is out of sight." Bili looked puzzled. "So what's up?"

"It's the hi-com. He's out of his league, but he had a meeting with the Frenchman. He's asked him to make a hit on you!"

"A hit. Why would he want to do that?"

"It's a long story, but they have a past going back to some black operations in Vietnam. The hi-com does not like the fact he is out of the loop on the status talks and wants to show someone in Washington that he is a player. He clearly doesn't know anything about the special relationship you have with us in that regard. He has threatened Gener that he'd pin some political killings on him unless he took you out and did it soon."

"Crap," Bili exclaimed, his eyes squinting. "I never liked him. So what do you think we should do, whack him first?"

"The hi-com, no; it is Gener we have to get rid of. Let's just scare him off the island if we can. So long as he stays out of Micronesia, I don't see any problem. The farther he goes away, the better. You agree?"

"Sure. I'll see what we can set up." *It should not be too difficult,* Bili thought. *With a history like Gener has, we can retaliate for the political killings the other night and pin it on Gener. We will just spin the hi-com's threat in another direction. He's no dummy. When he sees the handwriting on the wall, he'll run. When we catch up, we can do away with him and take the boat up to Taiwan where it will fetch a good price.*

"Fine," Johathan answered. "I don't need to know all the details. After that, whatever you have in mind for the illustrious high commissioner is your business. I just want to take care of the immediate problem first, and that means protecting you." It was a lie of course, but a convenient lie required at the time.

Jonathan Cartwright thought again, *Is this how it starts? Is this how they trap me into a dark world where you lose touch with reality, with right and wrong?* Bili would only remain valuable to Johathan and his bosses so long as the status talks continued. After that it would depend on whether the information Johathan was ordered to share with Bili resulted in Bili's being able to separate Palau and the Marshalls from what would possibly result in a federated state of Micronesia consisting of Yap, Truk, and Ponape. Ultimately, the decision concerning Bili's usefulness would be decided in the States, and that would be decided by the position Bili occupied in the new government. So long as he had power, he would remain protected and useful. In the meantime, could Johathan trust Bili?

Bili's eyes narrowed. "How do you know this?"

"Take it easy, Bili. A man in my position has to know many things, but how I get that information is strictly my business. Just know this: on this matter, I have your back. If I didn't, you'd undoubtedly wake up dead sometime in the next few days."

Chapter Sixteen

At half past one *Monique*, Beth, and I left Charlie Dock. My conversation with the high commissioner left me in an undecided frame of mind. I saw risk in doing what he proposed, but then there was also risk in ignoring him. Impulsive behavior was not my nature. I needed to reflect on my options. A few hours one way or the other would not make any difference. Besides, taking Beth out on the boat promised an immediate reward.

Tour groups were coming back from their morning outings. Their faces revealed little of their emotions, or at least so it seemed. What did they think? This island held such good memories for them, and yet in the end it represented one of the great failures of their culture— militarization, enslavement, unspeakable fear, horror, and death.

In the fifteen years since the island opened for outside travel, following the closure of the CIA base, only one or two Japanese cruise ships called each year. Some of those tourists must have lost family members here in

1944. Even the fact that I spent so many years of my life in Asia had not given me any insight into understanding the feelings of those people, a people who for the most part kept their innermost thoughts obscured by a mask of stoicism. Only when they were in extremis, happy, furious, and overwhelmed with grief, did they reveal anything at all. I now thought I could see pain on their faces, but I was not certain.

Hiroki had shown me the places of tragedy for them, the places where so many of their countrymen, soldiers and civilians alike, lost their lives during the war. I knew how I felt about Hanoi, the place where my father died, where my life had been turned on end. It occurred to me that may be how they felt about Saipan. If so, why had they returned? Why did they look for pain when pain found them out all the time? For that matter, why had I tried to return to Vietnam, opened the wounds of another life, endured grief at the girl's death, even torture?

Possibly they didn't know the answer to that any more than I could account for my own behavior, or else they came to recall the better days, before the war, when their country had a thriving culture here far beyond what America had built, even though both countries' occupation had been of equal duration. Certainly there was enough evidence of those good times with the little sugar train engine and old hospital building, now a ruin but classic in architecture, and the statue of the Sugar King.

Maybe visiting here was not painful to them at all. They may have been celebrating bushido, the way of the warrior, finding national and cultural superiority in fighting to the death for what they believed. I did not believe in that. I never had. France had surrendered to Nazi Germany during my lifetime, virtually without a fight. Then we collaborated through the Vichy government. We ran from Japan. We suffered defeat in Vietnam and lost in Algeria. Maybe we, I, just did not understand people who found honor in strength, courage in purpose.

The tourists waved to us; I say us, for Beth was with me on deck. I was in the cockpit steering *Monique* away while Beth stood to starboard and waved back. We motored out past the little island in the lagoon, and I took her out through the channel into deep water. It was after five when we returned to the dock, my conquest complete. I had repaid kindness with deception, generosity with seduction, charity with greed. No longer did I envy George. What he had, I now had. Lust had once more won the day. Before she left, we agreed she and George would pick me up later for the Las Vegas Night at the Inter-Continental Hotel.

I still had not made up my mind about what to do concerning the high commissioner's demand. I would see Bili at the hotel. I would just let things play out for the night and see where events led me. Clearly Bili was every bit as dangerous as the high commissioner, even more so. The danger from Bili and his associates was immediate while the high commissioner only threatened something in the future. Should I do as he demanded and kill Bili and then run, or should I ignore him and run now? For that matter, should I run at all? The idea of running again so soon after my experience at Vietnam galled me. No, I would wait and see where events took me. I could go either direction.

Beth and George were on the dock at eight o'clock that evening, the car horn honking to get my attention. I walked off *Monique* toward the car as if nothing had happened, watching George all the while. As far as I could tell, he suspected nothing. As usual he had been drinking; his appearance and slurred tongue testified to a dinner of vodka martinis, more drunk now than on any of the other occasions when we had been together. Thankfully Beth drove. He seemed excited about the prospect of gambling. Beth, on the other hand, looked radiant in a tight-fitting island dress that showed her form, a form I now knew intimately, to her best advantage.

"Hey, ol' boy," George began, "are ya ready to hi' the tables?"

"Sure. You were telling me about them the other day, so where's the best action?" I asked, not caring what he answered, just wanting him to keep talking. I shifted to the seat behind George so I could get a better view of Beth through the opening in the bucket seats.

"Ah you know. They're all the same. The oun-ly difernce is in who's runnin the table."

"Really."

"Yeah, I know all those guys. There isn't a real gambler in the bunch. They don' know what's goin on, so there's a lotta cheatin.' You know, movin' bets on the craps tables and stuff like that. Course there is a lot a' cheatin' goin' on everywhere these days. A lot a' cheatin' in a lot a' ways. Cheaters have to watch out though. Bad stuff happens to them, even here on Saipan." After that, he fell silent as we finished the mile-long drive to the hotel.

When we got to the hotel, George went directly into

the ballroom, now the casino, where he looked for the bar and got another drink before moving to the roulette table.

I lingered with Beth outside the main entrance to the hotel. "That last comment he made in the car, does he know you were with me this afternoon?"

"Sure he does. I told him."

"You did what?"

"I told him. You did not think it would be a secret on this island for long, did you? There must have been a dozen people on the dock he and I know when we pulled out."

"What did you tell him?"

"The truth, so far as I went. I told him you'd taken me out on your boat, and we went part way around the island and came back."

"What was his reaction?"

"He must have started drinking pretty heavy before he got home so didn't say much of anything. I have never seen him quite like that. He may have suspected something."

"Did he get rough with you?" I asked the question but did not really care so long as his violence, if he had it in him to direct violence toward anyone, was not coming in my direction.

"No, but then he had a load on when he got home from work or wherever else he had been. They don't drink in the office, you know, so he may have left early. The violence comes out when he is completely sloshed. That will come later unless he drinks so much he passes out."

"From the looks of him, that won't be too long now."

"Don't bet on it. He has an unbelievable tolerance; it comes from years of practice." An awkward silence followed. Then Beth said, "I suppose I should tell you he has a pistol, a .357 magnum from his police days."

"Oh? He seems to be all right now though. Do you think he suspects anything more than an afternoon cruise?" I repeated the question. The news about the gun worried me.

"Maybe; he has a suspicious mind. He would not be much of a lawyer if he did not. I just don't know what he'll do."

She paused again. "I've never cheated on him before. I don't know how he will react." This statement caught me by surprise. My expression must have shown it. She continued, "You seem to be concerned about George. You're not afraid of him, are you?"

"In France and other places I've lived, it strikes me more men are shot over infidelity than any other reason. Of course I am concerned. A jealous man with a pistol is not a man to be taken lightly." She would never know just how intimately I knew this.

"Well, you can rest easy; I hid the gun."

We had finished our cigarettes and walked into the building to where the tables were already crowded and noisy. Our absence had not been noticed, or so I thought. "Can I get you something from the bar?" I asked.

"A wine spritzer would be nice."

At the table set up to serve as a bar, the Micronesian waiter poured the California chardonnay and soda into the plastic cup and handed it across to me.

"Anything else, sir?"

I started to order for myself but then seeing the stock of inferior wine decided against it. As I turned to return to where Beth stood, Ferd Meier sidled toward me and with a grin on his face commented, "Well, isn't that cozy? I saw you with Beth outside just now with your heads together, and now you're squiring her around the tables." Nodding toward George, he said, "He know?"

"Does he know what?"

Ferd winked.

"Cut the crap, man," using an idiom I knew he would understand. "Whatever you think you know is just that."

"Ah, come on. Can't you take a little teasing; seems like it is all right when I am the one on the receiving end. I'm your friend, maybe the only one you really have on this island. Whatever George does or doesn't know is safe with me. After all, we all have our problems. In fact, I could use your help. Any chance I could catch a ride with you when you leave Saipan?"

The change of direction and odd request stopped me for a moment. What a strange way to approach someone. It had all the crude appearance of blackmail but without any of the subtlety. "Help you? Why would I want to do that? What's your problem?"

"Never mind that right now. I just need to know if I can go with you when you leave. You could drop me off on some other island. I just want to get away from the Trust Territory."

"Have you ever sailed before?" I asked.

"No, but I would stay out of the way and only do what you told me to do. I'd make it worth your while."

It only took a moment for me to decide. "No," I replied, "you can't go with me. I don't know for certain when I'm leaving or just where I'll go next, and I don't need any extra baggage along, especially not someone

who has never been on a sailboat before. Besides, I don't
like you. You have been rude, and I will not countenance rudeness. You don't know anything but presume
to accuse me of impropriety with a man who has shown
himself a friend."

"You don't think I know anything? I heard about your
cozy lunch at the Hafa Dai and trip out on your boat. I'll
bet Sydna is seeing red too. Did you take her out?"

"Mind your own business." I turned and walked away
to where Beth stood. "I see you were right about telling
George we went out on the boat. That imbecile Ferd just
approached me."

"Of course. That's why on a small island it is a mistake to believe you can keep secrets. The best way to hide
the truth is in the open."

With that advice, she moved across the room to
where George continued to pay out money at the roulette
wheel. She nuzzled his ear, said something. He turned to
her grinning, while I walked around the room watching
the games, picking out what I wanted to play.

I do not want to leave you with the impression I am a
professional gambler, but I tell you the men running the
tables and dealing blackjack were exactly what George
said, rank amateurs. I settled at last at a blackjack table
where the dealer handled a two-deck shoe clumsily. I
waited until he reshuffled the cards and began dealing
with the full shoe.

The table had a ten-dollar limit, small change by
my standards, but I was just passing time. As he dealt, I
started counting cards, keeping track of aces, face cards,
and tens, and, to the extent I could, the cards under the
five spot. There were five people at the table when I sat

down, and I could tell that not one other player had any idea how to play the game.

As the decks wore down, I could not believe my good luck. The dealer had no idea I was counting cards and so never questioned nor suspected anything when I failed to take a card when holding only twelve or thirteen in my hand while he continually busted drawing on fourteen. Of course, it was not luck on my part. I had counted a disproportionate number of cards lower than five in the first half of the shoe. That made it likely he would draw a card higher than a seven.

After sitting at the table while two shoes were dealt, I picked up my chips and moved away looking for something more stimulating. At that point, I had taken two hundred dollars from the Rotary Club, well not really the Rotary Club, from the cruise ship passengers. The Rotary and I were sharing the winnings.

As I passed near the front door to the casino room, Senator Bili arrived, accompanied by two men. One of them I recognized as the driver on Friday night, the same man I had the altercation with at the Palauan bar. The other man, better dressed, had a decidedly more nasty appearance. His round face and flat features were marked by wide set amber, penetrating eyes, eyes that had the same look as the Vietnamese jungle cats that dwelt in the high grassland. They were the eyes of a natural killer.

When Senator Bili saw me, he called out, "Gener, my friend, it is good to see you. I would like you to meet a business associate of mine who just arrived on the island today. P.D. Pollap, say hello to Henri Gener. P.D. owns a fleet of fishing boats that work the lagoon at Truk and the ocean area between there and the Marshall Islands."

"That's interesting. I have been hearing a lot about Truk since I arrived. It's a place I've always wanted to visit for a couple of days," I said. "So, where do you sell your catch? Surely there aren't any canneries at Truk or the Marshalls."

P.D. responded, "No, but most of my boats are small, and of course it depends on what you catch."

All right then, I thought, *he's a pirate taking whatever he can, someone to watch out for. I wonder why—*

Before I finished the thought, Bili said, "Come, play with us. It will be an enjoyable, interesting, and profitable evening." Senator Bili had a mischievous look in his eye.

We walked toward one of the two craps tables where a crowd of Japanese tourists was losing with every throw of the dice. Bili grabbed his driver by the arm, whispering something in his ear. The man muscled his way to the table. There he began making room for us as he pushed and shoved the smaller men and women aside.

Slowly many of the tourists began to leave the table until only one remained along with three or four of the Americans and Australians who lived on the island.

"Just place your bets beside mine," he said, "and we will both be a winner."

The croupier, a small, slightly built man, raked the dice back to his hand and gave them to a Japanese tourist on the far side of the table. The man placed bets on both the Pass and Don't Pass squares. The croupier shook his head "No!" then said, "You don't want to do that. You are betting against yourself."

The Nipponese did not understand and prepared to throw the dice. The croupier trying to indicate to the tourist that he did not want to place bets on those squares at the same time pushed his bet off the squares. The man said something I did not understand and pushed his bets back where he had placed them and threw the dice.

Senator Bili watched but did not place a bet. The haggling between the croupier and the Japanese tourist continued as the man continued placing money on the table with neither man understanding what the other was saying. At last, exasperated by the confusion, Bili said something to the tourist. The man's facial expression changed from stubbornness to confusion while he pondered whatever it was Bili had said.

Bili held out his hand. The driver began moving around the table toward the tourist who suddenly threw the dice onto the table toward Bili and walked away followed by his companions. Turning to the croupier Bili said, "I'll take the dice if no one objects." The remaining players, all American, stood silent. Bili placed his bet, a fifty-dollar bill, and nodded to me to follow his lead.

Taking the dice, rolling them in his hand, he slid them across the felt table covering. The dice did not roll nor bounce off the opposite table wall. When the dice stopped, he announced to the croupier, "Seven, pay me." Bets were collected and paid by the Rotarians, then Bili held out his hand to take the dice.

"Senator Bili, you know the dice are supposed to roll and bounce off the wall. Please shoot right. It isn't fair to the other players."

Bili did not respond but merely placed another fifty-dollar bet. I did the same. He once more slid the dice across the table, once again not rolling, once again not bounding off the wall. "Seven again."

"I'll pay, but that is the last time." The Rotarians working the table began looking around for help but saw none. The croupier, frightened, his face ashen, raked the dice back to his hand and held them. His voice quivering with fright and anger, he continued, "Senator, you're through playing at this table."

The people at the surrounding games all stopped and looked at our table to see what was causing the ruckus.

Bili responded, "You're all a bunch of suckers." Then louder, "Did you hear me? You're all a bunch of suckers." With that comment, he turned to us. "Let's get out of here." I followed Bili, P.D., and the driver out of the casino room, walking to his car in the dark. None of them noticed I left my winnings on the table as we left. Even I did not abide such behavior.

When we got to the parking lot, I noticed Mark Meriday's car, a dark blue Toyota Celica, parked nearby that of Bili with only an old pickup truck between the two cars. I had not seen Meriday in the casino, but then he had no money—I had seen to that. I thought nothing more about it, though if I'd been alert, the old pickup parked close by Bili's with no other cars parked even close, other than Meriday's, should have alerted me to something.

I want you to know that although I left with Senator Bili and his companions, I did not approve of his actions at the gaming tables. I had watched him cheat on two occasions. The first time was at the home of Senator Nakamura. Then we had both cheated, and the victim had not been observant enough to know how or why he continued to lose. This was different, power challenging. It was open and blatant, and although I could have profited too, I somehow felt cheapened and dirtied in the process. I did not need the money, and there was nothing for me to gain otherwise from his heavy-handed hooliganism.

It seemed to me then, but now with gifted insight I understand, the entire incident was not only a test of character but also a well-orchestrated plan to entrap me. Bili and his associates wanted to see how far I would go along with them, if I would align myself with them in opposition to the *haoles* on Capitol Hill, or so it seemed to me at the time. They had seen me follow their lead, they had seen me cheat along with them, and of course I had gone with them when they had been called out for the bullies they were. At the time, I could not hope to understand what they thought they would gain by my complicity. They knew I planned to leave the island in a matter of days. Nevertheless, I did not know then that they had a man planted watching our every move at the craps table. He had observed us as we walked away and had even seen me slip back my winnings to the croupier as I followed Bili out of the room.

The four of us walked across the dimly lit parking lot heavy with the smell of the island enhanced by the lush flora growing, sweet and musky, around the outside of the building. When we got to the car, the driver stopped to look over Bili's car at the blue Celica then slipped into the driver's seat while P.D. got in beside him. Bili and I settled into the backseat of the sedan.

We drove to a bar, one I had not previously seen, operated by a Trukese I did not know. There they met a group of men who had the squat, powerful build of the Trukese. They began talking politics, drinking beer, and smoking pot, all except Bili and P.D. that is.

Shortly after midnight, two men entered the bar, excited and agitated. They had the look of men who had just come from combat, eyes wide, sweating. They walked directly to our table. The larger of the two men spoke to Bili quietly, respectfully, a little afraid. His voice sounded familiar, but I could not see him clearly in the dimly lit room. Then I saw the droopy left eyelid and the scar that turned the corner of his mouth downward as if it had once been snagged by a fishhook then ripped loose. It was Xarkus. It was Hiroki's father.

"It's done, boss. We got two of Dr. Camacho's campaign workers. They are up on Navy Hill by the old generators. We left them where someone is sure to find them, hands and feet tied, one bullet each in the back of the neck, just like you said."

"And the other, did you leave the other thing?"

"Yeah, we did just what you said. Everything was left like you told us."

"Good work, Xarkus, a little tit for tat. There is nothing quite as exciting as a little trouble in the middle of a political campaign, even one where you have no apparent interest." Turning to me, he concluded, "Wouldn't you say?"

I did not respond but looked Bili directly in the eye, a little unnerved by the callousness of the situation. Political assassination did not bother me. What did bother me was the obvious disregard for secrecy. Why bring me here? Why talk about this in my presence? What did they gain by implicating me in the affair? I had no interest in their politics. I had no interest in staying on the island more than another day or two. Was their goal to frighten me? Why would they do that? These thoughts raced through my mind as the man spoke, but no answers came.

Jonathan had warned me about Xarkus and Bili. What did Bili know? How did he know it? *Of course, he wants me to run so he can take Monique. That is why he and Xarkus have had Hiroki crawling all over the place trying to get on the boat.* I am not a man who frightens easily but am wary of danger, and every fiber of my being screamed this was a dangerous situation.

"What about the gun?" It was Bili who had spoken.

"It's taken care of, just like you said."

"And the other?"

"They'll find it."

Xarkus looked at me but said nothing. A slight smile crossed his face, the first time I had seen him smile. He turned abruptly and left followed by the other man. I glanced at my watch. It was a quarter till two.

Bili watched them leave then addressed me. "Ah well, there you have it. You are a man of the world. You have no doubt seen many things like this over the years. It wouldn't surprise me if you had been involved in some yourself."

Involved, I thought, *you don't know the half of it.* I had accompanied him undecided on whether to do as the high commissioner demanded. If the chance had presented itself, I may have done so. Now, my mind returned to the last time I had been involved as Bili suggested.

The day had been perfect for what I intended to do. Rain in London is not at all uncommon, so it raised no suspicions when a businessman rose early at the Forum

Hotel, had breakfast, then walked the two blocks to the Gloucester Road tube station carrying his umbrella and caught the train to the central banking district.

The entire event had not taken two hours. I took the tube back to the hotel, gathered my packed suitcase that had not been unpacked but carried for the cover it provided, and rode the train from Victoria Station out to Gatwick Airport. No one paid me any attention. No one ever did when I was working.

The man had felt the prick of the needle, a sharp stinging sensation like a hornet's sting, as it pierced his flesh. The jostling in the crowd, the poking of the umbrella against his leg largely numbed him to what happened. Sure, he must have felt something as the sharp barb entered his leg. As I walked away, I noticed him rub the back of his thigh where I had inserted the ricin.

The papers two days later were full of the mysterious death of the World Bank official who had died of ricin poisoning. The autopsy disclosed the small wound in his left leg, the one I had inflicted as I walked along beside him in the mob of people scurrying to work that morning just before the rain started up again.

The autopsy showed a central puncture wound of about 2mm diameter and a circular area of inflammation to the left thigh. The results confirmed the diagnosis made at St. James's Hospital where the man had gone for treatment, septicaemia, due to the very high leukocyte count, 33,000 per cubic mm. A single metal sphere the size of a pinhead was excised from the wound. It was 1.52 mm in diameter and composed of 90% platinum and 10% iridium. It had two holes bored through it, with diameters of 0.35mm, leaving 0.28 cubic mm available for toxin retention.

Testimony presented had been to the effect the dead man had felt something and noticed a man stoop to pick up an umbrella as he looked back. The victim could not provide a meaningful description other than the man appeared to be a businessman on his way to work. When he got to his office, he noticed a spot of blood on his trousers and showed a friend a pimple-like red swelling on his thigh. When he returned home, he became ill with a high fever. During the early morning hours of the following day, he was admitted to hospital where he died two days later.

Now that, I thought, was the way a political assassination was supposed to be carried out, not in the crude manner they had used. There had been nothing to connect me to the London incident. Neither my name nor any of the aliases I used, ones I had reason to suspect had been compromised, were mentioned. The man who killed the official went by an entirely new and unrecognizable name complete with the best forged documents to be purchased in France.

I answered, "I don't understand. What do you mean?"

"Only this, in the world of politics it is sometimes necessary for people to die. Sometimes those reasons are better served when obscured by other events. Here, it is in our best interests for the elections for governor to be seen as something less than, shall we say, democratic."

It was after 2:00 a.m. when Bili had his driver take me back to *Monique*. This time, though, we did not take Bili's big car, one everyone on the island recognized. This time we drove back in an old Honda, so common it could have been one of a hundred Sablan Motors had sold in the last few years.

As we drove to the dock, I noticed an old pickup parked close by a security lamp at the Coca-Cola plant. It seemed odd to me that a vehicle was parked there when the dock had been deserted every night since I arrived. Even odder was the fact I had seen that same pickup before, once, that very evening, parked beside Bili's car at the Inter-Continental Hotel when we left.

The thought occurred to me, *Something is wrong.* The scene at the casino had been clumsy, maybe staged was the word, and the departure certainly drew as much attention to me as it did Bili and his associates. What was going on with them—and why now?

All was quiet at Charlie Dock; the cruise ship had sailed for Guam at eleven. Twenty minutes after the cruise ship sailed, two men drove two vehicles onto Charlie Dock. They left driving one, leaving the old pickup behind, under the light. Xarkus looked grim, jaw set with lips drawn taut over his teeth, his good eye squinting until the two eyes were balanced for a change, as he drove away.

Chapter Seventeen

The following morning Hiroki called to me, awakening me early. "Frenchman, it is Hiroki. I am at your service. Whenever you are ready to go, I will be waiting." He would once again settle for the daily stipend we had agreed upon five days earlier. Did he know about the events of the preceding evening? I doubted it. Bili and Xarkus would never have countenanced his leaving me the morning before while he ran off with Japanese tourists. He would never be included in something as important as murder. He was nothing more than a pawn in their game.

I lay in bed, alone, thinking he could just wait until I was ready to go and that would not be for quite a while yet. It had been a short night, and I was enjoying the quiet of the harbor. At ten, I awoke again from my light sleep, the heat of the day beginning to climb in the small cabin and the noise on the dock now returning to normal activity after the holidays stirred me. Remembering my appointment at the bank, I rose and dressed. Then going on deck, I had a few words with Hiroki to let him know what I thought of his actions the day before. He stood next to the car with his eyes downcast.

Once again, he was all apologies explaining it had been a misunderstanding. He had looked for me, he claimed, but when he could not find me, he thought I had gone away with someone else. After all, hadn't I often sent him away, he said, especially if I had a woman? As far as he was concerned, that settled the incident, only it was not settled in my mind. Such a clumsy, childish lie—could these people be as dangerous as I thought the night before?

I intended to see that Hiroki got what was coming to him; I stepped onto the dock and approached the car. No one had ever been allowed to treat me in that cavalier manner and then lie about it claiming a misunderstanding, and it would not begin now. It would be a misunderstanding all right, and he would be on the short end of it. I would see to that. I said nothing but, rather than getting in the front seat next to Hiroki as I had always done in the past, got in the backseat on the passenger side so I could watch him. I had no intention of taking a risk on not correctly assessing the relationship between this boy and his father and uncle.

Hiroki said nothing during the drive to the Bank of America, and I had said all I intended for the time being. When we arrived at the bank, Hiroki parked the Charger next door, in front of the Korean laundry.

True to his word, the branch manager had the verification and was prepared to hand over the cash. "How would you like to take the money?" he asked.

"Three thousand in fifties and the rest in twenties would be all right."

He left me alone in the room and a few minutes later came back with an envelope bulging with a hundred and sixty bills. He counted them out, presented a receipt for me to sign, and handed over the envelope.

"Don't spend it all in one place."

The flippant comment did not amuse me. I rejoined, "Thank you. I won't." I put the envelope in my shoulder bag, walked out of the bank, and found the car empty, Hiroki nowhere in sight. *Now where is Hiroki run off?* I wondered.

As I looked around, I heard two men, Micronesians, standing by the next car talking about two bodies being found on Navy Hill, murdered, executed, hands taped behind the back, one bullet each at the base of the skull. I knew news traveled fast on the island, but this... Had someone provided a tip on where to find the bodies? If so, who, and why?

Looking around, I couldn't see the boy anywhere. I waited for five minutes before he finally appeared around the end of the strip row building.

I see Hiroki now. He is in the laundry shop next door to the bank. He is on the phone talking to someone, his father at his job in TT Transportation. He has frightened everyone away from the phone so he can talk in private, but like everyone else on this island, they are lurking nearby so they can hear what he is saying.

"It's me, Hiroki. We are at the bank. Good news! The Frenchman went into a room at the back of the building with the manager, so I motioned to mother's cousin, Midori, to meet me out back. She tried to wave me off, but she came around when she saw I was serious. It's a good thing she works at the bank."

"What's the point, Hiroki?" Xarkus did not want to be bothered by any more petty news from his son.

"The Frenchman, he's loaded. Midori said the manager was handing over an envelope filled with money. There must be thousands of dollars in it."

"Good work, Hiroki. You stay with him and see what he does with it if you can. We know he won a bundle at the races. Either he will be carrying it with him, or it will be stashed on the boat. Either way, it is ours soon enough." He hung up.

As Hiroki appeared and walked toward the car, I whispered in a menacing way, "Where were you?"

"I had to answer a call, you know, 'the call.'"

He did not lie well. His eyes gave him away, looking away, down as he always did when he spoke words that were not true. I could not believe the difference between the boy and his uncle. The boy lied but could not pull it off. The uncle told the truth and did not care what you thought.

Now that I had my money, I saw no reason to stay on the island. In many ways the island had begun to bore me. At the same time, my heightened awareness of the danger that always existed on these out of the way places where culture and politics were alien to me said leave. The events at the end of the previous night did not surprise me. What did surprise me was the brazenness with which they had been discussed. As for routine life on the island, it held no allure. I had seen and done all that was exciting on the island. The only excitement that remained would be associated with the events of the preceding night, or so I thought, and I did not intend to stay around to see how that turned out.

The investigation on Navy Hill into the homicide of two political operatives involved in the gubernatorial campaign was wrapping up as Hiroki drove down the road toward Charlie Dock. A Capitol Hill police officer making a final sweep of the crime scene spotted something white caught in the underbrush. Reaching down he picked up a torn scrap of paper.

"What have you got there?" Lieutenant Reyes, the officer in charge, asked. Reyes had concluded his cursory investigation, location and bodies, their physical condition, expecting the others to get the details so he could review them later.

"I don't know," answered the other. "It is a piece of paper torn from a larger paper, and it has some writing on it, but I can't read it."

He handed it to the lieutenant who looked at it. "It looks like it is written in French," he said. "Where did you find it?"

"Over there," he answered, gesturing to a spot about twenty feet away, some fifty feet from the place where the bodies had lain before they were removed at the assistant coroner's instruction. The bodies had been taken to Dr. Torres Hospital to be held until the coroner could come up from Guam to conduct the autopsies if one was contemplated under the circumstances. After all, there could be little doubt as to the cause of death when you saw a wound like the one these two suffered. The only thing that bothered Reyes was the absence of blood. If they were alive when the gun was placed close behind their ears, where was the blood? That is, unless they were killed somewhere else and dumped here. Whoever did this had a very messy handgun in their possession. There would be blood residue and tissue on the barrel from the shooting.

"Bag it," Reyes ordered, "and be careful to maintain a chain of custody on it. Who knows, anything up here may be useful as evidence, although right now I'd guess this is just a political killing that will never be solved, probably nothing more than retaliation for the killing the other night."

Reyes secretly hoped the crime would not be solved if a political assassination was all there was to it. After all, the dead men had not been supporters of his candidate. Murder was not a common occurrence on the island, although the rate computed in terms of incidents per thousand people suggested it not be thought of as rare.

In the eleven years Reyes had served the public as a police officer, he had been involved in the investigation of more than fifteen homicides, some murder but more often manslaughter. The training he received at the Hawaii Police Academy had served him well. He held the distinction of being the best-trained investigator on the islands, a fact he was proud of though not conceited about. Nevertheless, he did not intend to bring down his candidate by solving this crime if the trail led back to that camp.

As he prepared to leave he turned to the group of residents on Navy Hill who lurked respectfully on the outskirts of the scene, having gathered once the bodies were removed. Gossip on the island, always at a premium and no one wanted to be left out, would be the topic of discussion for days, if not weeks.

"That's all there is, folks. Go home or to work. Go somewhere! There isn't anything to see here," the lieutenant commented as he got into his Jeep and drove away from behind the abandoned gasoline-powered electric generators where the bodies had lain. Moments later his comment about nothing to be seen was all too true. The spectators swarmed over the area like locusts. Any evidence that had been overlooked was soon destroyed in the frenzy of curiosity.

There is something a little too pat about this, he thought. For one thing, there were no shell casings. Every indication by his training suggested the murders had been committed during the night. If that proved to be true, then where were the casings? A professional hit man would no doubt police the area, but there were no professionals on the island, at least not so far as he knew. It seemed likely the killings had taken place somewhere else and the bodies dumped between the generators and the radio station knowing they would be found the following morning when the manager came to open for the morning broadcast. But why would anyone want to do that?

Clearly, if these were just political killings committed to affect the outcome of the election, whoever did it would want the bodies discovered. Maybe there was no more to it than that. If so, why not kill them here? Someone might hear the gunfire. Possible. After all, there were the Samoan houses on Navy Hill that had no air-conditioning. Maybe whoever did this wanted the bodies found soon.

The houses closest to where the bodies were found were concrete construction, with air-conditioning, windows closed against the humid night air. The house nearest the crime scene was vacant, the occupants on home leave to Australia. The house next to that was assigned to George Rowley. *I will have to check with George and Beth to see if they heard anything,* knowing it would be unlikely. George would undoubtedly be passed out. Beth, on the other hand, might have heard something.

Before heading down the hill, he turned right and drove two hundred yards then turned up the slight rise that led to George and Beth Rowley's house and stopped at the same place I had stopped earlier with George, to be greeted by the massive Bear. His luck held; Beth Rowley was preparing to leave for work at the Civic Center. Calling off Bear, she responded to his question concerning the events of the preceding night.

"No," she said, "we, I, didn't hear anything." She did not bother to state the obvious. George was in no condition to hear anything. "George and I returned home from Las Vegas Night a little after eleven, and I went straight to bed." She left out the part about George sleeping in the car until some time shortly before daybreak when she heard him in the kitchen mixing a drink.

"No," she continued in answer to his next question, "we didn't see anything unusual on the way home either."

"Can you account for your time from just about dark until you returned home?" he asked. Having Beth establish a timeline would help in the investigation. At least he would have the hours when the crime was committed narrowed down.

"Sure, we picked up the Frenchman, Henri Gener, at his boat tied up at Charlie Dock, at about eight last night. We went straight to the Inter-Continental Hotel and spent the entire evening there."

"What time did you take the Frenchman back to his boat?"

"Well, actually, we didn't. He left early with Senator Bili and some other men."

"Do you know who they were?"

"The guy who drives Bili was one of the men. I didn't know the other one."

"Can you tell me anything else, anything at all from when you left the Inter-Continental until you got home last night?"

"We did pass an old pickup truck coming down from Navy Hill. I think it was black. There was not much of a moon last night, so I cannot be certain. It was a dark color. I think maybe there were two men in it. No one up here has an old truck like that."

"I don't suppose you could identify them."

"Well, no. The moon was up, but there wasn't enough light to see in."

"Where were you when you saw the truck?"

"I had not quite reached the base of the hill off Middle Road when it passed me heading toward the Continental Hotel."

"Do you think you could identify the truck if you saw it again?"

"Maybe, but it was dark, and I wasn't really paying much attention to it. You know, it was just another old truck on the road. The only thing that struck me as odd was the time I saw it. Navy Hill is pretty quiet at that time of night, and you don't see much traffic."

Reyes thanked her for the information then made
another stop at the nearest Samoan house just across
the road and below where the Rowleys lived. If anyone
would have heard gunshots on Navy Hill, they would.
As he walked across the road, he noted the house did
not have any boards up or typhoon curtains pulled. All
that separated the inside of the house from the outside
were screens and diamond-shaped security mesh. A
couple with two daughters occupied the house. Inquiry
revealed they were all home all evening and no one heard
anything out of the ordinary. They had all turned in for
the night when the TV station had stopped broadcasting
at ten. *More evidence the killing took place somewhere else,*
he thought.

With nothing more to be done on Navy Hill, Reyes
drove down the hill then proceeded to police headquarters where he planned to go over the results of the
investigation. As he entered the building, he heard loud
voices. A local Chamorro man stood before the desk
sergeant complaining someone had stolen his 1971 black
Toyota pickup truck some time after eight o'clock the
preceding night. The lieutenant stopped to listen to the
report as it was being taken down.

"Calm down," the sergeant said. "We've located your
truck. It is all right and you can pick it up any time you
want. I will have someone drive you down to the Coca-
Cola plant. It was reported being there this morning by
the plant manager."

"Hold on a minute," the lieutenant interjected. "I want
to have a look at that truck before you turn it over."

"It wasn't damaged," the sergeant remarked. "Whoever
took it must have just been joyriding."

"I'm not so sure of that," the lieutenant answered. "A truck matching that description was seen going down Navy Hill last night, after most folks were at home in bed. It may have been implicated in the murder of the doctor's campaign workers."

The owner of the truck took a step back, away from the two police officers. Then in an excited voice, fearful that someone would blame him, he said, "I don't know anything about that. I just want my truck back."

"I'm sorry, but you will have to wait until we can get a close look."

Turning away from the agitated Chamorro and addressing the sergeant, the lieutenant said, "I want you to start making some calls to see if anyone saw that truck anywhere else last night. I think starting at the Inter-Continental Hotel parking lot would be a good place to begin. There was a lot of activity there last night, and just about everyone on the island was there at one time or another. Someone may have seen something."

The sergeant answered, "I'll get right on it."

Lieutenant Reyes then turned back to the man whose truck had been stolen, or at least so the man said. "What time did you notice your truck missing?"

The man looked worried. "Not until this morning when I got up. It wasn't parked outside my house."

"Was it there when you went to bed?"

"Yes. My wife and I went to bed as soon as it got dark."

"And you didn't hear anything?"

"No. We both sleep well."

I have told you before how gossip spreads on small islands. Within a couple of hours, virtually everyone on the island knew there had been a murder or murders and that the police were looking into the circumstances of a black pickup truck being stolen, the one owned by old Villagomez, and possibly used in the crime. To a lesser extent, the news about a scrap of paper with some writing in French was also circulated. I was probably the last to learn about anything other than that the bodies had been found, something I had expected.

I was not altogether surprised when the lieutenant came aboard *Monique* later that afternoon. Everything that had happened during the past fifteen hours told me I could expect an official visit from the police. I was below making final preparation for my departure from Saipan, not just because of the events of the night before but also because of my conversation with the high commissioner. Was this going to be more of his pressure?

My boat was well stocked all but for fresh water. I had been using the water liberally since I had gotten on island knowing I could easily refill my water tanks at the Coke plant. Gasoline, on the other hand, might be a problem. The jerry cans Hiroki and I had carried on board earlier were stowed away safely, and I had topped off the on board reservoir. Still, would it be enough? I planned to leave, slip away, during the night late when it was dark and no one would be moving about. I would have to use the engine, but I wanted to put as much distance between me and the island as I could before anyone knew I was gone.

"Mr. Gener," Lieutenant Reyes began, "I want to ask you a few questions about last night." He stood at the top of the ladder then proceeded to come below, uninvited.

"What about last night?" I responded.

"I have some questions about a pickup truck parked nearby. What time did you get home?"

I looked at him but in the dim light of the below deck passageway could not make out the name pinned to his uniform blouse. "Who did you say you were?"

"Reyes, Lieutenant Reyes. Now about my question. When did you get back here last night?"

"It must have been sometime between 2:00 and 3:00 a.m. Why?"

"Did you see the black pickup truck parked over by the Coke plant when you got home?"

"As a matter of fact, I did. It was parked near the security light. It seemed strange to me. There hasn't been any vehicle parked there all week. It looked like it would be in the way this morning when they opened."

"How did you get home?" the lieutenant asked.

"Senator Bili's driver brought me home. I left the Las Vegas Night gambling with him at about nine forty-five. We went to some bar, I don't know where, and he had his driver bring me back here several hours later."

"Did you see anyone around the truck when you got back?"

"No. I did walk up to see if someone was there. You know, I have made some, well, some people might say, enemies since I got here. It never pays to take too much for granted. I walked over and looked in. There wasn't anyone in the truck or anywhere near it that I saw."

"That is all you did; you didn't touch it?"

"I may have put my hand on it; I don't recall. Why?"

"We have reason to believe that truck may have been involved in two murders last night. There were blood stains in the bed, at least they look like blood stains."

"It was too dark for me to see anything like that."

"Mr. Gener, did you ride in that truck last night or any other time?"

"What is going on here?" I demanded. "I've answered all your questions. No, I've never been in that truck."

"Mr. Gener, we have information to the contrary. It is my duty to warn you that you have the right to remain silent; you do not have to answer any of my questions if you choose not to do so. I must also warn you that I will make a record of anything you tell me and that it may be used in court against you. Do you understand your rights?"

"Yes, I do ... " then reconsidering my outburst continued, "and I have no problem answering you; ask what you want."

"Mr. Gener, we have a report that you were seen driving away from the Inter-Continental Hotel last night at about nine forty-five. You weren't in the car with Senator Bili. Our informant says you drove away in a black Toyota pickup truck. We believe it may have been the one found over by the light pole, over there."

"Well, it's a lie. Who told you I drove that truck or any other truck?"

"I probably shouldn't tell you but ... Mark Meriday."

"What do you expect? He's just trying to get at me for taking his girlfriend and humiliating him at the races on Sunday. Surely you know that. Everyone on this island must know by now."

"That may be, then again maybe not," the lieutenant responded. "We've already checked up on those aspects of your story, and they square with what you've just told me. I don't suppose you'd be willing to give us a sample of your handwriting, in French, would you?"

"No, I wouldn't. As for my so-called story, it checks out because it is true. I don't know what's going on here, but it looks like someone is trying to set me up for something and I don't like it. I don't think I'd better say anything else right now."

Reyes left after that, warning me not to leave the island until the matter was resolved. I now see he thought, *This is too easy, too many leads, too fast. What's going on here?*

I walked over to the Coca-Cola plant where I first thought to telephone Hiroki and have him pick me up. Then thinking better of it, I struck out walking south. Three quarters of an hour later, I was at the Pink Apartments knocking on the door of Mark Meriday. He did not answer. I tried the door to the apartment and found it unlocked. I entered and waited.

A half an hour later I heard the long stride of Mark Meriday approaching along the outdoor walkway leading from the stairs to the apartment. When he entered, I hit him, knocking him to the floor, stunned but conscious. He started to scramble toward the end table by the rattan sofa. "Is this what you're after?" I asked, holding the pistol in my hand. "It seems all you law enforcement types have illegal firearms on the island. What should I expect? Who is there to prosecute you?"

Mark sat back on the floor, his back against a side chair, and asked, "What was that for?"

"I think you know," I hissed. "I had a visit from the police a while ago, and they tell me you have been lying about me driving away from the hotel last night in a stolen truck."

"Well, Frenchy, it's my word against yours, and I doubt they are going to believe you over me."

My blood was now up. "What you don't know is just how persuasive I can be." With that comment, I did a pivot kick, my foot striking him full in the face. Blood spurted from his nose. "I think you will tell the police you lied or I'll just keep going. What's it going to be?"

Mark had more guts than I had given him credit for. "Yeah, go ahead. You make a hamburger out of my face. That'll be sure to convince them I'm telling the truth."

"So you and Bili cooked something up between you," I said quietly, once more under complete control. "Well, it isn't going to do you any good." Grabbing him by the hair, I struck him a blow, knocking him unconscious. Then gagging him and tying him so he could not move, I took his keys. I locked the door to his apartment and drove his car down the hill to Middle Road following the path I had taken a few days earlier with George when he first showed me the island. I followed that road to a place where I could cut over to Beach Road without being seen by the crowd that always gathered at the Continental Hotel. I left the car beside some other cars and walked the final quarter mile to the dock.

It was obvious I had to get off the island fast. I had been set up to take the fall for killing the two campaign workers. I had never trusted Bili or Xarkus, and now I was convinced they were planning to rob me, kill me if necessary, and take *Monique*. Worse yet, they had the complicity of the law enforcement apparatus on the island. Of course getting off the island would now be a problem. I imagined they would be watching, if not now, soon.

As I approached *Monique*, I saw the orange Charger parked alongside. "What do you want?" I demanded.

"I want my money. You agreed to pay me for driving you. You said you'd pay me before you leave, and it looks to me like you're getting ready to leave."

"No! This joke is on you," I said. "It will teach you to leave me standing on the dock like a fool while you run Japanese tourists all over the island."

Hiroki had no intention of taking no for an answer. "I want my money. If you don't give it to me, I'll go to Uncle Bili."

I reached behind my back and, pulling Mark's pistol from my waistband, said, "Fine, you tell Bili anything you want. You and he can have some of this."

Hiroki's courage flagged in the face of the loaded pistol. He retreated toward his car, his face toward me. When he got to the Charger, he ran around to the driver's side. I had never seen him move as fast as he did getting into the car, driving away, spraying loose rock behind him. Just before he left, he flung something in my direction and shouted, "I already got mine, but you are the one who will be getting his." It was my money clip; I recognized the fleur-de-lis.

The sun was now setting, with just enough light for me to see my way out of the harbor, and so I set Monique free once more and started the seventy-five horsepower Volvo Saildrive engine. Pulling her away from the dock, I headed out past the island toward the open ocean. I could not wait for complete darkness. Undoubtedly Hiroki and his uncle would be back shortly. I had to risk it now. Once outside the reef with the sun now set and the crescent moon still not half-full, I set a course with the current northward toward the island of Anatahan.

When the sun rose the following day, the current

aided by my engine had carried me far to the north of Saipan. Then, with my fuel reservoir half spent, I killed the engine. Giving *Monique* all the sail the wind would carry, I took the next step toward total escape. I hoisted the mizzen and heard a loud noise. Something heavy fell from the sail striking the deck. The pistol used in the murders the night before, still sticky with the drying blood, fell harmlessly at my feet. It had been intended as the last piece of the puzzle to pin the murders on me. I checked the cylinder. Sure enough, two shots had been fired.

Chapter Eighteen

I must confess being at sea once more, as *Monique* fairly flew during the night carrying me along with the north current, gladdened me to the depth of my being, to be free of the tangling relationships that always ensnared me on land. I had not set out to find trouble. I had merely sought pleasure on the island. I suppose one could say I lived for the moment relishing the ecstasy, thrilled by the danger. My pleasure, my experience mattered, and no one else. For me, the mania of life on land was over, and peaceful hours at sea absorbed me.

When dawn broke and the sun suddenly appeared as if rising out of the water, a red semi circle at first, then a ball, I could not see land. I would have to wait until noon to take my navigation reading but knew I had to be well over a hundred miles north of Saipan. This I had calculated periodically throughout the night by fixing a weighted float to a three-hundred-foot length of lightweight line in which I had tied a knot every six feet. Then dropping the float into the water, I counted the seconds until the entire length was played out. Just less than fourteen seconds elapsed from the moment I dropped the float into the water until the entire line had extended through my hands.

Knowing that distance and the time involved, I computed my approximate speed, using simple arithmetic. It was a technique honored by time, going back to the days of Columbus. At one mile per hour, the line should play out at the rate of just under one and a half feet per second. At that rate, the three hundred feet of line would take two hundred seconds to unreel. I divided two hundred by fourteen and computed my speed with the current had been at just over fourteen and a quarter miles per hour. Nine hours had passed since I slipped out of the harbor at Saipan making my distance from that island about one hundred twenty-eight miles.

After that, I shut down the engine to save on gasoline; I checked my speed and found the time elapsed by the playing out of the line to be nineteen seconds and just more than twenty seconds. Averaging these, I determined my approximate speed to be just over ten miles per hour. One thing was for certain. Now that the sun was up, they could be looking for me from the air if they had access to a plane, and I wanted to get out of the northern current. It would make sense for them to follow that as one option in a plan of search and intercept.

I began to consider my options. I had no intent of going farther north to the Japanese islands. Sailing east would take me just south of Wake Island. No good; it made no sense to go there. The Pacific that far north offered few islands, and my supply of fresh water would not hold out until Hawaii. Truk Lagoon? A possibility. Senator Bili, P.D., and Xarkus were from there, and my sudden arrival might be reported to them, but if I was only there for a day or two ... my mind vacillated, drawn to the place yet wary of the danger.

Ponape though looked to be my best bet, farther but safer. If need be, I could always put into Truk, grab fresh water and gasoline, and then head out before my adversaries could react. Then too, Truk had always held a certain fascination for me, a diving paradise resulting from the ravages of war, a place where isolation had led to cannibalism in the last days of the war, two hundred Japanese ships of all sizes lying on the floor of the ocean. The allure of evil drew me forward.

Of course, Bili and his associates might not be my only adversaries. The high commissioner could not be counted as my friend, not that he ever had been, but what could he do? I doubted he would be willing to expose his unlawful proposal just to get at me. I had even less reason to worry about Mark Meriday. He would like to do me harm, but he would be limited to using the legal apparatus of the Trust Territory, and I was small fish to them.

Jonathan Cartwright—he worried me. By the time I left the island, I felt sure his real employer was the U.S. Central Intelligence Agency. I could not imagine any event, any cause, for that agency to be after me, unless, of course, the high commissioner revealed my activity during the second Indochina war and my duplicity. However, that too would be dredging up ancient history. Would they pursue me on that account? No, I now see their interest stemmed from their association with French intelligence.

Whatever, I was at sea and safe. Having calculated my possible distance from Saipan, they would have to look for me in a thirteen thousand square mile circle. That meant I was on a forty-foot long boat painted a color that did not show up well on the water. I had become that needle in the haystack so many people talked about, no, a small fish in a big ocean. I was at sea and safe. I could go where I wanted.

I turned *Monique* eastward, leaving the Kuroshio Current and catching the North Equatorial Current. I did not intend to go as far as Wake Island. I just wanted to put more distance between my adversaries and me. I figured that after a few hundred miles eastward the area for them to search would be so large the chances of finding me were nil. And so it proved.

The next two days were less than idyllic. There was work to do sailing the boat, and my days on land had cost me my sea legs. The motion of being at sea now left me slightly nauseous, a malaise that comes from mild seasickness, imbalance of the inner ear. I spent as much time as I could on deck, secured now by a safety line against the possibility my unsteadiness would pitch me overboard. The balance of the time I spent below deck in the salon lounging on the cushions taking what nourishment I could manage as my body adjusted, knowing that a working stomach would serve me much better than an empty one as far as the seasickness was concerned.

Two days later when my sea balance was restored, I turned *Monique* southward intending to work across the currents, with little wind to aid me until I reached the Equatorial Counter Current, and sail toward the islands that would allow me some degree of safe haven while I remapped my strategy.

The days occupied with work on the boat as we slowly

made our way to the south, now always being carried westward by the current, were filled with time to reflect on the events of my stay in the Mariana Islands. The old training, instruction in my church, came back to me as I considered my activity, and I resented the recollection of teachings I had long ago dismissed as foolish and for the weak only:

> Blessed *are* the poor in spirit: for theirs is the kingdom of heaven.
> Blessed *are* they that mourn: for they shall be comforted.
> Blessed *are* the meek: for they shall inherit the earth.
> Blessed *are* they which do hunger and thirst after righteousness: for they shall be filled.
> Blessed *are* the merciful: for they shall obtain mercy.
> Blessed *are* the pure in heart: for they shall see God.
> Blessed *are* the peacemakers: for they shall be called the children of God.
> Blessed *are* they which are persecuted for righteousness' sake: for theirs is the kingdom of heaven.
> Blessed are ye, when *men* shall revile you, and persecute *you*, and shall say all manner of evil against you falsely, for my sake.

Of the nine beatitudes I remembered, remembered even against my will, I could only say I had failed to trample two in the recent weeks. I had shown mercy to the little Vietnamese girl and had mourned her death, or at least would have done so had it not been for the events that followed. Certainly my ordeal meant much more to me than what had happened to her. At the time, I had sworn never to allow compassion to interfere again with good judgment. The next time someone needed my help they would have to wait until someone else came along.

Lying on the cushions or in my bed, other passages of Scripture came to my mind. Only when I practiced yoga was I able to empty my mind of those long suppressed memories and thoughts. I hated the priest for bringing them to my mind and swore an oath against him and all who followed him.

The commandments of Moses came to me one night:

> Honor thy father and thy mother, so that thy days may be long upon the land which the LORD thy God giveth thee. Thou shalt not murder. Thou shalt not commit adultery. Thou shalt not steal. Thou shalt not give false testimony against thy neighbor. Thou shalt not covet thy neighbor's house. Thou shalt not covet thy neighbor's wife.

Which of those had I not done in the past days? Certainly my actions as an adult brought no honor to my parents. Only when I joined the army had I acted honorably, and that soon became tainted. Murder, adultery, theft, false testimony, covetousness, greed were my way of life. It was in the pursuit of these things I found pleasure.

Later that night, they came, ghosts from my past, one following another until my mind swam in a sea of confusion as large as the ocean I sailed. First an old white-haired French woman came. In the beginning, I did not recognize her. She walked along a country lane holding the hand of a small boy of seven or eight. She looked vaguely familiar, but in the distance I could not make out her features. The boy, though, could not be mistaken. It was I. Then I saw her clearly; it was Mère-grand. "You must not play the truant from your catechism lessons. The priest will always tell us if you do. Why did you not go to your class?"

"It's boring, Mère-grand. I do not understand what he means. How can Jesus be God and man at the same time? He keeps on talking, but none of us knows what he means, so we do not pay any attention. Besides, some of the other boys wanted to look for frogs, so I went along."

"How will you ever know the truth if you don't go to your classes?" she answered.

I shrugged.

"You are a good boy. We know that, but it is not enough just being good. You must know Jesus and his mother the Blessed Virgin. Without them, you are lost."

"That is what the priest keeps saying, but I was baptized. You have all told me about it and shown me the white dress I wore when it happened. Isn't that enough?"

"Oh that it were, mon petit gars. Because it is not, you must promise me that you will not miss any more classes. Will you promise?"

"Oui, Mère-grand. I promise."

They walked on, but I can no longer hear what is being said. They have passed by me. As I look back, I see her tousle my unruly hair and hear her laugh. I understand the love she had was unconditional. Because she loved me that way, I wanted to love back the same way.

It is two years later. Now I recall; I am ten years old. We are in the church, and we are wearing our red confirmation robes. The priest touches our heads with oil. I watch as he comes down the line toward me. I wonder what will happen. Will I feel anything? I understand I will receive the Holy Ghost when he touches me and will become a soldier for Jesus when he slaps my face.

At last he stands before me. I lower my head and feel his hand on my hair but feel nothing except the weight of his touch. There is no miracle in-dwelling of the Spirit that I can feel. Nothing changed. Then, as I raise my eyes, I see that light touch lash out and feel the sting of his hand as it smacks across my mouth. Caught by surprise, I open my mouth just as the slap is delivered and my lip is cut. In that moment, rebellion rises in my heart, but I suppress the urge to lash back. The priest looks down at me. "You will be called upon to suffer many things, boy. It is well that you begin to understand now."

Obediently, I nod, but I do not understand at all.

Mère-grand has not been able to attend when I receive this sacrament. That afternoon, at a family reception, I see the look of joy mixed with concern on her face as I tell her about the oil, the slap, and the blood. I show her my lip, swollen and bruised but no longer bleeding. She is ill and dies a few days later. It is not the first time in my young life I have experienced death, and I question how a loving God could inflict this pain on me.

Now I am back in Vietnam. The mass of Christian burial has ended. My mother has aged years in the days that followed the news of my father's death. All the people in the legation came to express their grief, but I can see on their faces that they do not really care. It was not them; it did not happen to them. It was not any of their family. They cannot wait to get in their cars and return to work or to some other social event.

Only one man lingers to talk to my mother. Her face is drawn taut by the hours of crying, but now her eyes widen in disbelief. She raises her hand to strike the man then lets it fall to her side. She agrees but says nothing. Later when I ask, she tells me the man will help us leave Indochina. He will expedite the paperwork so we can return to France, but she refuses to tell me what the man said that caused her to raise her hand.

A week later when I return home from school, he is there in the house with her alone. He does not look at me but walks across the parquet floor and closes the door as I watch him go. It was a scene long repressed, but now I see it for what it had to be—all that talk of love and provision caught up in lust and deceit.

I recall his name as well as my own. He was called Political Officer Pham, and he was assigned to conduct indoctrination classes for some of the prisoners taken at Diem

Biem Phu. He speaks in excellent Colonial French. "I am your friend," he begins. "It is my earnest desire that you be repatriated to your homeland. But first, there are some things we must do. We have much to discuss, you and I. Although it may take some time, it will all work out. You have been specially chosen for this class. We want you to learn so that you may be free."

My image of Political Officer Pham changes, and now he and I are sitting alone in a spare office containing only a wooden desk and two straight-back chairs. On the wall behind the desk is a picture of an aging man with a stringy gray beard. A single window opens onto a courtyard where the grounds are immaculately kept. It is Hanoi, the home of my youth. "You have done well," he gestures with his palms opened upward. "Of all the students in the class, you are ready for the long journey home. You alone have embraced the truth."

I see myself accepting what he says. The settlement of Indochina by us, the imposition of Catholicism on this ancient civilization, had nothing to do with truth. It had to do with control, power, and greed. They have shown me that only through rejection of the old way can I gain my freedom. "Thank you," I lie, "for showing me the error of my way." I did not believe it then, though now I do. The seed of doubt was planted, and my belief, faith, was rooted in childlike understanding.

Now the faces come to me bright and illuminated against the blackness. My grandmother with her eyes open wide holding a crucifix before her telling me to stay fast, to believe, only to shrink before my gaze to become death itself, shriveled by decay. Her face fades and then that of the confirmation priest comes. He sneers as he slaps my face, his expression that of a cruel master enjoying some joke I am not allowed to understand.

Now faster and faster they come, the fat pigs who ate and drank at my father's funeral; the lusting, sweaty bureaucrat who turned my mother into a whore; my dead comrades abandoned in the circle of death, all betrayed by Catholic France. Political Officer Pham smiling and repeating, "You know I'm right; you know I'm right. I was right all along and now you know it. Remember what I taught you. Return to it now, accept yourself, and enjoy life. It is all you have."

The fool priest on Saipan only wanted people, me, to forego those pleasures because he had been forced to do so by his misguided religion. Why did I continue to dream about Scripture and the sacraments? Was it that I dreamed to remember or not forget? My mind would not give me any peace. I shouted out in protest waking myself. Rising from my bed, I opened a bottle of wine and drowned my thoughts.

Chapter Nineteen

At last the dreams subsided, and the rhythm of the water, as it rose and fell slipping along the hull of my boat with an almost imperceptible shushing sound, calmed my anxiety. I cannot otherwise account for the error that then followed. Instead of continuing on the course I have just outlined, I set a new heading that would take me to a place I should have known would spell disaster—Truk Lagoon, home to both Senator Bili and Xarkus.

I would be deluding myself if I told you my reason for going there was that the calm wind and strong current had carried me back toward that lake within an ocean. My desire to see the place where so much history had been made simply overpowered my reason. I had been days at sea. I was hundreds of miles away from anyone seeking my destruction. Truk Lagoon was a huge place with only primitive communications. It had become a famous place, one where my countryman Jacques Cousteau dove, one now made famous to a new generation of Frenchmen. Therefore, I ignored what should have been obvious warning signs.

As *Monique* approached the lagoon, reason once more

asserted itself, and I planned a cautious approach, going by the North Pass, skirting the western edge of the protective reef, and entering at Pieanu Pass near Tol Island.

I did not intend to spend much time inside the reef, but the many islands were intriguing, and so once entering the quiet waters of the lagoon, I began, early in the afternoon, a leisurely tour, first cruising around Lamotol Bay before entering Tol Harbor. The islands I noted were not high as Saipan and more nearly resembled elliptical green mounds half-floating in the azure water. From Tol I sailed on around Udot before going on to Fefan and Dublon.

It was nearing dusk when I finally arrived at the municipal center of the lagoon, Moen Island. Still mildly concerned for my safety, I anchored off the island rather than docking and spent a comfortable night on deck in the tropical waters. The moon and stars, the soft eerie music coming from the island, the warm humid deep tropical air, the lapping of water against *Monique*'s stationary hull soon lulled me to sleep.

I awoke once during the night but not having my watch did not know the time. The soothing music had stopped, and now in the distance I heard what sounded like American rock and roll, the kind of music the U.S. Army troops preferred during my time with them in Vietnam. I rose and looked about but, being anchored a quarter mile off shore, could see nothing and so soon drifted back to sleep once that strident music stopped.

Suddenly, it was morning and the sun was up, shining directly in my face. It had hardly cooled at all during the night. Even so early in the morning, the muggy warmth of the stillness promised another day; another adventure filled the air and I was ready for it.

I watched for signs of life on the island before setting out on my inflatable dinghy for the dock area. It was nearing nine o'clock in the morning before I saw people moving about and so with a small gasoline engine motored away from *Monique* to see what awaited me on Moen.

Truk had none of the sophistication of Saipan. If the latter was the "Paris" of Micronesia, then Truk Lagoon was more like the outer slums. The buildings were smaller, possibly no older but certainly less well maintained. There were no "skyscrapers" here, just low profile buildings of wood and metal, some concrete stained with lichen scattered willy-nilly along dusty dirt roads. One hotel of note, a motel-appearing structure of two stories with a dive shop next door, was located near the beach. It had the appearance of being the newest and most modern structure on the island.

When the dinghy approached the dock, an official greeted me. Pulling alongside the wooden dock, I grabbed the painter and tied the dinghy to land. Reaching a hand out, he helped me up and asked for my papers. I gave him a passport, but not the one with the name Gener on it. He gave it a cursory look and asked how long I intended to stay.

"Not long," I responded. "I may rent some scuba gear from the dive shop and try a little wreck diving if you or someone can suggest anything interesting."

I noticed a small boat with an outboard motor and two uniformed men aboard departed from the dock as we talked, heading in the direction of *Monique*, a fact that did not concern me. I had locked her down tight before leaving, so there was nothing for anyone to take or discover.

"Who's that?" I inquired.

"Some of our people who will only take a turn around your boat."

"You might have told me that without my having to ask," I answered, a little irritated.

True enough, the boat did not stop at *Monique* but merely circled and headed back to shore while we talked. The two men on board waved to the official talking to me though did not come over to us when they landed.

"I hope you have a nice stay," the official said. "Oh yes, and where did you say you came from?"

"I didn't. My last port of call was Majuro," I lied.

Then echoing his earlier question, "How long did you say you would be here?"

"Just a couple of days."

"Where do you plan on going then?" I thought the question unnecessary and wondered why the interest in my future plans. Surely his official interest was limited to issues of immigration and customs.

"Guam, and then over to Palau," I lied.

He thumbed through my passport then once again bid me a nice stay and departed, leaving me to walk down the dusty road to the hotel and dive shop.

I now see he returned immediately to the immigration/customs building where he met with the two men who had circled *Monique*.

"Is it him?" the official asked.

"The name on the boat is *Monique*," the smaller of the two men, yet the one clearly in authority over the other, responded.

"His name doesn't match," the official commented. "Maybe we should put in a call to cousin Bili just the same. He will be really ticked off if that is the guy and we don't let him know. People on some of the other islands have already noticed him. Word is bound to get back."

With that, he walked down the road to the Global Communications office and placed a phone call to Saipan, where after several minutes, he spoke to Senator Tobias Bili.

Minutes after the phone conversation between Bili and his cousin at Truk Lagoon ended, Bili placed a call to Jonathan Cartwright on Capitol Hill. Once he had him on the other end of the line, he spoke the words asking for a face-to-face meeting, "I thought you would like to know the price of yellow fin is out of sight."

Having spoken the words calling for a face-to-face meeting, Bili drove himself from his home near San Antonio across the south end of the island, turning right onto Middle Road just before reaching the turnoff that led to the new international airport. He then continued north the full length of the island.

The distance wasn't far, but the roundabout way to the meeting place at Naftan Point at the north end of the island below Suicide Cliff took almost a half hour.

When Bili turned down the tangen-tangen-chocked lane to the old airstrip, he saw Jonathan's car parked on the cracked tarmac, weeds growing up. The location had been well chosen. The combination of tangen-tangen and weeds located in this remote site left little likelihood of discovery. Jonathan stood beside the driver's side door. He was obviously perplexed by the sudden call for a meeting. In the thirteen months he and Bili had cooperated in achieving their mutual goals for the ultimate dissolution of the Trust Territory, it was only their third such meeting.

"What's up, Bili?"

"The Frenchman, he's on Moen. I got a call a little while ago."

Jonathan's head began to swim with the implications of Gener being caught and delivered to French authorities. Why had he been reckless enough to turn up at Truk Lagoon? He should have known Bili's people would be on the lookout for him there. Cartwright now understood the folly of merely attempting to scare Gener off Saipan. There was only one solution to the problem, the problem delivered by the cable from Langley days ago. The Frenchman had to die.

But how? Jonathan had missed his chance, and he had no connections at Truk other than his loose confederate Bili and there could be no way to know where or when he would strike out on his own. On the other hand, Bili had called and asked for the meeting. Could he count on him? Did he have a choice? Turning his eyes to look directly into Bili's, he said, "I suppose we both know there is only one solution to the problem of this Frenchman."

Bili nodded. "I thought as much. We are in luck; the Air Mike flight going east leaves tomorrow morning, and it arrives at Truk late in the afternoon. I plan to be on it. I will take P.D. with me. I've already alerted him to have some of his fishing boats in the area to be stationed off Truk so we can stop him if he runs again."

In a moment Jonathan responded, "I'll book a seat on that flight as well. I need to see that this is finished, no more slip-ups."

Bili nodded, and both men got in their cars and drove back to the extension of Beach Road and down island to the south toward the airport. At the first intersection, the two cars parted, each taking a different path ending with the same destination.

In light of my knowledge there were men after me and the questioning by the Trukese officials, penetrating though cordial, you may ask why do what I next did? The answer is simple. I did not know about the phone call to Senator Bili. After all, I had used a passport with the name Carlo Fosatti and had initially spoken to them in flawless Italian. I did not believe they made any connection between the fugitive from Saipan and me. Over seven hundred miles of open water separated the two locations.

Only now with the gift of seeing things as they were, not as they appeared to be, does my action seem reckless. Looking back, I see my failure to change the name on my boat gave me away, but how could I change the name at sea? I could not repaint the boat and in any event had no intention to do so. Besides, my desire to dive the wrecks of Truk Lagoon now had me firmly in its grip.

Diving could no more be passed by than when I had gone out of the Saipan grotto or having the pleasure of Beth's company that afternoon we had sailed outside the reef, beyond the reach of convention. Therefore, I went to the only place on the island where I could rent diving equipment. I only planned to stay on the island one or two days, and then I would be gone, lost in the ocean once more.

At the dive shop, I rented some reconditioned U.S. Divers equipment, an air tank and regulator, and inquired about the safety of the compressed air. Having seen an oily discoloration around the top of the tank, I questioned whether carbon monoxide might poison the air in the tank. The man cleaned the connection then showed me his compressor equipment. I decided to chance it.

He produced a map showing the location of the Japanese ships sunk in a vast part of the lagoon, focusing mainly in the area around Eten, Dublon, Fefan, and Moen islands. He seemed pleased when I bought the map for an additional ten dollars. One ship in particular caught my attention, the *San Francisco Maru*. She had been "discovered" by my countryman Jacques Cousteau a few years earlier and was reputed to be in excellent condition after thirty-three years on the bottom of the ocean. She lay upright in two hundred feet of water fully loaded with munitions of war.

It had been years since I last dove using scuba gear, but my training told me the *San Francisco Maru* was too deep for ordinary diving. Bottom time, the time counted from the moment you entered the water, dove down two hundred feet, and surfaced, could not exceed six minutes without suffering the effects of Caisson's Disease, the bends. What would be the point of diving all that way, only to have to blow and go to the top?

A half hour later, I left the shop having refused the offer of a dive guide, leaving a deposit equal to the inflated value of the equipment. The man in the shop insisted I should not attempt to enter any of the wrecks if I located them, especially not alone. Now loaded with the regulator and air tank and armed with a map providing me with the approximate location of some of the larger wrecks around Dublon Island, the trek back from the hotel where the dive shop was located to the dock took me over a quarter of an hour.

I moved *Monique* from Moen to Dublon and, by the time I arrived, noted my fuel gauge registered only one-half, diminished first by my escape from Saipan and then by my wandering around the lagoon. Nevertheless, I spent the balance of the day searching for the location of the shallow wrecks in blue water having a depth of under a hundred feet.

The sun was low in the sky, a red ball sinking toward the sea, when I located the wreck of the *Kansho Maru*, located nearly equal distance from Dublon and Fefan Islands, directly west of a point of land on Dublon and northeast of a rounded point on Fefan. It being late in the day and too late to dive, I motored along Dublon and found a shallow anchorage between it and Eten Island.

The next morning, with *Monique* dragging a sea anchor over the *Kansho Maru*, I donned my dive gear and went into the water. Even in the clear water, it took me several minutes to locate the wreck once more, and after a few more minutes passed, I descended to her. Swimming past the forward kingposts to the bow gun, I proceeded on around the fo'c'sl where there were some cables. I then swam back to the superstructure and considered exploring inside, but recalling the warning I had been given decided against it. After that I headed toward the stern, passing over the lifting gear and derricks.

By then my dive watch said I'd been down for forty minutes, and although I hadn't been below seventy feet, I knew I'd be pushing my luck to stay longer. I surfaced within my allotted dive plan time without difficulty and maneuvered *Monique* to Eten Island with the hopes of finding the two planes, an Emily flying boat and a Zero, known to be in shallow water at that location. Late that afternoon I located the Emily and dove down to her. She lay on her back in about fifty feet of water making my dive to her only forty feet. She was larger than I imagined, about ninety feet long with a wing span approaching a hundred and twenty feet.

I spent a third night near the spot where I'd stopped the night before and early the next day searched for the Zero but did not locate it. Concerned about conserving fuel until I determined the availability of more at Moen, I then sailed back to the municipal center arriving there shortly after noon. I loaded two of the empty jerry cans and the rented dive equipment I intended to return onto the dinghy and headed for the dock. By the time I returned the diving gear and hassled with the shop owner over the amount he would refund, it was mid-afternoon, and it appeared my life at Truk would be filled with conflict albeit not of the same severity as what I had fled on Saipan.

When I returned to my dinghy, I discovered one of my jerry cans had been taken. The nearest gasoline station, located at the end of the dock, filled my one remaining can as I eyed what appeared to be my missing can nearby. Deciding against any confrontation, I asked if that can was for sale. The response, a steely-eyed "no," left me with no alternative but to walk away wiser for my naiveté in leaving the cans in the open dinghy.

Not wanting to have my one remaining can stolen, I decided to return it to *Monique* and secure it before getting provisions. I had seen and done all I wanted at Truk, and the longer I stayed there, the more likely it was that word would reach Bili or someone else interested in my whereabouts. I had now been in the lagoon two full days, and I determined it was time to leave.

The gasoline safely aboard the boat, I once more returned to the dock and inquired about the possibility of buying some fresh fruit. In light of what I am about to tell you, you must wonder why I did not take additional empty jerry cans with me. The answer is simple. I did not want them stolen too while I searched about for the fruit.

My first stop was at one of the small local markets. The owner of the one-room store suggested I go to the airport when the Air Mike flight arrived. It had been rumored a load of fruit was on board. I could see for myself if that was true and then decide whether I wanted to wait around for it to be delivered to the local markets.

The suggestion sounded reasonable, and so, at a quarter till four, I followed a crowd walking to the airport at the end of the island. The crowd milled about waiting for the plane scheduled to arrive at four. The plane did not come. At four fifteen two American tourists on a diving vacation began grumbling about island life and the fact nothing came easy. I disassociated from them, not wanting to draw any more attention to myself than necessary. At last, the plane arrived, making a couple of passes before setting down on the coral runway amidst a cloud of dust and the roar of jet engines, reversing their thrust in order to stop just short of the water waiting at the end of the runway.

I stood near the back of the crowd just outside the area designated for security screening when the rear stairs to the Boeing 727 lowered and passengers began to debark. My heart leapt into my throat when I saw the first passengers reach ground and walk around the rear of the plane into sight: Jonathan Cartwright, Senator Tobias Bili, and P.D. What were they doing together? What possible reason could they have for traveling together other than *me*?

Following them, four passengers later, I saw Mark Meriday come down the stairs, his shock of red hair and gangly body looking about for someone he recognized. He did not look happy. Immediately behind him I saw Lieutenant Reyes deplane.

I do not want you to believe I ran away, although I certainly did beat a hasty withdrawal. In fact, my withdrawal was facilitated by the availability of a dilapidated pickup, once red now oxidized to a powdery coral, left unattended about fifty yards from the so-called security area. During the hubbub of passengers unloading and the personal freight coming from the front of the plane—chickens cooped in wooden crates, a goat, even a pig squealing, still frightened from the fright of the landing and no doubt having been knocked off its feet during the process—no one saw me steal back to the truck. The noise of so many people all talking excitedly together with the other racket drowned out the sound of the truck engine as I helped myself to a quick ride back to the dock.

Fruit would have to wait. I did not intend to stay in the lagoon where I had no defense against whatever the others had concocted. My mind was awhirl with conspiracy theories. If Jonathan was in fact CIA and the Americans had a preference in the outcome of the Saipan election, would they do something to fix the outcome? Would they get involved in political assassination? If so, why not kill the candidate—why kill some low-level campaign workers? Had they used Bili and his associates to do their dirty work and pin the killings on me? Would that make sense? Could they trust Bili and P.D.? Of course not!

The fact that Lieutenant Reyes was traveling with them suggested their appearance meant they were all together in the murders somehow, or did it? Moreover, what about Mark Meriday? Did he travel with them, or had he come for personal revenge?

I did not wait to find out at the time, although I now know the truth. They were not in collusion. Each acted on his own for his own reasons: for Reyes, it was law enforcement; for Mark Meriday, it was revenge. The fact that he happened to be a prosecutor was fortuitous. Reyes needed someone, a prosecutor, to authorize the arrest on Truk, and Meriday was delighted to volunteer for the task. It was not the revenge he wanted, but it would have to do.

Greed motivated Bili; the boat should have been his already, he reasoned, but I had stolen away in the night, and with his limited resources on Saipan, he had been unable to mount a proper search. Here on Truk, it would be a different matter. My disappearance would not be necessary. Here Bili was above the law. He could have me killed and still keep the boat. If I ran, he could hunt me down. The result would be the same. I would be dead, and he would have *Monique*.

For Jonathan Cartwright, it was more complicated. Motivated by fear that he had handled the instructions from his superiors badly, and with the arrival of French officials on Saipan just two days after my departure, he wanted to be certain I did not fall into their hands.

By the time the new arrivals cleared immigration, I had ditched the pickup and headed back on the dinghy to *Monique* and safety.

My pursuers were meeting with the local police and immigration officials. Lieutenant Reyes and Mark Meriday were talking to the man who had checked my papers two days before. He in turn kept glancing at Bili, wanting to give his cousin and benefactor a head start. They were all in an excited conversation, asking those in the crowd if they had seen me. One man told them I had been at the airport when the plane came in, but no one knew where I had gone. He told them I left in a hurry when all the passengers had disembarked. My pursuers concluded I must have left when I saw them.

Where was my boat?

It was last seen in the lagoon, just off the dock.

They all scramble for transportation, each trying now to get away from the others while they are all following me.

The ten-minute drive to the dock put them over a half hour behind me. *Monique* was already underway gliding through the water under the power of her engine at full throttle.

Monique was not fast, certainly not fast like a speedboat, but she had given me a head start of several miles. Reyes, the official whom I first met, and his two underlings departed the dock in the motor launch they had used to circle *Monique* on the morning of my arrival. Their boat sped after me, and before long, we were both mere dots on the water for those looking from land, heading rapidly toward the Northeast Pass out of the lagoon.

They gained on me, closing rapidly. With no other option open to me, I went below and retrieved the two pistols on board, checking to see they were both loaded. If necessary, I would shoot it out with them. After all, on *Monique*, I would not present much of a target while they, in a small open launch, were easy targets, easy to scare off even if I did not hit them.

As *Monique* slipped through the opening in the reef into deep water where the ocean swells worked in my favor, I looked back and saw the motor launch stop in the water rocking as a boat does when it suddenly ceases its forward motion. They were not going to follow me into the open ocean.

I now see the choice not to follow me was not their own. In the heat of the chase, they had not taken time to fill their gasoline tank, and now they were out of fuel. They were stuck, adrift, miles from shore and out of the sight of their friends on land. My lead just expanded by many miles.

I hoisted my sails, and now *Monique* surged forward under all of the canvass she carried and the gasoline engine at full throttle. I kept a watchful eye to both sea and air. Did they have a small plane they could use to look for me? I was free for the moment, but when would they next appear? Surely, they would, but not until the men on the dock discovered the motor launch sent to follow me had failed.

Monique seemed both faster than I had ever known

her, yet slow at the same time. Could I escape? My lead could not be nearly as great as when I left Saipan. Then I had the whole of one night, aided by current. This time I had hours at most, and the search area would be much smaller. For a fleeting moment my mind screamed at me, *You fool! Only your arrogance could have made you think stopping at Truk would not get you into trouble.* Then the danger at hand brought my mind back to reality. I had to get away.

Minutes passed, and I saw nothing. Hours pass, still nothing. Maybe I would make it yet. I killed the engine to conserve fuel and proceeded under sail. Four hours after my abrupt flight from Moen, as darkness began to envelope me, I saw the plane on the horizon and reefed my sails, trying to cut down on my profile, allowing the boat to slow so no wake would follow in the water. The dark green hull of *Monique* and her dark teak planking did not present much of an image on the dark gray ocean. The plane passed by well to the starboard and did not return. They had not seen me. Once more I hoisted sail and continued on my way setting a course to the southeast.

On the third day out of Moen, I began to feel secure once more. The plane had not seen me, and I could not then see anyone following to catch up to me. I looked at the barometer and saw the pressure falling. The weather would soon be changing. The sky changed from clear sunny blue to a slate gray. I saw no sign of serious storm, although that would have not been altogether unwelcome. Bad weather affected everyone more or less equally at sea. It might just make me even more difficult to find—if they were still looking.

Then I saw it. It was just a speck at first, but it headed directly toward me. As the hours passed, I watched as it grew larger and larger—a fishing trawler, one of P.D.'s? Through my glass, I made her out clearly. The hull rusted, the way I would have expected P.D. to maintain one of his boats. I had seen boats like it before, maybe a hundred feet in length, maybe a little more—just two or three times the length of *Monique*. Few of them had been capable of more than about ten knots. They were built for fishing, not racing.

The trawler made a slight course correction, and she now came directly toward me. Looking away from the approaching vessel, I saw what appeared to be light fog ahead of me, moving slowly in my direction. It might be enough with my engine. My only chance was to head directly into the coming weather; the race was on. Would I be able to reach the safety of the fog before the trawler caught me? For that matter, could she catch me?

Armed and ready, though not nearly as confident in a fight as I had been against the motor launch, *Monique* slipped toward safety. I started the gasoline engine, and now proceeding under power and sail, we picked up speed and moved quickly toward the fog. As I watched during the following half hour, I could not tell that the trawler had gained on me.

Chapter Twenty

As the fog enveloped *Monique*, I felt her slow, the lack of wind ceasing to urge her forward, almost as if she were caught in an invisible net. *Safe again*, I thought, just before the gasoline engine sputtered and stopped. The lack of engine power did not pose any immediate threat. I knew the crude navigation and radar equipment on board the boat trailing me could not find me in the fog. Any signal sent would be hopelessly clouded by the "noise" created by the wall of air, air heavy with the moisture that had enveloped me.

Taking advantage of the cover, I poured the last precious gallons of fuel from a jerry can into the fuel reservoir and restarted my engine. Knowing the engine of my pursuer's boat would drown any sound made by my small motor, I set a course at an acute angle away from the direction I had last seen taken by my adversaries. I calculated my lead at the time I had entered the fog to be something less than three miles. Nevertheless, speed was no longer an imperative. It was time that mattered, time while the engine would continue to run creating a greater search area for the trawler.

I set my speed for the maximum engine time and went on deck to watch. A few hours on this course using all that remained of my precious fuel should take me well beyond the ability of those sailing the other vessel to find me. I tried to reef my sails to cut down on the drag, sails being of no use in a fog, but something stuck. At last, to my relief, they came free.

The only question was where to go. Majuro or Kwagalein were too obvious. If the fog lifted while I continued on course for those atolls, I would surely be found. Tarawa and Nauru were better choices. From those I could slip on below the equator to either the Gilbert or Solomon Islands. Surely they would not follow me that far. There were just too many places for me to hide. Of course, they might assume that is what I would do.

I went below, covered the portholes in the main cabin, lit the oil lamp, pulled my charts of the central Pacific, and began to work out a solution. *It's a big ocean, and their radar probably can't pick up something as small as* Monique *for more than a few miles without a lot of luck. It is also almost certain they will have connections to people on either Tarawa or Nauru. I should not go to either of them, but where should I go?*

There it was, Banaba. There had to be a few people remaining there, but even so they wouldn't have any connection to the Micronesian islands. I quickly calculated the distance. *I can get more gasoline there. The phosphate mining operation on the atoll will have something.*

After an hour looking at the charts, I made another course correction, this time for Banaba Atoll. Secure now in the knowledge I was safe for the time being, I broke out a loaf of bread, some camembert cheese from a tin, and opened a bottle of wine. Turning the oil lantern down until it merely gave off a ghostly glow in the salon, I began eating the first meal I had had in over two days of flight. The bread had gone stale, but the cheese and wine soon warmed me, filling me with hope. I would escape once more. I opened a second bottle of wine. Soon fatigue and wine caught up with me, and I felt myself drifting off to sleep, a sleep troubled by the confusion between what is and was, what is past, present, or future, made ever more horrible by alcohol and by my present troubles.

The man has been following me all morning. I first noticed him after I left my home in the Toulon suburb and walked to the bus stop. He kept a respectful distance, so I did not know with any certainty how long he had been behind me. Even with my suspicious mind and background, it did not initially concern me that he was there. However, when he transferred from one bus to another, the same one I boarded, he took on a new importance. Later, when he waited at the Metro station, fifty feet down the platform from where I stood, and entered the car just after I did, he became very nearly menacing. He said nothing and did nothing to cause me to take any action.

I met the woman at a café in the old part of town, the historic section visited by tourists, a small affair with doors that open giving the place that airy feeling you only get at such places. We are in Paris. I arrive first and sit outside at a table for two against the wrought iron railing. She came shortly after, dressed in a gray hip-fitted skirt and white blouse, making her ebony hair seem all the darker. The cotton sweater she wore was now draped around her neck, the arms tied loosely. She is spectacular. She is everything I desire. She is someone else's wife.

As she enters the café, she approaches from behind me, nuzzles my ear, then kisses me lightly on the lips. Pouting, she says, "I've missed you. Where have you been?"

"Away," I respond vaguely, "on business. I am sorry I could not call you before I left. The timing was bad. You'd have left the office, and I couldn't risk calling at your apartment."

"I forgive you. Now that you are back that is. Where did you go?"

"It's not important. I'm back, and we can spend the entire afternoon together if you like."

"I like. My husband is busy with clients until late this evening, some people from the States, company lawyers. They come over a couple of times a year and stay a few days. Their meetings last all day, and their dinners never end until after ten. So what did you have in mind?"

"You! All of you! Over and over again!"

We finish our lunch, and as we walk away from the café, there he is, he—the man, the same man who followed me all morning in Toulon. Now he is in Paris. How can that be? He stands across the street, a half block away, not staring but watching, watching as if he wants me to notice him.

"Let's go this way," I say, leading her in the direction of the man. As I do so, he enters a little shop, but when we get to the window, he has vanished as if into a fog.

"Look at that," I exclaim, thankful for the exquisite piece of embroidered linen in the window. With that, I drag her in after me. The shop is small, a room not much more than twenty feet square without a rear door. The man is simply gone.

"Oh, it's not so nice once you see it up close. I thought it was worthy of you but now see it would be like placing plain cotton on the Mona Lisa."

"You say the prettiest things. I do not for a moment believe you really were interested in that linen. You were just using it as a prop."

"No, no, how can you think such a thing?" I pull her toward me and kiss her, not the peck we shared before lunch but the warm, slow, moist kiss of lovers.

We walk from there down the narrow angling streets until we come suddenly out at the Place de la Concorde. Crossing it, we stroll hand in hand along the Champs-Elysees. The sun is warm, but the avenue, cooled by the shade of the trees, makes the setting idyllic. At last we turn off the avenue and walk to a small hotel we have used before. Entering, I sign my name, not my name but the name I use, and we walk up one flight of stairs to room number six, the same room we always use, with the small balcony off the interior courtyard.

Suddenly a man, the man, stands in the room beside the bed where we lie naked and content. His eyes glow with hatred as he looks at the woman. I leap to my feet, standing between him and the woman. It is then I see the knife, long thin blade, in his left hand. He slashes at me but misses. I grab his hand, and we struggle. The knife falls to the floor, and he is gone. Once more, he has vanished. He does not leave, I tell you; he has simply vanished. Throughout the entire struggle, the woman sleeps peacefully and untroubled.

Now the scene changes; it is no longer Paris—it is once again Toulon. As I watch the woman sleeping, I am aware of a man lying on the bed beside her. I had fought the man. It was he making love to the woman, not me. The woman is my wife. Enraged I reach for the knife, but it no longer feels like a knife—it is a gun, a pistol. I press the barrel of the gun against her temple and pull the trigger. I can smell the cordite. She does not move. The man sleeps on. I place the gun against his temple, and as I pull the trigger, he opens his eyes. They are my eyes. It is not I with the gun, it is he, the man—but it is I, I am both men. He is smiling the smile of a victor.

The explosion in my dream has awakened me. No. It was not a gunshot. There was someone on the boat. Still woozy from the wine and sleep, I climbed the ladder to the deck. It was dark. I could not see anything for the fog. *Maybe I'm imagining things. There is not anyone or anything here. Could it be the shark, the one following me for the past two days, has he bumped against the hull?*

I leaned out slightly to look but in the darkness saw nothing, then something came flying toward me. I felt the awful blow to the side of my head. Dazed from the blow and the effects of the wine, I lost my balance and fall, striking my head. Disoriented but conscious, I staggered to my feet then fell headlong into the water, into the eternity we know as death where there is darkness and the gnashing of teeth, and as I fell, I cursed whatever God there is that caused this to happen.

Chapter Twenty-one

It was a half hour after dawn when I awoke in the second-floor bedroom of my comfortable chateau outside Toulon, startled by the reality and brutality of my dream. The boat, the places, events, they all seemed so real. Much of the dream had indeed been real, the events of my life as they had happened. But where had the rest come from? Micronesia, I had never been in the islands. I wondered about the confusion of things that had been and what else, the things that might be, would be. What about the woman in the dream just before I had awakened? She had resembled my wife so much I would have sworn it was she. In my dream I killed her in a fit of violent rage. In light of the double life I had led since my discharge from the colonial army and sojourn as an employee of the American intelligence service, it seemed odd to me that anything related to violence could bother me. I took a deep breath and tried to relax, to think about how well I lived, much better than I could have afforded off my earnings as an importer. I marveled that I had been able to keep my secret life away from my wife. Why had she never asked more? Of course, it had never occurred to me to ask about her activities while I was away on one of my errands.

I looked out the bedroom window toward the edge of my estate some hundred meters away just as the sun rose over the trees, thankful it was Saturday. I did not have to endure the commute into the city nor rush to Mass, a duty I endured for the sake of my marriage. After a minute pause, I dragged my trim forty-year-old body from the bed.

Lying on the bed was a woman of like age, small, voluptuous, snoring quietly, wearing a sleep mask and earplugs against my snoring—never her own. We had been married for five years and were still deeply in love with the mature concern and commitment to the other's happiness that comes with age and experience, so I believed.

I smiled as I recalled our lovemaking the night before. The passion was still there. After all these years, we still found the other desirable, unlike my other relationships, especially those in Asia. There I had only been interested in my own satisfaction. Had my wife ever wondered about those occasions when I traveled and did not call home, where I went, what I did? Certainly since my return from that business trip to Great Britain, the instances were infrequent, though they had increased during the past three years.

I could not get the dream out of my mind. I had no idea where it had originated and pondered its meaning. Surely the activity of my subconscious mind could not portend the future, could it? Perhaps I would discuss it with the old priest tomorrow following Mass. It seemed to me that there was much about heaven and hell, not that I really believed in either, about the way we all live our lives, only a priest, one well versed in theology, could answer.

We'll see, I thought. *I can always frame the question without revealing the details. It will be fun to taunt the old man. He believes I am so sincere.* I repressed the urge to laugh, not wanting to awaken my wife. There was enough to do today. After all, there was the garden to tend and the afternoon visit by my wife's new friends, a man and his wife. The man seemed familiar, almost like someone in my dream.

I went downstairs and put coffee on to brew. Fifteen minutes later the aroma of fresh-ground beans steeped in steam filled the room. I looked out the window and saw the mail carrier leaving the front of my house. I was fortunate to be among the first on the man's route and, therefore, frequently got my mail before leaving for the office.

I walked across the parquet floor of the foyer to the great door of the house and bent over to pick up the morning post. On top, I saw an advertisement that nearly caused my heart to stop. On the back cover of the sailing magazine was an ad for the sale of a boat, a sleek jade-green ketch with brass fittings and teak decks, a sailboat with luxurious appointments below deck—a boat named *Monique*—and I knew I must have it, regardless of where she took me or what happened.

Epilogue

Twenty-one months after Henri Gener awakened from his frightening dream, twenty months and three weeks after he purchased the sailing yacht *Monique*, the frigate *Daniel Stone, USN*, saw *Monique* as a blip on her radar well before they made visual contact with the derelict boat. Minutes after noticing the blip, the radar operator concluded it must be some vessel in need of assistance. Immediately, the captain, Lieutenant Commander John P. Merritt, ordered his ship to alter course to investigate.

Half an hour later, the *Daniel Stone* lay off the *Monique*, the small boat drifting in her lee. After hailing to no avail, Merritt dispatched a motor launch to investigate. She was obviously a vessel under some distress, her main sail and mizzen reefed, sheets flapping ever so slightly in the gentle morning breeze.

An ensign, bo'sun, and three ordinary seamen carrying side arms crossed the two hundred yards separating the two vessels. Once on board the sailboat, the investigation revealed only a giant flying fish dead beginning to decay in the cockpit. No one was on board. I had fallen into the sea just as I had dreamed, lost forever. I had ignored the dream and followed my course of arrogance and denial to the very end. My pride in going my own way, my unbelief had been my undoing. It had all happened just as I dreamed it.

The ensign ordered pictures taken and radioed back the circumstances after which *Monique* was placed in tow for the return trip to Kwagalein Atoll. Three days later word reached Saipan. The boat had been found adrift south and west of the Marshall Islands, somewhere between the Marshalls and Banaba Atoll, and towed into the naval base. Among the people who knew the Frenchman, reaction varied. The high commissioner revealed only that he had known the man during the U.S. war in Vietnam, during the early days. He refused to reveal what the two men talked about that afternoon before the Frenchman fled the island saying only that an opportunity had been lost when the Frenchman had stolen away in the night.

Monsignor Boulanger crossed himself and promised to pray for the man's soul, believing God would truly have to be gracious to forgive not the worldly sins of the Frenchman but his spiritual sin. Those nearby heard him say, "At sea, all alone, with no one to intercede for him; to stand before Christ like that. Oh, that God might grant him some measure of hope, of mercy."

Bili, Xarkus, and P.D. resented that somehow the *Monique* had escaped them. The fishing trawler had been so close before the fog closed around the little sailboat and she was lost to them forever. The Frenchman was of no consequence whatever. The boat, ah yes, the boat, that was a different matter. So close yet not to be.

The deputy high commissioner commented it served

the Frenchman right. He deserved whatever he got. He was an arrogant opportunist who had no right to live a high life while the DHC remained stuck on this island, leading nowhere, just because the voters in Arizona thought he was a crook.

George Rowley and Mark Meriday were determined to go on with life. George never found out about the truth of the afternoon cruise. Beth hardly commented on my death and remained with George, who continued to drink. Sydna left the island, physically and emotionally damaged, returning to her family in the States. Mark moved rapidly in on her replacement. He did not intend to repeat his mistake by seeming to be chivalrous.

Ferd Meier heard the news in his jail cell on Guam where he awaited trial in U.S. District Court on charges arising from his many illegal activities. Just as he suspected, they were on to him. The Director of the Micronesia Bureau of Investigation arrested him a week after the Frenchman left Saipan. His reaction contained a strange mix of emotions, sorrow that the Frenchman had refused to take him to sanctuary, thankful that he had not—a sanctuary Ferd felt certain was beyond redemption, thanking God that he understood the difference.

Jonathan Cartwright, more than any of the others, slept easy knowing that he had had nothing directly to do with the death of the Frenchman. Nevertheless, he would have to answer to his superiors at Langley concerning his involvement in the sudden departure of the man from both Saipan and Truk Lagoon. It bothered him that somewhere in that story there was enough to trap him into the dark world of covert activity. Would there be enough there to turn him into a man much like the Frenchman, a man he'd liked but sold out in the end in order to advance his own career?

A week to the day after the *Daniel Stone* began towing *Monique* toward the harbor at Kwagalein Atoll, Lieutenant Commander Merritt, a Naval Academy graduate from a seafaring New England family, re-read the written report. He reflected this was not the first derelict boat he had come across, nor was it likely to be the last. A boat, at sea, with no one aboard was rare but not without precedent.

What happened? Clearly whoever had been aboard was either French or spoke French fluently. Was it possible the book by Moitessier provided a clue? "Since I have gone too far" underlined in the text; "No, 'because I have gone too far'" scribbled in the margin. What could it mean? He wondered as he read the physical description of the ship's contents, *Camembert, from a tin? How very odd. I thought it would be in a small balsawood box. Ah well, I suppose there are some things we will never know.*